The Protocols of Uma

By John Brage

The Protocols of Uma – The Journeyers' Tale Book 1
Copyright 2015 by: John Brage
Written by: John Brage

Book Cover Design: keithdraws@wordpress.com

ISBN Number: 978-1-940155-27-2

10 9 8 7 6 5 4 3 2 1

Published by: Castle Top

Printed and published in the United States of America.

FOR ERIN AND CADEN – THE ARROWS I
FIRE AT THE WORLD.

Acknowledgments

First and foremost, I'd like to thank my family for allowing me all the time it took to write this. I apologize. It took a lot longer than I thought it would.

I appreciate the time taken by my test readers, Mike O. and Kris G., to look over the text and for the feedback they provided.

Dr. G., thank you for all your input and commentary throughout this process, as well as your constant encouragement to "publish!" I know I still owe you a mocha.

Finally, special thanks go to KeithDraws for the great cover art.

PROLOGUE

Four men drove the canoe silently across the water's surface. At the stern of the boat sat a young woman with her head bowed. The infant girl she held was wrapped in a dull cream cover. The child babbled happily as she tugged at her mother's long straw-colored hair.

As the canoe bottomed the men stepped out and pulled the craft onto the beach. They each wore a simple hooded red robe. Noting the anxiety on the men's faces, the woman tentatively followed. Their eyes uneasily scoured the land extending beyond the shoreline. She slowly bore her child down the beach away from the men and their boat. She knelt at a cluster of shallow-rooted bushes and set the baby on the ground between two of the plants. The woman hid behind her trembling hands as her daughter bawled with displeasure, reaching out for her mother. Trying to run down the beach, her legs failed and she toppled into the sand.

"Come!" called one of the men. The others watched impatiently.

The woman shuddered as her eyes released a deluge of tears. Her grief deprived her of breath until she finally managed a desperate gasp. Struggling to her feet she staggered back to where her baby sat.

The child's lower lip quivered, her face reddening as she sounded her displeasure. The woman knelt down once more, carefully re-securing the child's wrap. As she rose to leave, her daughter again seized her hair, this time with both hands. A thunder of anguish poured from the mother's breast as she pried at the child's fingers and began a slow retreat. She tore herself away and ran as fast as she could back toward the boat. Her daughter's wails quickly drowned in the din of the incoming waves.

CHAPTER 1

The man stood, arms crossed, staring out of the portal. Outside, innumerable chunks of rock hurtled by. Most were larger than the ship itself. At its current speed, the vessel would be obliterated by a collision with any one of them. Although he was a master of the technology that prevented such a fate, he remained uneasy.

"Min?" Another man stood in the doorway. Min had not heard him enter.

"Sol," he said with gentle recognition. "Come in old friend." Min held his hand to his mouth and began coughing.

Sol took Min by the elbow and led him to a nearby chair. "You should be resting," he noted. "You aren't the most cooperative patient I've ever had."

Min sat down. "I suppose not." He motioned for Sol to sit in an adjacent chair. "You have the results?" He asked the question having already found the answer on his friend's face.

Both men were slightly built with pale skin that was nearly without pigment. They had cream-colored hair that was speckled with white. Min's skin was a bit more wrinkled, his hair a bit whiter. Sol sat down.

"I do," replied Sol soberly.

Min was calm. "Not 'if?' is it? But 'when?'. How good are you at 'when?'?"

Sol leaned forward slightly. "I'm pretty good," he replied. "I'm also pretty good at delaying 'when'."

Min looked down at the table. "I'm done after this trip, aren't I?"

"Yes. There is no doubt. Another period of repose and your death is almost certain. The process I was working on isn't tenable." He looked away. "I'm sorry."

Min reached out and squeezed Sol's forearm. "No apology needed," he said. "If I could pick anyone to try and

3

resolve this issue, it would be you. The fact that you haven't done it yet is simply evidence of the problem's difficulty."

The "problem" was called Repose Termination Syndrome. It had been an issue for as long as the Journeyers had been traveling in space. Even at the speeds they employed, the Journeyers had to place themselves into a state of repose sleep in order to cover the area of space required by their mission. Emerging from this state of dormancy was very hard on their bodies. Their ability to regulate their blood gases sometimes became compromised. When this condition became too pronounced, a Journeyer had two choices – stop employing repose sleep or die. Sol had been attempting to devise a cure since he first came aboard all those ellipses ago.

"I was hoping that Hab's autopsy findings would provide me with some additional insights," said Sol with a sigh. "He was exceptionally old. Do you realize how many repose cycles he put his body through?"

Min shook his head. "Eight?"

"Try fifteen," said Sol. "For some reason, his cells just refused to break down for a very long time. I wish I knew why."

"It is a question for another day," said Min. He sat back in his chair. "So, assuming no repose cycles, how long?"

"If you lead a fairly sedentary, low exertion lifestyle......... maybe twenty ellipses. Less if you don't."

Min began coughing again. "I have some ideas on how to accomplish that."

Sol debated internally before responding. "Eve?"

Min considered Sol's answer and then broke out into a grin. "What, do you think I'm planning on just having her serve me hand and foot until I die? I hardly think she would agree to that."

"Don't be so sure," Sol said solemnly. "If that isn't what you want, then don't ask her," he advised.

Min took a deep breath and closed his eyes. "What I want…….." he echoed. "Any chance you would be interested in becoming Command Agent?"

"Would that solve anything?" Sol asked rhetorically. "I wish I could tell you that I am interested and qualified. But I am neither."

What I want…Of course, Sol was right. This was Min's last journey. He needed to assign a new Command Agent. Eve was by far the most suitable choice. But if Eve became Command Agent, she would have to leave with the ship when it departed from Uma the next time. Min would have to remain behind. He had no other choice.

"You don't give yourself enough credit," said Min.

"What about Jack?" offered Sol. Min *had* considered Jack despite all of his instincts telling him that it was ridiculous. As talented as Jack was, he was barely an adult. He had only served as Technical Agent since Hab's transition two ellipses prior. Jack was too raw to serve as Command Agent. But if he did…

"That would allow the crew to have one person serving as both Command Agent and Technical Agent," continued Sol. "I would think that there would be certain efficiencies with such an arrangement, at least until another Technical Agent could be trained. The panel could manage the data analysis until the next Data Agent was ready. And Eve. . . . . ." Sol allowed his thought to complete itself.

Eve could stay with me. Min saw the direction of Sol's logic. "I'm tired," said Min. "I need to rest."

"Sure you do." The trace of sarcasm in his voice was not lost on Min. Sol stood up and walked to the door. "I'll check back with you later. If you want to talk anymore……."

Min nodded. Sol turned and left, leaving Min alone with his thoughts.

The young woman stood at the bottom of the steps. She could hear the buzz of the crowd on the far side of the platform. Eight steps upwards and she would be facing them.

She wasn't ready. The announcement she was about to make was not going to have the impact she wanted. Disappointment had created doubt. The people had embraced her message before only to find it empty and unsatisfying. She had little expectation that they would give her a second chance.

"Shu?" said a man standing next to her. He was much older. Both wore dark red robes with hoods pulled over their heads. A light rain sprinkled down upon them. "Do you really intend to go through with this insanity?" he asked earnestly. His condescension stung her ears. "You are going to lose them for good!"

"It is NOT insane, Bal!" Shu snapped. She drew back her hood exposing her off-white hair to the rain. After a few brisk steps she was atop the platform behind a wooden podium. In front of her, most of the island's able-bodied residents stood waiting for her appearance. Once they saw her they began to quiet down, anxious to hear what she had to say.

Shu swallowed hard. Reaching behind the podium, she withdrew a small wooden megaphone and pressed it to her mouth.

"People of Atla!" she called. She thought she sounded confident. "I have called you here to share wonderful news! In our time of need, a Journeycraft approaches! It will be here before the morning!"

She paused, partially for effect, but primarily to gauge the crowd's reaction. There was a great deal of murmuring as the people bantered back and forth about what they had just heard.

Their level of enthusiasm troubled her. It was almost as if she had just announced the size of the mushroom harvest.

"Again?" came a voice from somewhere in the back

The crowd responded with weak laughter trimmed with irritation. They had been called to hear this?

"This time is different!" insisted Shu. "This time . . . . ." *This time they are really coming.* The crowd's murmur rose in protest. "By the morning, they will be here!" she said, mustering as much volume as she could. "For those of you who wish to wait by the rings, you will be rewarded with a spectacular vision. A Journeycraft nears!"

The crowd's energy quickly waned. They were slowly beginning to disperse. Bal climbed the stairs and watched as the people moved off. He removed his hood.

"They don't believe you," he said in a low voice. "That is very . . . .troubling. Is it not?"

Shu turned towards him and scowled. "It doesn't matter if they believe me or not, Bal," she snapped. "Because the Journeyers **are** coming. There is no doubt. And once they arrive, they will help us deal with this illness."

"Which illness?" said Bal. "The one that makes the people cough and burn and die? Or the one that affects their minds? The one that has eroded their faith in us? Which do you think is more dangerous?"

"Both will be eliminated, once they arrive," said Shu, sounding more hopeful than confident. "One will lead to the other. And once they leave again, all will be well."

Bal remained expressionless. He looked out at the area in front of the podium. Only a few of the Atlans remained. Shu's assessment had to be correct. The absence of the Journeyers was manageable, at least for a time. But if they returned now, and failed? That would derange his entire plan. Their confidence in him was a reflection of their faith in the Journeyers. Without that, he could not rule.

7

Shu hurried away from the meeting ground. Bal followed behind along with another pair of red-clad individuals.

"Shu!" hissed Bal. "You need to continue speaking. You can't just dash off like that!"

Shu stopped abruptly and whirled towards Bal. "Bal, for the last time," she said through clenched teeth, "you need to remember your place, even if you don't like it. I am your Chief Chronicler. I am not answerable to you, or to anyone else. I'll not explain that again."

Bal glanced around, a bemused smirk rising on his face. "Or?" he asked. "What will you do?"

Shu glared back at the older man, her chin quivering. She struggled to sound defiant. "Care to find out?" Bal's expression remained unaffected. "Now, any further discussions must take place in the Hall." She anxiously checked to see if their spat had drawn anyone's attention. It appeared not.

The Chroniclers' Hall was a large pyramid in the center of the island. Two huge Guards flanked the entrance. While the Guards had the same light skin and hair as the other inhabitants of the island, they were almost twice as massive. They stood passively, arms at their sides, making no acknowledgment of the pair's approach. The Chroniclers strode past and entered the building.

The interior of the pyramid consisted primarily of one broad open space. At the far end was a huge display that covered most of the wall. A number of people in red robes stood watching it intently. Most of them turned upon hearing Shu and Bal enter.

"Anything?" snapped Shu. They all shook their heads. She stared up at the display, willing it to do *something*. It remained dark.

"Shu, what are you going to do when your silly ruse is exposed?" asked Bal. "I don't think the people can bear a second failure. I should have been consulted."

Shu bristled at the word 'silly'. "They said they are coming," she insisted. "This time is different."

This time. Slightly less than an ellipse earlier, a Journeycraft had abruptly appeared in the sky without notice. The Atlans, at least those who were physically able, swarmed towards the landing area to watch its descent. Then, they waited. Nothing happened. The Journeycraft had sat there, inert, ever since. Rotations passed and the plague continued to ravage the people.

It was a slow, uncomfortable death. Initially, the stricken began to cough. The cough became more and more pronounced until the subject developed a raging fever. The Rearers tried to treat them with poultices and concoctions made from herbs, but more often than not, this simply resulted in the Rearer falling ill as well. Once stricken, no one survived. No one knew how to combat it. The appearance of the Journeycraft was a miracle. Its failure to produce its crew upon landing assaulted the deepest hopes of the Atlans. Then the message appeared on the display. Another Journeycraft was on the way.

Shu approached the figures standing by the display. "When they contact us again, be sure and advise them of the plague. They must immediately begin working on a cure."

"Again?" repeated Bal. "They didn't contact **us**. They contacted **you**, or so you say. Odd that no one else was present at the time." He studied the reactions of the other Chroniclers. By his judgment, most of them did not believe Shu at all. "Imagine what the Portentists will do once this sham is exposed. Didn't you give that any thought at all?"

The Portentists. They had lost their reverence for the Journeyers generations ago. The Journeyers had become a fable to them. Instead, they saw signs in everything. Signs about the future. The empty Journeycraft was a powerful omen.

"Enough!" snapped Shu. "This is no sham!" she asserted fiercely. "They approach. And when they arrive, they will end the plague." Her fellow Chroniclers appeared to be rather unnerved by her outburst.

Bal shook his head. "But how . . . . .?" Just then, the display produced a faint hum. A glow gradually arose on its face. Then they saw her.

"Chronicler Hall, this is Data Agent Eve. Can you hear me?" An excited murmur rushed through the gathered Chroniclers as they all drew around the display.

Shu looked over at Bal. Her relief was unmistakable. "Yes, Eve," she replied to the display. "This is Chief Chronicler Shu. I can hear you."

"We anticipate landing in just under one rotation. That should be shortly before dawn for you. We have to execute a return ceremony first."

"We eagerly await your landing," injected Bal. "But know that we have a situation here. A plague. We desperately require assistance."

"Of course," said Eve. "I will ask Life Agent Sol to address it as soon as we disembark. We look forward to seeing you."

A new weight settled on Shu's countenance. "Despite our plight, you must delay your exit from the craft for two rotations after landing," she said sullenly. "Your adjustment to the surface takes time, does it not?"

"Yes, but not much. If we........."

Shu cut her off. "We can't have the other Atlans see your crew stagger out of the ship on the edge of collapse," she noted. "Do not disembark until you are strong and well-adjusted to the surface."

Eve looked away from her monitor momentarily. "Very well," she said, attempting to hide her disapproval. "Two rotations."

———————

Min sat at the far end of a small elliptically shaped table. Sol sat to his left. Directly across from Min sat a woman with the same light hair and skin as the two men. Eve's cheek bones were high and delicate, her skin smooth. She watched Min attentively. To her right sat a young man, barely an adult. He was eagerly consuming the contents of a report on the small display in front of him. The young man was Jack, the ship's Technical Agent.

"Within the rotation," Min began, "we will be landing on Uma. I have called you all together to be sure that everyone knows what is expected while we are on the surface." Sol's eyes were closed as he was clearly uninterested in what Min had to say. This was his seventh trip back to Uma.

Jack looked up from his report. "The preparations for Hab's return are done," he said enthusiastically. "Do you want to review them?" His question was laden with hope. While he suspected Min would review the preparations, as important as they were, he wanted to hear that Min trusted him enough that such a review was unnecessary.

Sol opened his eyes as Min studied the expression on Jack's face. Min sat back in his chair, pretending to contemplate the inquiry. "No," he said finally, "I'm sure your arrangements are satisfactory."

Jack beamed and his cheeks turned red. "Well," continued Jack, "I have done the calculations concerning optimal thermal . . . . ."

Min raised a hand, silencing him. "It's fine, Jack. I'm sure it's fine." Jack shrugged, wrestling with his wish to explain everything to his mentor.

"You were going to explain our behavioral guidelines?" said Eve. Min looked at her from across the table. She was incalculable. He had at least twice as many physiological ellipses as she. From the moment she had come on board as a student, her presence had distracted him. He had distanced himself from her tutelage as much as practicable, but their interactions were unavoidable. Despite numerous consultations with Sol, as well as a thorough study of the *Starshine's* resources on Umae emotional responses, he could not fully comprehend his feelings for her. That want of understanding unsettled him. She expressed the same emotional attraction to him but did not share his discomfort.

"Of course," he said finally. "Sol, Eve and I have all returned to Uma before, but you haven't, Jack. It is absolutely vital that you do what is expected, and allowed, while we are on the surface." As usual, Jack closely followed every word Min said.

Jack frowned. "I'm not sure I understand."

"I'm sure we will be housed in our own pyramid," explained Min. "You must remain there unless accompanied by one of us."

"I can't circulate by myself?"

"No." Min's answer came quickly. "Not unless some unusual situation arises. We have to err on the side of caution." Jack shook his head, trying not to reveal the sting of Min's reply.

"So, what shall I do?" he asked quietly.

"Our fellow Umae expect us to solve problems for them," said Min. "Our visits are extraordinary. We must leave an impression that we are willing and able to help them. When we leave, they must be left with a sense of wonder. Journeyers must maintain an elevated status in society, even though we are rarely here."

Min imagined Jack's mind racing through all the possible purposes of such an endeavor. Apparently, none met with his satisfaction. "Why?" he asked finally.

"The Chroniclers hold themselves out as our agents on Uma. If we maintain our revered status, then their ability to maintain order is augmented. Without that . . . ." He let his voice trail off to provide emphasis on his message.

"The Journeys are scheduled so that a Journeycraft returns to Atla at least every other generation," explained Sol. "That way, everyone has at least seen a Journeycraft personally or knows someone who has."

"We have to avoid exposing them to our technology though, isn't that right?" said Jack. "But how can they be left with a sense of wonder if we do things for them without them even knowing what we did?"

Eve reached over and patted Jack's arm. "They will know what we did," she said. "They just won't know how we did what we did."

"There's your wonder," added Sol.

Min resumed his discussion with Jack.

"Jack, Umae society is locked into a specific level of technology. That is by design of the Directors, may they guide our way." Min uttered the last phrase with a minimal amount of enthusiasm.

Jack frowned. "But . . .why? How? That seems so . . . ."

"We don't know 'why'," said Min. "Although I hope to gain a better understanding of the rationales behind all the Protocols. I have always suspected that the Cataclysm was caused by some misuse of technology. The Directors, may they guide our way, implemented a protocol that arrested Umae technology at its current level. It could be that the developmental ceiling placed on the Umae is intended to prevent whatever occurred from happening again before we find Haven. 'How' is a bit easier to explain. The way things are done – the way boats are made, food is grown, anything you can think of – is offered to them by the Chroniclers as a gift from us. That is why it is so important for them to view us with wonder. That wonder . . .or reverence . . . .prevents them from trying to improve upon technological methods. It would be . . . .blasphemous . . .in a sense."

So many questions raced through the young Technical Agent's mind that he didn't know where to start. "You don't know the nature of the Cataclysm?"

"No, we don't," admitted Min. "The Chroniclers have simply taught that it led to the Directors issuing the Protocols. We don't even know for sure when it happened."

"Who *does* know what happened?"

Min hesitated before offering his theory. "The Chroniclers might," he said finally. "But I'm not convinced."

Eve turned towards him. "You don't think they know?"

"I'll believe it when one of them explains it to me."

"When we provide assistance," interjected Sol, "it is imperative that no surface-dwelling Umae see any of the technical aspects of that assistance."

"But, I don't see how that could hurt anything," Jack protested. "Could it?"

"Jack, first and foremost, this is a Protocol from the Directors, may they guide our way." Sol was barely more enthused than Min had been. "It is their wisdom which will provide our salvation. Second, imagine what would happen if the Umae saw how we were able to do something. What do you think the consequences would be?"

Jack thought for a moment. "Well, they would know that there was a better way to do something – better than the way they do it, I mean."

"Exactly," continued Sol. "And then?"

"They would want to know how it was done," said Jack. "I know I would."

"And if we didn't tell them?" asked Sol.

Now Jack understood. "We wouldn't be seen as special anymore, would we? Instead, they would wonder why we don't just give them everything we have."

"Exactly," said Sol. "And once we leave?"

"I suspect they would try to figure out how we were able to do what we do," said Jack. Min was once again impressed by Jack's mental agility.

"And that would result in technological improvement," said Sol, concluding the thought. Jack's protest was cut off by Sol's last comment. "Violating the Protocols of the Directors." He paused for a moment. "May they guide our path."

Jack sat back in his chair, still trying to determine all of the possible consequences of such a protocol.

"It is hard for us, too," said Eve. "But it is crucial that we follow the Protocols."

"You really intend to delve into the reasons for the Protocols?" Sol asked Min. "Since when?"

"It has been an interest of mine for some time," said Min. "An interest Hab would not let me pursue. He found it......profane."

"Do you think the Chroniclers will just explain it all to you?" asked Sol doubtfully.

Min shrugged. "Unlikely."

Sol stood up and stretched. "Come on Jack," he said as he walked towards the door. "I have a few things in the Life Lab that might interest you."

"Just remember," said Min. "He's **my** student."

Jack's ears flushed. "I know that," said Sol grinning. "Lucky." As Sol and Jack departed, Eve rose from her chair.

She is leaving? No. She walked over and sat down where Sol had been seated. Min had long struggled with the anxiety he experienced in her presence. She excited him in so many ways he couldn't explain. She reached out and took his hand.

"Has Sol completed his tests?" she asked. As usual, she didn't engage in any unnecessary delay.

"He did." Min knew that his simple response would instantly convey Sol's bad news to her. "We have a lot that we need to discuss."

———————

It was still dark and there was very little activity at the docks. A man and a woman inspected a medium-sized canoe, assuring themselves that it was ready. Behind the canoe was a much larger barge, attached to the smaller boat by a collection of thin hemp ropes. The latter craft was wide and shallow, essentially a broad floating platform.

"Looks fit to me," said the man. The woman was seated at the stern of the canoe, staring off into the distance. "May?"

She smiled. "Sorry. I was just thinking about Dom. Are you sure it is a good idea to take him with us?"

"Yes. If I didn't, I wouldn't have suggested it." He walked down the dock and knelt down next to her. "But that isn't what you were thinking about, was it?"

The woman shook her head. "No, it wasn't."

"Let me guess," said Cap. "Dom's first trip to shore means that he is getting older. And . . . .you don't want him to get older. Am I close?"

May flushed. "Mostly," she confessed.

"But even when he has completed his rearing age, it isn't as if you will never see him. After all, the island is just so big."

May stood up and Cap assisted her as she stepped onto the dock. She stood facing him, holding on to his hand. "It's different you know. Rearing your own. It is difficult to explain in such a way that you would understand."

Cap studied her face. "I can't imagine," he said. "It is hard enough when any group completes their rearing age. They become our own, in a way, don't they?"

May looked down. "It isn't the same," she said quietly. "I know that sounds awful, but it is true."

"Like I said, I can't imagine. Maybe . . . . "Cap abruptly stopped speaking. "Wonderful," he said under his breath.

"Good morning, Rearers!" It was Bal. He was striding down the dock trailed by two of the enormous Chronicler Guards. "I trust the ship is adequate."

May turned away and rolled her eyes.

"Yes, it appears to be," answered Cap without enthusiasm. "I'm sure it will be fine."

Bal reached inside his dark red robe and produced a small sack, handing it to Cap. "You are familiar with this?" he asked.

Cap knew what it was without opening it. "I've used it before, if that is what you mean," he replied. He untied the top of the bag and looked inside. There was a small oblong black box bearing a series of small multicolored lights. The lights seemed to go on and off in a random pattern. As always, Cap found himself fascinated by the device.

"Take excellent care of that," said Bal sternly. "It is a gift from the Journeyers!" His last statement was so full of false enthusiasm that Cap almost laughed. He had heard that same exclamation more times than he could count. The crops. The pyramids. The canoes. All were "gifts from the Journeyers" and all generated an inordinate degree of enthusiasm from Bal. The other Chroniclers weren't quite like that. Only him.

"I will," said Cap. He always had before. Surely Bal knew that.

Cap saw a quintet of youngsters walking down the dock towards them. They were his Wards. He and May had served as their Rearers for the last several ellipses. Today, they would be crewing the canoe to the mainland. The eldest girl had been there before, the others had not. Trailing along behind the group was a boy, the youngest of the lot. He looked annoyed.

17

"Good morning Dom," said May. The boy stopped and folded his arms in front of him.

"Do I HAVE to go?" he whined. "I want to see the Journeyers come." Like the other Wards, Dom had heard the news about the return of a Journeycraft.

May went to him and placed her hands on his shoulders. "I don't think you'll miss anything," she told the boy.

"May!" protested Cap. "Enough! You are going to create problems for yourself."

"Why would they send us on a trip to the mainland if a Journeycraft is coming?" she asked quietly.

"We will be back soon, and then we can see the Journeyers," said Cap. "Wait and see. And believe."

"How long do you think you will be gone?" asked Bal. Neither of the Rearers had heard him approach. It was impossible to tell what he may have heard.

Cap began directing the Wards to their respective positions in the canoe. "We should be back not long after nightfall," he said. "It always takes a bit longer when we are towing the barge."

"Excellent," said Bal. "We will have the signal drums prepared."

"We'd appreciate that," said Cap. He looked over at May. She was ignoring Bal. "All right everyone, let's get ready to go."

The Wards settled in and took hold of their respective oars. May sat in the bow, and Cap sat in the aft with Dom. The two Guards gave the canoe a firm shove, and May began calling a cadence for the rowers to follow. As they pulled their oars, the canoe skimmed away from the dock.

———

Min and Eve could barely see one another, even though their bodies were pressed together. Eve rested her cheek on his chest, listening for the beating of his heart.

"It's still there," said Min assuredly. "I'd think you would know if it stopped." Eve looked down into his eyes and smiled.

"I'd know even if you weren't here. With me," she said quietly.

"Eve........." She held a finger to his lips.

"Even though I know, tell me what Sol told you," she said. Looking into her eyes, Min thought he could see tears beginning to gather.

"This was my last journey," he said finally. "I can't take another period of repose."

Eve slid slowly off of him and onto her side. She tenderly stroked his cheek with her thumb. "I had hoped otherwise," she said. "So, what happens now?"

Min closed his eyes, soaking in the ticklish sensation of her finger on his face. "I won't be permitted to stay on Uma," he said. "It is against the Protocols. I can either go back into space on the *Starshine* and serve until I die or go somewhere else."

"Somewhere else?" she asked.

"The moon," said Min. "The Citadel. I am taking Jack there anyway for his tour. I could stay there and do some research until I passed. At least that way I could be doing some good."

Their eyes locked, neither of them willing to blink. It was Eve who finally broke away. "Good? You could be with me. Wouldn't that be good?"

Min gently grasped her chin, trying to bring her eyes back to him. She didn't put up much resistance. "You know the answer to that," he insisted. He wanted her to believe. It wasn't that simple.

"Then let me go with you," said Eve. She had said this to him more times than he could remember. Even before Sol completed his formal research, they all knew what the result would be. Min's illness was pushing him towards death, and no one could do anything to stop it.

"What about the *Starshine*?" asked Min. "What about Haven?"

"What about that?!?" snapped Eve. She rolled away from him, breaking all contact. "Critical Closure is still far, far away," she protested. "There is still plenty of time to find Haven and relocate our people. I won't be needed for that." She rolled back towards him, wrapping one of her bare legs over his. "Your career as a Command Agent may be ending," she said in a whisper. "We don't have to be."

Min brushed a stray strand of her straw-colored hair away from her light pink eyes. He had seen as many different star systems as almost any member of his race. None of those memories contained anything as beautiful as Eve. Min closed his eyes as a tear cautiously made its way down his cheek to the corner of his lips. He held his mouth to hers and then sat up.

"I need to think about this some more," he said wearily. "I'm sorry. In all likelihood, the projections about Critical Closure are still valid. If they are . . ." Eve looked at him hopefully. "Well, your argument is pretty . . . . Compelling."

Eve slid out from underneath the thermometric covering and walked over to retrieve her clothes from the floor. "I know this isn't easy for you," she said without turning around. "You know what is so difficult?" Min remained silent, honoring the rhetorical nature of the question. "If your decision were an easy one, I wouldn't care about you nearly as much." She slipped into her clothes and walked to the door.

"Eve?" said Min.

Eve turned around and looked back at him. "Yes, dear?"

"We will figure something out." He was trying to sound reassuring. She was probably right, as usual. Critical Closure was still thousands of ellipses away. The loss of one data Agent, no matter how talented, would have very little impact on the chances of a successful relocation. Besides, if that minor compromise somehow caused the effort to fail, no one would survive to remember.

CHAPTER 2

The journeycraft **Starshine** sped past a huge, gaseous planet, its engines easily compensating for the giant's immense gravity. The ship was an elongated cylinder, slightly flattened at each end. Its twin wings rose broadly from its spine about one-third of the way along its body, arching high above the ship before nearly touching one another directly above the center fuselage. They bowed parallel to one another before reattaching to the main body of the ship near the tail.

The crew sat scattered at various stations, monitoring a variety of displays. "We can terminate beacon tracking," said Min from his seat near the center. The ship's sensors were locked onto a repeating wave of electro-magnetism, the beacon signal. It served as the ship's tether to its homeworld.

"Min, beacon tracking is terminated," said Jack. "Turn full navigation over to the ship?"

Min rose and walked over to the far wall. A tiny portal allowed him to see into the darkness of space. "Yes, Jack. We need to prepare for Hab's return." He turned and walked past the other crew members, stopping at a raised platform covered with a metallic sheet.

Min stood over the platform for a moment, resting his hand atop the sheet. "Fine," he muttered before finally pulling it back. Underneath was another man lying prone on the platform, very similar in appearance to the crew. He had the same white skin and creamy hair, but his face was more deeply wrinkled. His bushy eyebrows were pure white. The man was completely naked.

"Hab, how many journeys did we make together?" asked Min. "You happened with me," he said quietly. Looking about, he said more loudly, "He happened with me." The others responded.

"With me as well."

"Me, too."

"I wished he'd happened more with me."

Eve walked back to the platform and stood next to Min. She reached down and took Hab's hand in hers but remained silent.

"Is the bay prepared?" asked Min.

"Prepared," she said quietly.

Min waited for Eve to release Hab's hand. She did and smiled warmly as she brushed the prone man's cheek with her thumb. She then recovered him with the sheet and returned to her position.

Min engaged a mech assist, directing it to push the platform to a nearby egress tube. The medium-sized robot easily rolled the platform over to a circular opening in the far wall. It was just large enough to enable the mech to ease Hab's body inside. Once that was done, the opening was resealed with a circular hatch and locked into place. Min then returned to his chair. They would be home again very soon.

As the ship neared the planet Uma, it came to a virtual stop. Its fusion thrusters matched the tug of the planet's gravity to prevent the ship from falling. Uma was a large, gray, rotating ball. The shades of gray in its atmosphere were subtle in their distinctions. A single moon orbited in the distance, its bright surface pocked by small, irregular blotches of darkness.

Min peered through the portal. "Prepare for return," he said, maintaining his attention on the planet. "This is one I want to be sure and remember."

"Rotating ship to optimal angle," said Jack from a nearby console.

"Let me know when rotation is complete," said Min. He folded his arms and lowered his head for a moment. "Hab, you were a great teacher, and friend. Your guidance allowed us to make many great discoveries, and to add to the knowledge base of our people. While those who remained below may not fully appreciate your contributions, your fellow Journeyers surely do. Now you journey alone, an honor you well deserve."

"Rotation complete," said Jack, almost as if on cue.

Min took a long slow breath. "Initiate return," he said.

A hissing sound came from another part of the ship, and Min could see Hab's body, still wrapped in its metallic shroud, as it fell towards the planet. It gradually grew smaller and smaller until it disappeared from sight.

Min continued to watch, actually pressing his nose against the portal. He could soon pick out a green, phosphorescent ball growing larger and brighter in the atmosphere below. Hab's shroud had absorbed a tremendous amount of heat from friction created by the atmosphere. Once the temperature reached the shroud's tipping point, it burst into a huge, green flare that instantly consumed Hab's remains. The light was so bright that it could be seen from the ship, despite the fact that Hab's body was more than halfway through the atmosphere when ignition took place.

The view from the ground, Min thought, would be spectacular for anyone who happened to be looking.

———————

"Pull . . . . . . pull . . . . . . .pull . . . ." May provided her Wards with a regular tempo. There were only four of them, adolescents of various ages. They sat single file, drawing their oars back in response to the rhythm of May's direction. At the aft of the boat, Cap sat, looking ahead. He had rowed with them for a bit but stopped once the canoe reached a steady pace. The physical fitness of his Wards was a part of his charge.

The lake's surface was smooth save for the furrow cut by the boat. A patchy fog rose from the water. The rowers all had sweat dripping down their faces. Cap held the small, black, triangular-shaped box presented to him by Bal earlier that morning. He studied it closely, watching the colored lights on its surface.

"Hold!" he called without looking up. The mainland was visible now, even through the fog. The rowers stopped, thankful for the reprieve. Just then, a bright light streaked over their heads before bursting into a brilliant green ball over the lake. A rumble that echoed back over their heads towards the land soon followed the sight of the explosion.

"What was THAT?" asked Dom excitedly. "Did you see? Did you see that?" Cap and May both focused on their attentions on the gray billows overhead. "Is there more?" asked Dom. His eyes eagerly studied the clouds. "Did the Hek do that?" His last question was offered in a quieter voice as he looked out over the water.

"No!" insisted May. "Of course not." The other four youths were plainly rattled. They all stared at their Rearers, hoping for an explanation.

"It's fine," said Cap. "I'm sure of it. It was probably just . . . lightning or something. It's gone now. Come, there is work to do." He took one last quick peek upwards, trying to hide his unease.

Cap held the box up in front of him. On its face was a single, steady blue light. He didn't know a lot about the Hek, but he had never heard that they knew how to fly through the clouds. The steady light calmed him somewhat. Dom reached up and tugged at Cap's plain gray smock.

"What is that?" he asked, looking at the box.

"I don't know what it is called," Cap admitted.

The child was not satisfied. "What does it do?"

Cap looked at May, who simply shrugged.

"Well," Cap began deliberately. "It . . . . looks for things."

"Like what?" Dom leaned forward, his eyes widening. "The Hek?"

Cap turned and looked ahead again. There was a sandy beach, with a rocky rise beyond. The boat continued to drift towards the shore.

"Yes," said Cap, trying to assure the boy. "So we know that it is safe to go ashore."

The child stared out towards the beach. "Are they out there?" he asked. He squinted as his eyes searched the landfall ahead. Dom had drawn the attention of the other Wards. They were filling with apprehension.

Cap looked once more in May's direction. "No," he replied. "The Journeyers have given us this . . . .," Bal's exaggerated words trespassed on his thoughts, "gift to make sure we are safe. If the Hek were nearby, this box would tell us," he announced loudly. "They are not."

"Pull!" called May, cutting off Dom's next question.

The rowers responded to May's demand. Soon, the boat's keel came to rest on the sandy bottom of the shallows. The rowers all climbed out into the thigh high water and began pushing the boat towards the beach. Once the canoe was ashore, Cap joined his students in pushing the much heavier barge onto the beach as well. Cap drove a number of stakes into the sand and secured the barge as best he could with lengths of rope.

"Where are we going?" asked Dom.

"Be patient," said Cap, as he started up the beach. "You might find this interesting."

The rowers strode along the beach. Once more, Cap studied the metal box. The steady blue light shone as before. Dom tugged at his sleeve and pointed. A short ways away, a group of lake birds were running along the sand, searching the incoming waves for food.

"Why aren't they afraid of the Hek?" said the boy in a nearly accusatory tone.

Cap nodded towards the birds. "Because the Hek aren't here. They know that."

Not surprisingly, Dom continued. "But what if they *were* here?" He pulled himself closer to Cap.

May gathered the other rowers together on the beach. "We need to move quickly," she said seriously. "Come with me and stay together." She began jogging down the beach, not needing to look and see if anyone was following her.

Cap looked down at Dom. "Hear that? 'Quickly', May said. Want to ride on my back?" Dom frowned at him and ran off after the others.

Just beyond the beach, the land sloped steadily upwards to a plateau. The group followed a narrow, rocky path until they reached the top. Most of the rowers stopped to catch their breath, leaning on their knees. Dom stood, hands akimbo. "Let's go! Why are we stopping?"

"A moment," said May sternly. "Patience." Dom folded his arms in front of him and frowned.

"How much farther?" asked one of the other boys. Cap patted him on the shoulder.

"Soon. It is worth the trip, believe me."

The plateau yielded to a flat, grassy plain. They maintained a steady pace, stopping intermittently to catch their breath. Despite his initial enthusiasm, Dom quickly tired, causing the rest of them to move much more slowly than they would have otherwise. The Wards were not entirely displeased by this. At every opportunity, their eyes scoured the landscape ahead of them.

In the distance, they could see a forest of immensely tall trees. Already the group had to tilt their heads to see the treetops. They moved on into the forest. Just as many of them were ready to stop again to catch their breath, it came into view.

The trees opened up into a huge clearing. Within the clearing was a stone wall about three times Cap's height. May waved them all forward. In their excitement, their fatigue was forgotten and they soon reached the base of the stones.

The wall stretched as far as they could see in both directions. Its carved stones were set together without mortar. The seams between the stones were almost invisible. The rowers were awestruck at the sight of the structure.

"Did . . . . .we . . . .build this?" asked one. "It sort of looks like our pyramids."

Cap smiled. "Well, yes and no. You didn't. I didn't. It is . . . . .." He nearly choked on the phrase. ".......a gift from the Journeyers."

"Why?" asked the youngest girl.

"You will see soon."

They walked along the wall. Soon, they saw a huge wooden door. A large crossbeam was fit into the stone to hold the door securely shut.

"How do we open it?" asked one.

May removed a narrow metal circlet from her pocket. As she held it next to the crossbeam's jam, there was a distinctive pop from inside the jam itself. She looked around to be sure that everyone was watching. She then held out a finger and easily pushed the crossbeam out of the jam, sliding it back the length of her arm with seemingly no effort. She then pushed on the huge door with the same finger, causing it to open inwards.

The rowers suspended their welling amazement in favor of seeing what was inside. Neither Cap nor May impeded their efforts to go through the door. Once they were inside, May closed the door behind them.

Inside the door were rows and rows of lush, green plants of varying shapes and sizes. Some were no more than a few inches off the ground while others stood well over Cap's head.

Beyond the walls, the Wards could see the huge forest trees towering above them.

"What is this?" asked Dom.

"Food," answered Cap.

"We came here to eat?" asked Dom.

Cap tussled Dom's light-yellow hair. "No. We came here to work." Dom frowned at him. May pushed the huge door shut and secured its crossbeam on the inside by performing her prior actions in reverse order. "This way," she said. "This way to the tools." Dom groaned. He didn't like the way this rotation was developing.

———————

Min gave the display of pyrotechnics every opportunity to make an impression in his memory. He stood at the portal pondering Hab's passage until Eve appeared at his side.

"We must initiate landing sequences," she said quietly.

Min turned towards her. "Of course."

"Initiate landing sequences," he said generally.

"Initiating," echoed Jack from his position nearby.

The modest hum that had pervaded the ship stopped completely. "Fusion in repose," said Jack. "Friction thrusters ready."

The ship slowly began to drift into the planet's atmosphere. Without its fusion-based propulsion, the ship was in free fall. As the ship accelerated into the atmosphere, its nose began to glow. The jet-black shields on the front of the ship began channeling the heat created from the friction of re-entry towards a set of thrusters on either side. As the temperature rose, the thrusters automatically compensated by slowing the ship's descent. Min reviewed a small display in front of him. The heat energy was being converted to power for use by the thrusters. The faster the ship fell, the more thrust energy it generated. The equilibrium was perfect.

The ship broke through the thick atmospheric cloud cover. Directly below was a huge, freshwater lake with an island near the center. A large land mass could be seen in the distance.

"Alignment?" asked Min.

"Minus naught naught . . . . .three," said Jack, a hint of disbelief in his voice.

"Not bad, Jack, for your first time off of the simulator." Jack's ears burned scarlet.

The ship smoothly lowered itself towards the island. There were dozens of 4-sided stone pyramids of varying heights. There was also a series of circles carved into the ground. Within one of the circles sat a ship very similar to the **Starshine**. Min moved to a nearby portal and looked down.

"There is another Journeycraft down there!" he exclaimed excitedly. Eve and Sol rushed over to look through nearby portals.

"I don't believe it," said Eve, smiling broadly. "Do you know what the odds are?"

"No, and I'd rather not," said Sol. "It would kill the wonder. Are there any special Protocols for such a situation?"

"I doubt it," said Eve. "If there were, Chief Chronicler Shu would have said something."

Min could see a collection of boats gathered alongside one side of the island. In the center of the island, one large pyramid loomed over the others. It had a long, thin needle projecting upwards from its apex.

"Welcome back," said Min to the crew. "Per the Chief Chronicler, we have to remain aboard for two rotations. Then we can see what has been going on since we left."

He could already feel the heavy tug of the planet on his legs. Despite the ship's technology levels, the simulated gravity they employed in space was not quite the same as the gravity from the planet. The ship sensed when any individual might function more efficiently with a slightly lower gravity and compensated accordingly. The planet offered no such mercy. Min was sure the others would become fully acclimated within two rotations. He was not quite as confident about himself.

Cap, May, and the rest of the rowers spent most of the rotation tending to the Garden inside the stone wall. The harvest season was near so their job was to determine how soon a full complement of harvesters could be sent. Cap, May and Lin, an older girl on the threshold of adulthood, gathered as many harvestable plants as they could. They rolled the stalks into bunches and tied them off with hemp straps. The younger members of the group helped as they could, mainly by uprooting weeds.

Cap finally looked up at the sky and gathered the group together. "It is time to go back." The rowers returned their tools to a covered alcove in the wall. Each person bore as many of the harvested plants as they could. Cap made a quick check of the light on his box before giving his assent for them to depart the confines of the Garden.

The burden of their harvest made the return trip much more difficult. Dom was exhausted and eventually dropped what little he had been asked to carry. He complained about his fatigue repeatedly until Cap picked him up and carried him, divesting himself of part of his own load in the process. While they didn't stop to rest nearly as many times, their overall pace was much slower. The remnants of the rotation's light were nearly gone before they made it back to the beach.

They reached the top of the rise above the beach just as it was becoming difficult for them to see. "Be careful on that path," warned May. Even under the best of conditions, she knew it could be tricky. Cap set Dom down. The descent would be safer for both of them if he wasn't carrying the boy.

As the first Ward started down the path, Lin looked behind them. She dropped her bundle of stalks and stumbled slightly. "C-Cap??" she stuttered, her voice betraying her. "What is.......?" Unable to finish she pointed.

Cap turned. In the distance, he saw three balls of light bobbing across the darkness of the plain. The lights were coming directly towards them. Growing whooping sounds arose on the wind. Everyone froze.

"Go! Now!" screamed Cap. His students had never heard that tone in his voice. "Drop everything and get to the boat!" The Wards fell all over themselves trying to dump their bundles and start down the rocky path to the beach. Cap grabbed Dom by the arm and hoisted him over his shoulder. "May, go!"

May tore herself away from the sight of the approaching lights. Her Wards had started down the path so she scrambled after them. In the dark, and in their haste, the path proved treacherous. The first two Wards made it just over halfway down before tumbling forward in the darkness, leaving their knees and hands torn and bloodied. Lin was just behind them and quickly got them to their feet as they bawled in terror. She ushered them forward until all four made it to the beach. The whooping sound from the plain was growing louder.

May managed to make it down without losing her footing. Once she reached the bottom, she looked behind her. In the darkness, it was impossible to tell where Cap and Dom were.

"Cap?" she called.

Cap was still at the top of the rise, trying to gauge how long May and the Wards needed to make it to the boat. The lights were close enough now that he could see the vague outline of figures running towards him. Judging from May's voice, he guessed she had made it down. Now he had to get Dom to the bottom.

Cap started down the path, his feet sliding in the darkness. He tried to keep his weight back, towards the face of the rise, to minimize any spill he might take. He could hear the stones freed by his descent skipping down ahead of him towards the bottom. It seemed as if he had been sliding forever.

Finally, his feet hit the sand. May and the others were just standing there, looking up. Dom kept his arms locked tightly around Cap's neck, his face hidden in the man's hair.

"Get to the boat!" he implored. He turned and looked up. At the top of the path were six figures. Three of them held torches. Their lights flickered back and forth, giving Cap his first good look at them. They were short, but thickly muscled. They wore only brief cloths that covered their loins. Each of them bore a long spear half again as tall as they were. Two of them began beating the butt of their spears rhythmically on the ground as they stared downward at the group on the beach. Another approached from behind the others who stood aside to let him though. He was taller and thinner than his mates. He folded his arms and calmly looked down at Cap as the others banged their spears and bounced about.

May and the Wards dashed across the sand towards the canoe. Cap backed up slowly, waiting to see if the figures would try to come down the path. He had to make sure the others had time to get into the water and make their escape. The taller figure seemed to be studying the way down, but none of them moved. Cap turned and ran towards the canoe.

The rowers could hear them begin to yell from atop the rise. Their hooting and howling were incomprehensible. They pounded their spears together and the sound echoed across the beach. They made no effort to come down the path.

"Quickly!" screamed Cap. "Leave the barge! Man the canoe!" He tucked Dom under one arm and splashed into the lake.

The figures on the ridge continued to howl and bang their spears. Two of them frantically waved their arms as the crew of the canoe made a hasty retreat back to the lake. Cap dropped Dom roughly into the boat before producing a fragment of sharp flint from his belt. He quickly sawed through the ropes connecting the canoe to the barge before climbing aboard next to Dom.

Once they were all aboard, May demanded a furious pace. The rowers matched her requests for as long as they could. Soon, only a couple of them could continue rowing at all, so Cap bade them to stop. The boat floated along, adrift on the dark waters. Sprinkles of rain began to fall.

Cap peered into the darkness. He couldn't see the beach or the people on the rise anymore. The rowers were exhausted. They sat, hunched over in their seats, glancing questioningly up at Cap. He knew what they wanted to know. He didn't have anything to offer them. They were the Hek, but they weren't supposed to be there. At least not according to the Journeyers' box. A single blue light still shone steadily on its face, as before.

"We can rest a bit here," said May finally. "Then we will continue until we hear the drums. We aren't far from home."

Dom leaned up close to Cap. He put a comforting arm around the boy's shoulder. "Were they the Hek?" Dom asked quietly.

"I . . . .yes," Cap said finally. "I think they were."

Dom tried to close his eyes but could not. He kept staring back in the direction where he thought the rise was, the rise with the strange looking figures. He squinted at the darkness, but he could see nothing. He had only his imagination, and it pressed him tightly against Cap's warm body.

CHAPTER 3

A crowd gathered near the landing area. The return of a Journeycraft was a sacred event. The Umae could hear the hiss of the friction thrusters well before the craft appeared from beyond the heavy gray cloud cover. Its twin wings arched back from the main body of the ship. They were both outlined by bright red light – their metal highly agitated by the vast amount of friction energy they had absorbed. The mass of people moved back from the landing platform as they began to feel the heat radiating off of the ship's hull. They stood as close as they dared, waiting for something to happen. A faint rumble rolled through the cloud cover, and then it began to sprinkle. Each drop sizzled on contact with the ship. The rain built quickly into a steady downpour. Undeterred, the crowd remained.

They had seen the same thing before, not long ago. Another ship had gently lowered itself from the sky and sat there, motionless, within a circle inscribed in the stone. It had been there ever since. No one had come out. The Chroniclers had watched the ship faithfully every rotation. Nothing changed.

Once this ship set itself down, the people's anticipation surged. Surely this time would be different. The Journeyers would emerge, bringing word of the new paradise, Haven, where everyone would live. They would save their people from the sickness that had plagued them for the last ellipse. Yet, for the first two rotations, nothing. This ship sat quietly, just like the other. The people of Atla returned each morning and stayed well past dark. Their patience began to wane. The Portentists spread amongst them, offering vague guarantees of peril. The Guards moved into the frustrated crowd, trying to disperse it. Each time they succeeded, the crowd returned. This second ship had become the focal point for all their frustrations.

Towards the end of the second rotation, Min and his crew finally began to exit. As the egress ramp lowered to the ground, the raucous crowd fell silent. The Portentists slipped silently away, returning to their homes to reassess their prior conclusions. Each crew member walked briskly down the ramp, waving towards the gathered crowd. Min moved slowly, using the railing on the ramp to support himself. He tried not to betray his level of fatigue. When Min reached the bottom, he bent over at the waist, hands on his knees. As the crew waved, the people cheered ecstatically. Their Journeyers had returned to them!

Shu, Bal, and a dozen of the large Guards awaited them at the bottom of the ramp. "We will take you immediately to your quarters," said Shu. "I trust you are prepared to address the plague?" Eve and Sol couldn't take their eyes off of the Guards. Sol's mind was already racing through a list of possible explanations for their enormous statures. They were, by far, the largest Umae he had ever seen.

Min stood up straight and grimaced. "Yes, of course," he said in a strained voice. "Can I have some help getting inside?"

Bal shook his head. "I'm afraid not," he said forcefully. "You must not be seen to struggle by the crowd. I thought two days would be sufficient time?"

"I'm sick," said Min. "The rest . . . . are fine."

Shu gestured towards the Guards and issued some quick directives. Each crew member was hoisted onto the shoulders of a pair of Guards, who began to bear them away from the ship. Shu produced a small megaphone and turned towards the crowd.

"Our Journeyers have returned, as promised!" she declared. "Now we give them the welcome they so deserve." The crowd cheered madly, many of them weeping like children.

The group left the landing area and started towards a nearby pyramid. The spectators followed along at a respectful distance, their urge to embrace these saviors attenuated by the presence of the Guards. Like the other pyramids, this one was made of stone blocks. The work was so skillful that the seams between the blocks were almost invisible. Above the opening into the pyramid was a sign composed of three squares aligned horizontally. The square on the left was empty. The middle square had a single, centered vertical line with ends that didn't quite reach the edges of the square. The square on the right was like the center square, except there was also a centered horizontal line that crossed the vertical one. The inside of the pyramid was rather sparse. There was a collection of bland-colored cushions near the center. A number of lit torches extended from sconces on the walls. The Guards carried the Journeyers inside and carefully set them down on the floor. Min knelt down and sat on one of the cushions.

"Ohh......" he groaned. "I don't miss this part."

The Journeyers were noticeably smaller than their island counterparts. Min was a half-head shorter than Bal and much slighter. The Guards towered over everyone and were easily twice as heavy as any of the Journeyers. Bal and Shu remained standing as the Journeyers tried to make themselves comfortable. Bal was much older than she and his face was burdened by the weight of an intense earnestness. Shu was a rather young adult, yet she appeared prematurely troubled. She was doing her best to maintain a forced smile.

"I am Chief Chronicler Shu," she announced. "Is something wrong? Are you sick?" She studied the crew, all of whom were now reclining on the floor.

"Just me," said Min. "And I am Min. I am the ship's Command Agent. Our prior C.A., Hab, transitioned a couple of ellipses ago. Did you see a bright light in the sky two rotations back?"

"Yes!" exclaimed Shu. "What was that?"

"It agitated the Portentists a great deal," noted Bal.

"Friction activated crematory return," said Min. The Chroniclers looked at him blankly. "That is how we got rid of the body and paid tribute to him." Another group of red-garbed figures were now entering the pyramid. "As for them," continued Min indicating his fellow crew members, "they aren't sick. It is just that between the artificial gravity and the time spent in repose, our bodies have a difficult time readjusting to being on Uma. It is preferable and customary for us to remain in repose for some time after we actually land, but we had to attend to Hab. We couldn't do that this time."

"Why have you been gone for so long?" asked Shu. Her smile had disappeared and her voice was laden with concern. Min noted that her garb was somewhat different from that of the other Chroniclers. Her robe was a slightly deeper red and its hood was lined with black. "Almost five hundred ellipses."

"Our search for Haven has extended a long ways out into space," Min explained. "Each successive journey is longer than the prior one. But" he added as a fresh concern weighed on his tone, "there haven't been any other ships besides ours? What of the one that is here now?"

The Chroniclers, now huddled in a red mass, conferred with one another.

"According to our records, there have only been two returns since your ship last departed," said Shu. "And both Journeycraft are here now."

"Only two?" replied Eve. "But......there should have been others. There are eight other Journeycraft based here at Atla. Where did they.......?"

"Where are the Journeyers from that other ship?" Min's crew followed along, reflecting his concern.

"They haven't come out yet."

"When did it land?"

Bal conferred briefly with Shu. "Just over three-quarters of an ellipse ago."

"That long?" Min passed a concerned glance to Eve, who shared his expression. "All right. Once we are up and about, we'll see what the situation is."

"What of the plague?" asked Bal. "That should be your priority."

"I'll need to examine someone who is sick," said Sol. Bal turned towards the Life Agent, apparently disturbed by his interjection. "I'm Sol, the ship's Life Agent. I'm sure I can prepare a remedy, but I need to know what it is that I am remedying first."

"Very well, we shall bring someone here as soon as possible. You should address the illness before concerning yourself with the other Journeycraft."

Min leaned back, releasing an exhausted sigh. "That is our intent."

———————

The rowers had all pulled their coverings tightly around them in an effort to avoid as much of the rain as they could. It had begun drizzling steadily upon them just after they left the beach. Dom remained near the aft, staring out in the darkness. His thoughts were still of the figures from the rise. He expected one of them to leap up out of the water at any moment.

They were surrounded by complete blackness. The deep gray clouds had darkened to pitch before releasing the rain. Neither the sky nor the water's surface offered even a shimmer of light.

Cap felt around in front of him, finding Dom's shoulder. He leaned in close to the boy's head and listened. "Dom? You all right?"

"Yes," he said finally.

"Are you scared?"

"Not really."

"Are you cold?"

"I'm fine."

"We should be hearing the signal drums soon," he said. "And then we can go see the Journeyers."

They had seen the glowing craft descending from above earlier. Not even the rain, distance, or the depth of this night could completely conceal its light. Now the Wards were conflicted. They were still rattled by what they had seen on the beach but were anxious to see the Journeyers.

Dom turned to face Cap, even though he could barely make him out.

"Will there be Journeyers this time?" Dom asked. Cap remained silent for a moment. "Will there?!?!?"

"Shh......" Cap implored, giving his shoulder a squeeze. "I'm sure there will be."

"You don't know?"

"Dom," interjected May, "we don't know anything about the Journeyers for sure. The last Journeycraft was empty. I'm afraid that doesn't bode well for any of us."

Cap's scowl was lost to the darkness. "Not now, May," he growled. "You speak heresy."

"And we were nearly caught by the Hek!" she added. "Cap, even you should admit......."

"Quiet!" Cap snapped at her without intending to. May was, in his opinion, too free with her Portentist opinions. Cap pulled his collar more tightly around his neck and folded his arms.

Dom looked out in the direction he thought the land was in. "I hope there are Journeyers this time," he whimpered. "I hope they can protect us."

Cap placed an arm around Dom's shoulders. "Nothing will happen to you," he said, trying to sound assuring. But the earthquake, the plague, the empty ship...... and now the Hek. Cap felt guilty promising the boy anything.

Dom leaned back against one of the benches and closed his eyes. The light hiss of the rain hitting the water failed to soothe his irritation. He rested his chin on the side of the boat, unable to free himself from the jabbering figures atop the rise.

Eventually, the rain eased and the Wards were able to shed their hoods. They were wet, but that was a condition to which they were accustomed. Soon, they could hear a heavy thrumming sound repeating itself in the distance.

"Signal drums," said May. The Wards immediately took their positions and waited for May to begin her cadence. The sound of the drums lifted their spirits and they were eager to renew rowing. Once they heard May's directives, they began to row, propelling the boat in the direction of the drums.

———————

The *Starshine*'s crew slept. Their fatigue was such that they took no notice of the curious Chroniclers who stopped by periodically to peer into the pyramid. Outside, a steady drizzle continued for most of the rotation. Only when the last vestiges of light had nearly disappeared did the rain finally stop. Shu entered with Bal and a half dozen others bearing water, fruit, nuts, and other foodstuffs. The Journeyers sat up stiffly on their cushions and surveyed the meal.

"Careful," said Sol. "Start slowly."

Shu frowned and looked nervously at her helpers. "Is something wrong?"

"No," said Min, attempting to reassure her. "It's just that we consume so much alternative sustenance while we are in space, our bodies have to readjust to eating . . . . this." Shu nodded, despite her lack of understanding. She sat down next to

Min and stared.   "I suppose you have a lot of questions," said Min.

"Yes, is that all right?"

"It always is. What would you like to know?"

"What's wrong with you?" she asked bluntly.

"All of us have been Journeyers since we were young. While the ship provides an artificial field of gravity, it isn't quite the same as what you have here.   We are also in physical repose for most of our journeys.   That causes a certain degree of muscular atrophy and compromises our cardiovascular systems."

Bal removed a nut from a nearby bowl. "We . . . . don't really understand that."

"Where have you been?" asked Shu.

Min took a small sip of water. "I suspect that what you really want to know is if we have made any progress in locating Haven."

"Yes, of course." She leaned in closer to Min.

"No, no progress," he said finally.

"So you will have to leave again soon?" asked Bal. Min looked over at Eve, but she avoided his eyes.

"It takes a long time to find another planet that could potentially sustain us," said Jack. "The chances of finding one that is within the range of modification on any particular journey are rather low."

Bal turned slightly towards Jack but remained silent. Shu stared at the young Journeyer. "This is Jack," said Min finally. "He is our ship's Technical Agent."

"But" countered Shu, "he is just a boy."

Jack's cheeks flooded crimson. "I have more ellipses than you......" he began.

"Jack!" said Min, cutting him off. The young man sat back, holding his tongue.

"How long do you think it will be before you find Haven?" asked Shu.

Min drew a deep breath. "Based on the projections provided to us by the Directors, may they guide our way, and the number of Journeycraft involved in the search, the statistics say we should have found it already," he noted soberly. "But Journeycraft should be returning about every 50 ellipses or so. You said there have been only 2 in 500 ellipses?"

"These statistics strongly suggest their absences are not the result of random chance," noted Eve. "There must be something in common with the other missing Journeycraft."

"What does that mean?" asked Shu, picking up on Min's concern.

"The estimates I gave you are based on a total of approximately 240 Journeycraft being involved in the search," said Min. "If the other settlements are also losing ships likes Atla is…….." he loosed a disheartened sigh. "The chances of finding Haven in time become very unlikely."

Bal cleared his throat. "There is much we don't understand. Is it like this every time you return?"

"My situation is unusual," said Min. "I also suffer from a chronic condition resulting from our repose cycles." Bal plainly did not understand. "I've gotten sick from flying too much," clarified Min. "I can't fly anymore."

"How many ellipses do you have?"

"Chronological ellipses or physiological ellipses? Chronologically, I have ……… about 900 or so. Physiologically, I would estimate about sixty."

Shu studied Min. "You have . . . .900 ellipses? But . . . . how?"

Min plucked a nut from one of the bowls in front of him and studied it. "We travel extremely fast in space. While we do that, we are in physical repose about nine rotations out of ten." Noticing the woman's confusion, he added, "We are asleep. Essentially. The fact that we are . . .asleep… in conjunction with the fact that we are traveling so fast means that we age more slowly than you do. It also means that we are smaller than you are and have a hard time with physical activities when we are on planet. I know that doesn't make any sense, but that is the best answer I have."

Shu was obviously disappointed and more than a little frustrated with Min's reply.

"How long will you stay?" asked Bal.

"We need to address this disease," said Eve. "We need to supplement our crew, so we will need time to do evaluations of some of the younger members of the community to see which are suitable as Journeyer trainees. They will then be trained by us on the ship. The evaluation process should take roughly twenty-five rotations."

"We also need to check on that other ship," said Min. "And we need to do that soon, since you said it has been here for quite a long time already. Even if they were still in repose when they set down, someone should have come out by now. Did you check your histories to see who is on board, when they left, that sort of thing?"

"It is not from this settlement. That is all we could determine."

Min slumped back onto his cushion. Despite his rest, this conversation had taxed him. "At first light tomorrow, we will take a look. I doubt that any of us are up to it just now."

"And the subject Sol requested should be here soon," said Bal. "We have quarantined anyone who has become ill. When we did not, it seemed that anyone who came into contact with someone who was sick became sick themselves. If a Journeyer were to become ill, it would create a great number of difficult questions for us."

"How so?" asked Jack. He had recovered from Min's earlier rebuke. Min preferred that he remain silent but allowed this question to pass.

"You are supposedly here to save us," replied Bal. "How can you save us from something that you can't even save yourselves from?"

Sol couldn't remain quiet any longer. "Your concern for your people is touching," he told Bal. "They are a 'patient' or a 'citizen', not a 'subject', can we agree on that much?"

Bal was unaffected by Sol's comments. "Certainly," he said, turning to leave.

"I have already provided the crew with a general immunity phage that will protect them from any pathogen that wasn't already in their bodies when we landed," said Sol. Shu cocked her head. "We won't get sick," Sol assured her. "I took care of it."

The beating of the signal drums grew steadily louder as the canoe drew closer to the island. The lake was frequently covered with fog. Trips to the mainland were rare. Groups would go occasionally to tend to the plants in the Garden, but those trips were kept to a minimum. Perhaps a dozen times during harvest, the barge was taken to the shore to collect the ripened foodstuffs. This was the first such trip of the season. As it was expected that few plants would be ready for harvest, only Cap's small contingent was sent.

As the canoe neared the docks, the fog parted enough for them to see the Guards lined up waiting to meet them. Two other men, distinctly smaller than the Guards, slowly pounded the drums, which were made of wood with leather drawn taut on their faces. The sound of the drums could travel across the top of the water for a long distance. They served as a beacon for those traveling by boat in the dark.

Cap tossed the mooring lines to one Guard who then secured them to a thick wooden post. As the canoe drew next to the dock, the Wards began climbing out, taking their gear with them.

"We were told you had the barge," said one Guard. His tone was almost completely flat and he spoke without emotion.

"We did. But there was a problem. I need to speak with a Chronicler."

Bal was walking down the dock just as Cap spoke up. He conferred briefly with the Guard before addressing Cap.

"Where is the barge?" Cap could tell that he was rather irritated.

"We had to leave it behind," said Cap. Before he could continue, Bal interrupted.

"You what?!?" raged Bal. He clapped his hands at one of the Guards. The large man lumbered over and Bal whispered into his ear. The Guard then jogged off down the dock. "All of you must remain here for the moment. I must confer with Shu."

"Shu?" asked May. "Why would she care about this? I'm sure she is too busy to be bothered."

Bal glared at May. "You do not understand the gravity of what has happened," he said. "You will remain here." May turned towards Cap and noted that he appeared to be as concerned by this turn of events as she was.

Dom walked up next to Bal and tugged at his sleeve. "Are the Journeyers here?" he asked excitedly. "Are they?"

Bal stared down at the boy with disdain, yanking his sleeve from Dom's grasp. "Unhand me!" he spat. One of the Guards moved over and interposed himself between Dom and Bal.

"Move back," growled the Guard in a deep baritone.

Dom stared up at the Guard, who was more than twice his height. "You aren't going to tell me?" he asked Bal, trying to peer around the Guard.

"You there!" snapped Bal at Cap, "take charge of this boy. He must know his place."

"Dom, come here," said Cap calmly. "Now."

Dom was hesitant to abandon his hope that Bal would answer his question. But now the Chronicler was intent on watching the end of the dock instead of talking with him. Reluctantly, Dom turned and walked over to Cap. Cap placed a comforting arm on his shoulder.

Before too long, Shu appeared at the end of the dock along with another half score of Guards. Cap subconsciously pulled Dom closer to him. The other Wards migrated towards May. Shu and her legion quickly closed the distance to where they stood.

"You are the Rearer?" she asked Cap.

"I am one of them," he replied. Shu noted May's presence. "We must speak with you immediately. We will take you to a building where that will be done. You must not speak to anyone on the way there, upon threat of exile. Understood?"

The Wards began murmuring nervously. Dom looked up at Cap. "What's 'exile' mean?"

"Not now," he said quietly. "Certainly, Chief Chronicler. Tell us where we should go."

Shu waved at the Guards and they assumed various positions around the Rearers and their Wards. Shu turned and walked back up the dock, the entire group following along behind her.

———————

The Journeyers slept well into the morning. Bal had checked in every so often to see if any of them was stirring.

Once they were awake, Bal and the others once again presented them with fresh water, nuts, and fruit.

Min was reluctant to rise. He sat up and stretched, drawing little relief from a deep groan. Hesitantly, he rose to his feet. "Moons," he muttered. "This makes me miss the repose chamber."

His fellows were much less lethargic. They had been sleeping for almost a full rotation. As expected, their bodies were acclimating more quickly to the planet. Shu entered the pyramid. She studied Min and the others as they stretched and finished eating.

"Good waking Min of Olg and Bek."

"I have not heard those names for quite some time," he said warmly. "Thank you, Shu." Olg and Bek had been his Rearers until he had about 8 ellipses. Then, he began his studies with Hab.

"I have not had time to review any additional genealogies," she said apologetically. "But I thought that might make an appropriate greeting. I rechecked the pedigree of the other ship," she said finally. "It isn't in any of our chronicles. I can vouch for their maintenance. If the pedigree isn't in there anywhere......"

"Then it doesn't belong to this settlement," finished Min.

"But why would it land here?" asked Eve. "Unless its nav system was overridden."

"And it received its re-entry directives from one of the beacon satellites instead of the crew," offered Jack. "That is the only way it could have happened."

"All right." Min rotated his head, trying to stretch his neck muscles. "We will have to get on board then. Ideally, the crew is still in repose and they can get us caught up." Once more, he pushed himself up to a standing position. "I hope this doesn't take very long."

"The sick man Sol wanted to see is outside," said Shu. "Should I have him brought in?"

"Absolutely!" said Sol, jumping up from his cushions. His head spun slightly, reminding him of how brief his visit had been thus far. He found his pack and began searching through it.

A Guard cradle carried a man inside and set him down on the floor. The man was middle-aged with the same off-white skin and creamy hair as everyone else. He was shivering and wracked by a violent cough. He was obviously feverish and seemed oblivious to what was going on around him. The stricken man babbled senselessly.

Sol produced two metal circlets slightly larger in circumference than his wrists. In the center of each circlet stretched an opaque membrane. Sol pressed his hands into the membrane and then pushed the circlet up his forearm, locking it in place just below his elbow. He repeated the process on the other arm. The membranes adhered to his hands like a second skin. They became completely invisible. Sol then placed his hands on the man's face and closed his eyes.

Shu was intrigued by the procedure. She desperately wanted to ask questions, but didn't, noting Sol's intense concentration. Sol opened his eyes briefly, frowned, and then closed them again. Perspiration began to bead up on his forehead. Finally, he removed his hands and pulled the circlets from his arms. He was plainly shaken.

"When did this plague start?"

"Not long before the other ship landed," replied Bal.

"We must move quickly," he said, struggling to his feet. "This is an exceptionally dangerous pathogen. It is a micro strand of protein directors that takes over its host's cellular activities. If we don't do something soon, it will kill everyone on Atla."

Shu only understood the last part. "Can you . . . .stop it?" she asked fearfully.

Sol ignored her for the moment and instead addressed his fellow crewmates. "I wouldn't have thought this possible," he said. "Umae protein templates are extremely stable. That's why there is so little variation in our appearances and physiques," he added, glancing at the hulking Guard. "But those templates have a structural characteristic that this pathogen is perfectly suited to exploit. Once a certain portion of the cell's genetic material is modified, a cascade effect takes place. Change then becomes rather simple, and fast. That's why we have to act immediately. Fortunately, it isn't highly communicable or every Atlan would be dead already."

Shu was no more enlightened than she had been. "What will you do?"

Sol continued speaking to the other Journeyers. "I need to get back on the *Starshine*. I should be able to create an oral medication that will destroy the pathogen responsible for this."

"But how can we give it to our people?" asked Shu.

Sol turned, finally acknowledging her presence. "They'll drink it."

Shu shook her head. "Impossible. That would violate the Protocols. There must be some other way."

"What?" said Sol indignantly. "Weren't you listening?" The Guards in the room immediately moved forward. "If we don't do it, everyone will die."

Shu composed herself in the face of Sol's anger. "Then you must find a way to administer it to them in such a manner that they do not know it is being done," she said. "The Chroniclers will provide the explanation for what has happened."

Eve moved next to Sol and put her arm around his waist. "Do what she says," she said softly. "You can do it, right?"

Sol continued to glare at Shu. "Yes, I'll just put it into a flavor augmenter or something," he said finally. "You can sprinkle it on their food."

"Excellent. Start immediately."

"In the meantime," said Min, "Eve, you and I will try to access the other ship. We need to know what has happened there as well."

"Can I help?" asked Jack.

"Not yet, Jack. But you will soon. I want you to stay here for now."

Jack sat down on a group of cushions and stared at the floor. Bal folded his arms, noting Jack's distress. He watched silently as Shu and the other Journeyers took their leave.

"'Jack' is it?" asked Bal. Jack looked up, not realizing Bal was still there.

"Yes, that's right," he answered. His voice was weighted with disappointment.

"Do you know how long it will be before Min returns?"

"No. It depends on what they find."

"Oh my......," said Bal. "I had a question for him but didn't want to delay his departure to the other ship. Well, I suppose it can wait." Bal turned and took a slow step towards the exit.

"What sort of question?" asked Jack. Bal smiled momentarily before composing himself and turning back around.

"Do you think you might be able to help?" he asked.

"I can try." Jack's spirits were lifting.

"I'm not sure I understand what is meant by 'Critical Closure'," said Bal. "Can you explain it to me? There are references to it in our chronicles."

Jack hesitated for a moment. Min had told him not to discuss anything with the residents of Atla. Surely that didn't include a Chronicler. Jack didn't see how it could hurt anything.

"We are trying to find a new planet for our people," Jack began. "And we have to do it before the Hek reach a certain level of development. Once that happens, our projections show that they will overrun our people."

"Development?" echoed Bal. "Like what?"

"They don't raise crops, use fire, or build their own shelters," continued Jack. "Someday, far in the future, they will do all of those things. Once their technology reaches a certain level, they become a serious threat."

"They aren't a threat now?" Noting Jack's enthusiasm, Bal was playing along. "It is my understanding that they are very powerful physically, much more so than we are."

"All of the Umae settlements on the planet are protected by some sort of physical barrier. Atla, for example, is in the middle of a lake. It is far enough away from shore that the Hek can't even get here. Once they achieve the technology to bypass those barriers, they become a threat because of their physical superiority and aggression."

Bal recalled the missing barge. "So, Critical Closure just happens all at once?" Jack was motivated by Bal's confusion to provide a better answer.

"It will be very gradual," said Jack. "Before they can develop any technology, they have to evolve themselves. From what Sol has said, they shouldn't be smart enough yet to figure any of these things out. Evolution is slow."

"But how long will it be before Critical Closure happens?"

"We rely on projections from the Directors, may they guide our way, for their expected rate of development. I don't know for sure what the exact projection is. You would have to ask Eve. She is the data expert."

Bal was still confused. "So, on the day Critical Closure is reached, we should expect an armada of Hek to appear on our beaches?"

"It isn't that precise. Prior to Critical Closure, a period called 'Looming' takes place. Once Looming starts, Critical Closure could follow anywhere from something like a few hundred ellipses to a few thousand. Every group's technology, even the Heks', is accelerated by the work of a few exceptional individuals. It is impossible to predict how often such an individual might arise in a particular society. If it happens at a relatively high rate for them, the Looming period will be much shorter."

"So, once Looming starts, what can be done?" asked Bal. He burdened his voice with worry.

"Well, it means that we Journeyers will need to accelerate our search for Haven. We work on the assumption that Looming will be very short to error on the side of relative safety. In addition to finding Haven, we also need time to prepare a fleet to transport everyone. That will require us to train a great number of Umae. Because of your rules about technological improvements, we can't do that until Haven has been discovered."

"I am fully aware of the Protocols," said Bal. His words were out before he thought to censor them. He hoped they hadn't served to dull Jack's enthusiasm.

"Of course," said Jack.

Bal again turned towards the door. "It will take me some time to digest all of this information," he said. "You are very bright for your age."

Jack frowned. "I think I'm just very bright," he muttered.

Bal smiled inwardly and left the pyramid without turning around.

———————

Min and Eve returned to the landing area. A pair of Guards stood watch near each of the Journeycraft. Even with a long night's sleep, Min was still having great difficulty getting around on his own. Min entered an access code into the second ship's hull doors, and a walk ramp lowered itself down to the ground. He and Eve walked slowly up the ramp, stopping halfway to rest. At the top of the ramp, Min reactivated the walk ramp, causing it to return to the closed position. He waved his hand over a nearby panel, and the interior of the ship filled with light.

It was nearly identical to the **_Starshine_**. There were a variety of task panels spread throughout the ship, each with a chair in front of it. In the center was a larger seat that was slightly elevated. On one wall were a dozen transparent repose tubes large enough for someone to stand inside. They were all empty.

"There's no one here," said Eve quietly. "No one." Min walked over to the repose tubes. They were all sealed up tight.

"Let's see what the logs show." He sat down next to the central panel and entered a directive. He frowned as a stream of information appeared on the display. "A lot of the logs are missing," he said. "Everything from the time of the ship's last launch is gone."

"I'd like to run a bit scan," said Eve.

"For Haven data," confirmed Min. "Good idea."

The two of them traded seats and Eve placed her hand on the display. A thick blue horizontal line scrolled down the display, highlighting the perimeter of Eve's hand as it passed underneath it. She closed her eyes and concentrated. She wasn't searching for data generally, as Min had. She was trying to find any specific reference to Haven. Her training as a Data Agent enabled her mind to readily sort through and identify data relating to a specific topic. The tactile interface on the display was feeding information directly into her nervous system. Her face was a mask of concentration as she searched and searched……..

"Nothing," she said pulling away. "For whatever reason, the logs are completely clean. I don't understand it. I did get the ship's name. It is called the *Aurora*."

"This will give Jack something to do," suggested Min. "Just because the logs are wiped doesn't mean the information isn't recoverable. I'm not up to the job right now, but he might find something." He stood up slowly. "Let's look around a bit more."

They moved deeper into the interior of the ship. All of the task stations appeared to be in order. The environmental controls were undamaged and functioning properly.

Min sat down in one of the nearby chairs. "What would cause them to abandon their ship and send it back unmanned?"

Eve sat down at the station next to him. "The information agendas would prioritize the ship, and its log, over the crew. But that doesn't explain the missing log information. If they had a bio-emergency of some sort, they should have secured their data before abandoning ship, and they certainly wouldn't have wiped the logs. But the environmental controls are fine, so I don't see how that sort of emergency could have arisen."

"I wonder how much data they sent back through the tether beam," Min mused aloud. "We might be able to access some of the log information from their Chronicler Hall. It isn't far."

"The Land Bridge," noted Eve. The ship's settlement of origin had been discovered by both of them during their respective searches. "It is only a few rotations away by boat."

Min was focused on her face. She could tell his thoughts had drifted away from this ship and its data logs.

"Eve . . . . ." Min began. "I . . . .still haven't made my decision. It's hard. I hope you understand."

Eve went to him and he took her in his arms. She rested her cheek atop his shoulder. "What if all of this is for nothing?" she asked. "There are no guarantees that Haven even exists, at least not within a workable distance." She pulled him tightly towards her.

"We have to assume that it does," said Min. He took in the scent of her hair. "Because if we assume it doesn't, and do nothing, our race's destruction is simply a matter of time."

"Isn't that true anyway? Does any race last forever?" Eve held him for a moment and then withdrew. It was a clumsy, selfish question that she wished she could take back. She stepped away and lightly caressed his cheek. "We keep going in circles."

"It seems so," he said as he started for the exit. "Let's go talk to Jack."

They returned to the egress area where Min reactivated the walk ramp. They slowly walked back down to the bottom where Shu and another pair of lesser Chroniclers awaited them.

"Well?" asked Shu anxiously.

"The ship is empty," said Eve. "We need to run some tests to see what happened to the crew. That's all we know now."

Shu studied the ship as the walk ramp closed above them. "How did it land if no one is on it?"

Min leaned up against the ramp's support beam. "We will convene a council soon when my crew and I are feeling better. We will tell you what we can then."

The walk back to the pyramid proved very difficult for Min. He had to stop several times to catch his breath. Outside their pyramid, a group of people had gathered. Most of them were standing at the entrance, trying to see inside. The crowd parted for the Guards as they cleared a path for Min and Eve to enter.

Min practically collapsed onto his cushions. Eve moved over next to him, her face betraying her concern. "You need to rest. I'll have Jack go and look at the other ship."

"Remind him not to talk with anyone," Min began.

"I will," said Eve.

"And Eve?" She smiled at him as she stroked his hair. "We will figure this out. I promise." With that he closed his eyes, took a couple of deep breaths, and drifted off towards sleep.

CHAPTER 4

"Get your vacuum suit on!" implored Gull. "The docking ports aren't responding. We'll have to land on the surface. As soon as we stop, we'll need to get inside!" Olm fumbled with the connections around his head and feet. He stopped, opting to watch as Gull donned his own suit. It was jet black and covered his entire body. A round transparent helmet enclosed his head. Upon seeing Olm just standing there, Gull quickly moved over to him and secured Olm's suit for him. Gull consulted a nearby panel. "We are still holding our distance. We had a good-sized head start."

In pursuit was another, somewhat larger shuttle. Except for the size difference, it was identical to theirs. It was a perfect dark gray sphere. Ahead of them a bright crescent moon grew larger as they approached.

"Brace for landing," said Gull. "I'll get us as close to the Citadel as I can. After that, we'll have to go on foot. Without a docking port, there isn't any other way."

The shuttle's navbrain took over the controls, set for Gull's mark. Once the moon completely filled the view port, the craft began to spin. Powered by the undiluted sunlight, the thrusters deployed along its equator slowed the shuttle's descent. Just prior to contact with the lunar surface, the thrusters retracted. The craft began rolling along the smooth ground. Gyro dampeners inside the cabin kept Olm and Gull spatially oriented.

The rolling gray sphere left a stream of moon dust in its wake. It bounced repeatedly, the moon's gravity unable to maintain constant contact between ship and surface. Once it stopped rolling, Gull initiated the egress sequence and released his restraints. Olm stayed in his seat, so Gull released his restraints for him.

"Where are we going?" asked Olm into his com-piece. He was trembling.

"Follow me!" replied Gull. Another set of directives caused the shuttle's egress ramp to lower to the moon's surface.

The pair stepped down and employed long strides, taking advantage of the low gravity to bound along with steps four times their body lengths. In the distance, the hard gray walls of a large building rose from the dusty surface. Pumping their arms in synch with their strides, the two men quickly covered the ground to the base of the structure. Gull entered a code into a small panel on the exterior and a heavy door slid to one side. Once they entered, the slab then returned to its original position sealing them inside.

The area on the far side was entirely dark. Gull began activating the controls on his wrist lamp. "We need to be sure that this place is sealed. Then maybe we can......."

The floor heaved beneath them, throwing them both to the ground. The echoes of an explosion rattled around the insides of their helmets. Gull blinked hard, trying to regain his senses. Finally, he managed to activate his wrist lamp. He saw Olm trying to pull himself to his feet.

"What happened?" asked Olm.

Gull looked up at the ceiling, mindful for any falling debris. "The other shuttle . . . ." he said finally. "It must have crashed into the side of the Citadel."

Olm seemed unphased by Gull's announcement. "Where?"

"We'll have to go see. A better question is 'why?'" He shined his lamp down the corridor. "I doubt anyone could have survived that."

"We should find out," suggested Olm. "Don't you think?"

"We don't have much choice," he conceded, quietly assured that his belief about their survival was correct. "That way," he said, pointing in the direction of the explosion. The two men walked off down the darkened corridor, uncertain about what they were going to find.

Jack stood in front of the alpha panel of the *Aurora*. He pulled up a diagram of the ship's schematics on the screen. This ship was very similar to the *Starshine*. The efficiency of its fusion thrusters was a bit lower. The augmentation array for the beacon signals wasn't as powerful. This ship also didn't have quite the same range as the one he journeyed on. The *Starshine*'s technology was much more refined.

He tried to access the logs. As Min had described, the logs were gone except for those recorded prior the ship's last liftoff from Uma. He opened a box and began searching through the various implements inside. He had to determine whether the logs were overwritten with junk or simply erased. That would dictate his approach to recovering the information.

"Moons," he grumbled under his breath. They had been erased. Retrieving buried data was a much simpler task than "unerasing" the logs. The signature on the erasure command was given not quite an ellipse earlier. It originated from . . . the forward shuttle?

Jack left the panel and walked towards the front of the ship. The doors to the shuttle dock were closed, as he expected. He opened them and looked around. The shuttle dock was empty. He activated the voice command function of the alpha panel.

"When did the forward shuttle depart?"

The ship was silent momentarily. "No information," replied the hollow voice of the ship.

"How many crewmen were aboard?"

"No information."

"Moons!" he cursed. There were three other sets of shuttle dock doors next to these. "Did any of the other shuttles depart?"

"No information."

Jack groaned. "Current status then. Are any other shuttles missing?"

Again, momentary silence. "This vessel is fitted with 4 shuttle craft. The forward shuttle and the port shuttle are currently . . . . .unaccounted for."

Jack moved to the doors for the port shuttle dock and opened them as well. The port shuttle was absent. "Well, at least the ship's processor seems to be working all right," said Jack. "I can guess where this is going, but . . . .did the shuttles leave at approximately the same time?"

"No information."

"Based on schematics, how many crewmen can each missing shuttle hold?"

"The forward shuttle has a maximum capacity of 6, and the port shuttle has a maximum capacity of 2."

Jack walked back to the alpha panel. He was concerned about how recently the erasure command had been entered. There was some chance he could retrieve ghost images of some of the older data since its imprint had been in place longer. The newer information, say, anything less than a dozen ellipses, would likely be gone for good. Jack dug into his box and set his tools on the panel. If the data was there, he was going to find it.

———————

Olm's nostrils twitched in protest. The stimulant being added to his air supply had a sharp, stinging odor. As the frequency of the electrical waves in his brain increased, the ship lowered the ratio of the stimulant in his repose tube. His eyes opened. As always, there was an indeterminate period of complete disorientation. His heart rate slowly increased and his vision started to focus. He turned his head to one side, then the other. He was waking up. He was still in his repose tube. Beyond that, he knew nothing.

He took a deep breath. The ship was stimulating his major muscle groups to encourage circulation. He could feel a weak, tingly sensation sweeping over his arms and legs. He flexed his hands and tried to clear his throat.

"Status?"

A small panel lit up in front of him. "Seventy-eight percent. Are you experiencing any unusual sensations?" read the panel. The ship's directives limited the *Aurora's* communications with someone just awakening to solely visuals as one of its checks on neurological status.

He took another deep breath. "No," he said. "Why am I being awakened?"

The panel erased its prior message. "Eighty-six percent." He wouldn't get any answers until he was fully awake.

Olm closed his eyes and waited. Aside from the dryness in his throat, which was typical, he felt good. "Ninety-nine percent. Prepare to exit."

The transparent door in front of him slid quietly to one side. He stepped forward onto the ship's deck. It was mostly dark, although his vision was beginning to adjust. It was quiet and he saw no one else. He looked at the repose tubes next to his. There were four and another crew member occupied each.

Olm walked over to his panel. As the ship's Life Agent, there were a very limited number of reasons why the ship would ever awaken him first. He activated his panel and made another status request.

"There are five crewmen, four are in repose. Only Life Agent Olm is currently conscious." Unscheduled repose termination only happened if the ship determined that a situation existed requiring action from a crew member. Ninety percent of those situations were priority circumstances for the Command Agent. The others involved ship functions requiring the Technical Agent. The Life Agent almost always stayed in repose longer than any of the other crew members.

"Why did you end my repose?" he asked finally.

The ship switched to audio communication. "The ship is encountering a life form. There is a ninety-six-point seven percent likelihood that it is attempting communication."

Olm leaned back in his seat. A light flutter skipped through his chest. "Why . . . .how . . ?" he stammered. "Why have you determined a likelihood of communication?"

"Ordered electro-magnetic waves directed at the ship's hull consistent with communication patterns. They are not sufficiently energetic to compromise hull integrity."

"Can you show me what the form looks like?"

"Negative. It is not currently within the range of the ship's exterior scanners."

Olm frowned. Even as a Life Agent, he appreciated the tremendous distances the ship's scanners were capable of reaching. "If it is so far away, why did you end my repose? Why didn't you end it when it got closer?"

"It is not within the minimum range of the ship's exterior scanners."

"The minim-"........ Olm stood up and apprehensively studied the interior of the ship.

"Where in the moons is it?"

"Based on the energy levels of its emissions, and its absence from the minimum range of the ship's sensors, there is a 99.2% likelihood it is attached to the hull of the ship."

———

Fortunately for Jack, the crew of the *Aurora* hadn't followed maintenance procedures to the letter. When a shuttle departs, the launch sequence should have included a command to the mother ship to dissipate the gasses emitted into the bay by the shuttle's thrusters. Jack scanned the interior of both empty shuttle bays. The gasses had not been properly cleared and now atoms from the gasses had formed weak bonds with the atoms on the inside of the shuttle bays. There were standards available that allowed him to more accurately determine the amount of time that had passed since the bonding took place. The shuttles had both launched within the past eight-tenths of an ellipse. That was very close to the time when the Chroniclers had said the *Aurora* had landed on Uma. However, that told him very little about where the ship was when the shuttles launched. A Journeycraft could cover a lot of space in that time.

Once he was done analyzing the bonds on the bay walls, Jack walked back to the bay's ladder so he could re-enter the main area of the ship. A small brown spattered pattern at the foot of the ladder caught his eye. He knelt down to examine it. He didn't want to risk touching it until he knew what it was. He passed his sensor over it.

"Is this a maintenance substance of some sort?"

The sensor was inert for a moment. "There is no such substance required to operate and maintain a Journeyer starship."

"Well, tell me what's in it then."

"It is an entirely-desiccated mixture. The principal component was liquid water. It also contains a significant proportion of proteins and a complex molecule surrounding a central iron atom."

Jack poked at the stain and then rubbed his fingers together. His fingers were still clean. He had endured enough of Sol's life science training to recognize the sensor's description. The stain on the floor was dried blood.

———————

Olm stood outside Kat's repose chamber, waiting for her to regain consciousness. As Command Agent of the vessel, she had to be advised of the situation. Her eyes opened and she blinked a few times, shaking off the lethargy of repose. Once the chamber door opened, she stepped down to the deck.

Olm repeated to her the information the ship had provided him. "Have you done any supplemental scans?" she asked.

"No, not yet. Whatever it is, it is inside the effective range of the ship's sensors. I'm not capable of modifying them."

"I'd rather not awaken Gram until we have to. Hopefully, Gull can do it. Panel, how close are we to Uma?"

".43 average planetary distances." Kat's eyes widened at the reply.

"We are practically home!" said Kat. "We don't have a lot of time. We'll have to awaken Gram, we can't risk it otherwise. Gram can do the sensor modifications faster than anyone. And you say the panel thinks it is communicating?" They both turned and looked at the second repose tube. Inside was a young adult male with bright white hair.

"I can't tell you what to do about Ath," said Olm, looking at the young man in the tube. "He is unpredictable."

Kat entered the commands to terminate Gram's repose. "But he is also best-suited to determine if this creature is trying to talk to us," countered Kat. "Is he dangerous?"

"Psychologically, maybe. Physically, hard to say. There are four of us and only one of him."

"I don't think we can count on Gram," said Kat. "She was rather debilitated before we last entered the repose cycle."

Olm watched as Gram's repose tube began the gradual process of waking her from her deep sleep. "And she won't be any better now," he offered quietly. "You are the Command

Agent. I can be sure to have some counter measures prepared in case Ath acts up again."

"Very well," said Kat finally. She entered the command to awaken Ath as well.

Gram was significantly older than the others on board. Her hair was long, nearly reaching the middle of her back, and pure white. Her face bore deep lines around her eyes and her neck was covered with loose skin. Gram had been the Technical Agent on this ship since before any of the others had come aboard. Once her cycle was completed, she stepped hesitantly from her chamber, grasping Olm's arm for support. Her student, Gull, was already out of his repose tube and looked on with concern.

Olm looked her over and took a quick series of readings. "Sit," he told her.

"I'm fine . . ."began Gram.

"Sit!" Olm insisted.

"Yes Gram," agreed Kat. "Sit."

Gram hesitantly complied and Olm began a more detailed examination. As he finished, he sat down next to her. "How do you feel?"

She looked at Kat before glancing suspiciously at Olm. "Like I have been in repose for two hundred odd ellipses."

"Two hundred forty-six" said Olm. "Your respiration is severely compromised. Your metabolism is breaking down."

Gram's demeanor remained unchanged. "So what do we do about that?"

Olm lowered his eyes. "There isn't much we can do, I'm afraid. I would estimate that you have about 5 rotations. But" he added quietly, "we should reach Uma before that."

The old woman leaned forward in her seat and smiled. "Well, that's something. I've missed that sea air. Why am I even awake?"

Ath's chamber signaled that his cycle was nearly complete as well. Once the door opened, he stepped out and surveyed those standing nearby. He was obviously displeased at seeing the other crew members. Ath was rather tall for a Journeyer. His eyes darted back and forth from person to person. He was the ship's Data Agent. Information analysis was second nature to him. He had already determined that everyone looking at him was full of hostility.

"In sum, we have a life form attached to the hull of the ship," said Kat. "It is apparently trying to talk to us," she added, looking at Ath.

"Have you activated any of my translation matrices?" he asked eagerly. His countenance brightened immediately. "I would suggest . . . "

"Don't suggest," interrupted Kat. "Just do. I want to know what this creature has to say."

Without a reply, Ath bounded off towards his panel.

"As for you," said Kat, turning towards Gram. Kat hesitated for a moment. She detected no fear or worry from her elderly crewmate. "We need for you to reduce the effective minimum range of our scanners. Before we try to talk to it, I want to know as much about it as we can."

Gram rose, still a bit unsteady, and placed a hand on Kat's shoulder. "Consider it done." She slowly shuffled off in the direction of the Tech panel as Kat and Olm watched.

"Olm, once the scanners are ready, I want you to gather as much information about this creature as you can. I don't even care if you can't analyze all of it, we can do that later. We need to figure out how to detach it as soon as possible. We still have to prepare for that short-range data transfer to the beacon satellite. Everything is secondary to that Haven data. Everything."

———————

Jack finished his work inside the ***Aurora*** and began walking back to the pyramid where he and his fellow Journeyers were housed. Although it had been almost 500 ellipses since he had been on the island, the nature of his travels and the repose cycles made it seem like weeks. The daily activities of his people looked exactly as he remembered them. Some tended small gardens, maintaining a number of fruit and vegetable plants to contribute to the island's food supply. Rearers monitored groups of children. As he passed, the children stared openly. His small size and unfamiliar dress made him stand out. The adult Rearers tried, but mostly failed, to remain more subtle in their own observations.

There was a group of men standing outside of one pyramid, watching him closely as he approached. There were four of them, two plainly older than the others. The two older men stood with their arms folded in front of them. They both coughed repeatedly. The younger men seemed fit. Jack guessed that the older two must have the plague that Bal had spoken about. Jack was surprised when one of the younger men stepped out, blocking his path. The man, albeit younger than his companions, appeared to be older than Jack. Jack stopped, waiting for the man to say something.

"You are a Journeyer?" asked the man. He was plainly nervous. That made Jack nervous in turn.

He wasn't sure what to do. Eve had warned him against interactions, but he couldn't just walk away. "Yes. My name is Jack."

The man relaxed a bit. "Are the Journeyers going to come here?" He gestured towards the opening to the pyramid.

"Here?" asked Jack, seeking clarification.

"Inside," said the man.

Jack stepped around the man. The other three were watching him with great interest. Jack looked inside the pyramid. He was immediately met with a strong odor of wood smoke. It was difficult to see very far, as a haze hung in the air within. There were a half dozen men standing around a pair of long tree trunks that had been stripped of their limbs. They were adding coals to the top side of the trunks, slowing burning away an interior cavity. Now Jack remembered. This was how his people fashioned their canoes. He stepped out, giving his eyes a moment to recover from the sting of the smoke.

"Well?" said the man.

"I don't know," he said hesitantly. "Do you need something?" The older two men immediately began coughing. Jack gave them a moment to regain their composure. "We are going to . . . .remove . . .the plague," he said finally. Jack wasn't confident in his ability to remain within the bounds of his directives. He had likely said too much already.

"Plague?" said the young man. "Oh. Yes. But, they don't have the plague," he added, gesturing to his companions. "They have been like this for . . . ." he looked to his companions for assistance.

"Two ellipses," said the first.

"Not quite two," said the second.

The younger man continued. "Those with the plague don't last more than ten rotations or so," he explained. "Can you help us?"

Jack needed to think quickly. Now he understood why Min was hesitant to let him circulate through the settlement alone. "Help . . .will be provided," he said finally. "But we must determine the best way to address this need. I will consult with my fellow Journeyers. How many of you are stricken?"

The two older men took heart from his answer and nodded. Seeing their relief, the two younger men smiled as well. "Eighteen," said one. "Please, can you hurry?"

"Of course," said Jack, trying to sound reassuring. He moved past the men and continued back to the pyramid.

When he arrived, the entire crew was present. Min was asleep. The others were resting. Another collection of foodstuffs and water had been delivered. In addition to the nuts and fruits from before, there were mushrooms, fresh vegetables, and flat squares of brown crackers.

Eve looked up as Jack entered. Sol was closely examining one of the crackers.

"Well? Any success?" asked Eve.

Jack sat down and poured himself a cup of water. "Some. The logs are mostly unrecoverable. The crew disembarked in two of the shuttle craft. I was able to calculate a range within which I would expect to find them. It's a big area though."

Eve cocked her head. "Really? Shuttle craft? Why would they leave the ship unmanned like that? It doesn't make any sense."

"I agree. The logs weren't much help. I did find traces of blood in one of the shuttle bays." He reached into a small bag at his waist and withdrew a clear vial. Inside were some scrapings he had taken of the blood stain.

"Can I see that?" asked Sol, pointing to the vial. Jack handed it to him.

"The scanner I had could only identify its chemical composition. I know it is blood, but that's about it."

Sol opened the vial and scanned it with his own apparatus. "It's Umae blood," he said. "And its genetic markers are intact. It belonged to a woman."

"I was able to recover some residual entries from the logs," said Jack. He looked over and noted that Min was still sleeping. "Of the information that I could recover, it seemed like there was an unusual amount devoted to their search for Haven."

"What do you mean?" asked Sol.

"The more information that was recorded about a specific topic, the more likely information about that topic would be recoverable, assuming the purge wasn't targeted to any information specifically," noted Eve.

"Simple probabilities," added Jack. "But most of the data that gets logged involves ship functions, crew health, research — that sort of thing. It seems strange that so many references to Haven were made."

Eve looked down at Min. "Unless they found it," she said quietly. "Then it would make all the sense in the world."

"You are suggesting they found Haven?" exclaimed Sol.

"IF they did," said Eve, emphasizing merely the possibility, "they would have recorded the data as redundantly as possible. It would have been recorded numerous times, and in numerous ways, within the logs. It would have been transmitted multiple times through the tether and then multiple times through the short-range transfer beam. That information, if they had it, is the entire reason why we are doing what we are doing."

"They weren't close enough for the short-wave transfer. I can tell you that much," said Jack. "So if it went through the tether, it's in the panel of the Land Bridge's Chroniclers' Hall."

Eve stood up. "Let Min sleep but fill him in as soon as he awakens. I'm going to go and talk to Shu. She will need to know this immediately. Jack, was there any detail to the data, or just simple residual references?"

Jack shook his head. "Nothing specific at all. Just the references."

"All right," said Eve as she walked towards the door. "I'll be back soon." She then departed for the Chroniclers' Hall.

Jack sat down and examined the offerings for dinner. "A group of Umae stopped me on the way back," he told Sol. "They asked for help."

"What kind of help?" asked Sol. "I hope you said all the right things."

"So do I," Jack replied. "A couple of the older men had some sort of sickness. They coughed a lot but said it wasn't the plague. That's what they wanted help with."

"Boat wrights?" asked Sol.

"How did you know?"

"Another price these people pay for all of these directives. They make their canoes by burning out the insides of the boats. They have to do it inside because of the rain. Exposure to all of that smoke damages their lungs."

"Why do they make canoes like that?" asked Jack. "Even with rudimentary tools........."

"You tell me," interrupted Sol. "Keep in mind, preventing technical advancement is the goal."

Jack thought some more. "Well, fire is . . . .fire. It is always the same. There aren't really a lot of ways to improvise or advance that technique."

"Exactly," said Sol. "And tools?"

"What sort of tools?" asked Jack. "Axes, scrapers, chisels . . . .all could be used. You could use wooden tools, stone tools . . . ."

"Some are better for certain jobs than others?" asked Sol.

"Of course."

"And how would they know which tools were better for what purpose?"

"Trial and error." Jack was beginning to see Sol's point. "That would tend to encourage innovation though."

"Right again," said Sol. "And like you said, 'fire is fire'. No innovation possible, even if it means that the boat wrights eventually die from respiratory diseases."

Jack's shoulders slumped. "You figured all of that out pretty well for a Life Agent," he said.

"No, I didn't," he admitted. "Min explained it to me. But" he said standing up, "after I check on the plague remedy I'm making on the *Starshine*, I'll pay a visit to the boat wrights' pyramid to see if I can help." For a moment, Jack thought he could see a hint of despair in the old Life Agent's eyes. "I always do."

"He said there were eighteen," said Jack.

"Eighteen?" echoed Sol. "Eighteen what?"

"Eighteen boat wrights who were stricken. They said it wasn't the plague."

Sol frowned. "That can't be correct," he said. "There can't be that many boat wrights on Atla. Why would they need so many?"

Jack shook his head. "That's what he said."

"I don't doubt you," said Sol. "Eighteen? And that's just the sick ones." He picked up his bag. "I wonder what they are doing with all of those boats."

———————

Gram had settled into her station and started to work on decreasing the minimum range of the ship's sensors. The technology wasn't the problem. Great technological advances had been required to extend the maximum sensory range to its current limit. There had never been much of a need for minimum range scans, so the issue had been given much less attention. Gram had few problems in making the necessary adjustments.

Ath's situation was a bit more problematic. He had done as much as he could in attempting a translation of the beam of electro-magnetic radiation that the creature was bouncing off of the ship's hull. There was still a significant amount of static that he couldn't attribute to the creature outside. Since the organism was completely unknown, what he viewed as "static" could actually be intrinsic to the communication. Ath needed to know exactly what was coming from the creature and what wasn't.

Kat moved up next to Ath and looked at Gram's display. "Any progress?"

Gram drew a deep breath and returned her attention to her work. "Yes. I decided to try a wave fold routine to recalibrate the sensor range. By reducing the maximum range by approximately 3%, we can now actually scan the interior of the ship with the exterior scanners." She looked back up at Kat. "How is that for minimum range?"

Kat couldn't help but smile. "Outstanding. So, Olm and Ath can begin now?"

"No. I did a preliminary test scan on whatever that is out there. The test results suggest that it is coated with something that causes the sensor's waves to scramble once they interact with it. I have never seen anything like it."

Kat summoned her Life Agent. Olm rose from his station and joined his three crewmates.

"Are we ready?" he asked.

"The creature is coated with something that interferes with the scans. Are you familiar with anything like that?" asked Kat.

Olm looked at Gram's display. "Only in theory," he said after a moment. "If this creature spends a significant portion of its life cycle in space, it would have to have some sort of ability to counteract all of the radiation it would be exposed to. The sensor waves are just another form of radiation. It may be that it reflects all radiation except those frequencies that it needs for its life functions."

"How difficult would it be to scan at different frequencies?" Kat asked Gram.

Gram leaned forward and rested her head in her hands, bracing her elbows on the surface of her workstation.

"Gram?" Olm took a quick scan of her.

"I'm . . . . .fine," the elderly woman said, sitting up. "Tired."

Olm looked at his scanner. "Not surprising."

"We can scan at almost any frequency," said Gram. "Some are just more efficient. But I don't know . . . .which ones this thing doesn't like."

Olm patted Gram on the back. "That's it! Since all of this is theory, it may be that it isn't the frequency of the radiation involved, but the total energy. If this creature's metabolism is flexible enough, its 'defense' may just kick in when the total energy of the radiation around it reaches a certain level."

"So we would need to reduce the radiation that it is experiencing so that it wouldn't 'defend' against the scans," said Kat.

"Exactly."

"Any suggestions on how we might do that?"

Gram shifted the display from a schematic of the sensors to one of the interior of the ship. "We can't just turn down the general level of radiant energy in space, so we will need to shelter it somehow."

"With the ship," said Kat.

"Yes, with the ship."

"You aren't suggesting that we bring it aboard without knowing anything about it?" asked Olm.

"No," replied Gram. "But we could try to get it into one of the shuttle craft hangar bays. That would provide it with almost complete insulation from radiation outside the ship. If your theory is correct, we should then be able to scan it all we want."

"And if it's not?" asked Olm.

"Then," said Kat, "we would need a way to get rid of it."

"We can't get rid of it now," said Olm. "We are supposed to be home very, very soon. Are we supposed to land with it still perched on our hull?"

"What do you mean 'we can't get rid of it?'" asked Kat.

"This creature managed to attach itself to our ship while we were traveling, how fast?"

"Seventy percent of light," said Kat.

"And we know it has a huge resistance to radiation and that it is intelligent enough to attempt communication," added Olm. "I'm not a Technical Agent, but I'm guessing we don't have anything aboard that is likely to remove it without outright killing it."

"I doubt we could remove it at all," said Gram wearily. "Alive or otherwise, and I AM a Technical Agent."

Kat folded her arms and closed her eyes. "All right," she said finally. "Let's see if we can get it into a hangar bay. I want the bay door's seals examined before we do that. I don't want an *electron* to be able to squeeze through those doors if we don't want it to. At least if we have to land while it is still on board, we can keep it contained."

She again gently placed her hand on Gram's shoulder. "I don't want you to do any of that manually. Have the ship automate as much of the work as possible and ask someone else to do whatever else needs to be done. Including me if you have to."

Gram started to protest. Her fatigue and the resolute glare in Kat's eyes convinced her not to. She began entering directives into her panel.

"Olm, a word," said Kat.

The two walked back to Kat's alpha panel. Kat sat down and made certain no one else was within hearing range.

"Doesn't it seem astronomically unlikely that this creature just happened to run into us in the dead of space?" she said in a low voice.

"Yes, and no," he replied. "Again, speaking theoretically, this creature necessarily has adapted to deal with the reality of a high-radiation existence. Such a creature would necessarily have to be very sensitive to radiation of all sorts."

"I'm not following."

"We are following the beacon signal," said Olm. "It is simply a high-powered beam of ordered radiation. My best guess is that this creature was doing the same thing."

"What? Like . . . .following a scent?" said Kat.

"Something like that. The frequency of the signal might interest it for some reason. It could be attracted to it, or . . . ."

"It could be hungry," added Kat.

"Yes. That is another possibility. But without the scans, we can't be sure." Olm looked back at Gram as she entered her directives.

"Do we have any ideas about how long it has been out there?"

"No," said Olm. "Not really. The ship didn't awaken me until it detected what it believed to be an attempt at communication. The organism could have been out there enjoying the ride for quite some time until it decided to start talking for some reason."

"This creature is sentient and hasn't taken any overtly hostile actions against us," said Kat. "So we can't just kill it. But we can't make any determinations about its intentions without scanning it. And we can only scan it if it is inside the hangar bay."

"That is about the size of it," concurred Olm.

"Any suggestions about Gram?"

The Life Agent sighed. "Not any based-on science. Aside from her fatigue, she isn't in much discomfort. She seems resigned to the situation. It may be best to just let her do what she can. At least she will get to see Uma one last time."

Kat tapped her finger absently on her chair. "Very well. Get your scans ready. As I told you before, I want to know every last detail about that thing. Don't leave anything out. We don't have that much time before we are supposed to return. I'll start preparing for the short-range data transfer. If ever there were a worse time to encounter a sentient life form..........."

Olm turned and walked off towards his station. The information they had was far too important for anything to go wrong now.

It was a long walk from the Journeyers' pyramid to that of the Chroniclers. It was easily the tallest pyramid on the island. Unlike the others, it had a long metallic needle projecting from its apex.

Eve was conscious of all the glances that were directed at her as she walked along. Umae engaged in conversations suddenly stopped upon her approach. She tried to make some attempt at eye contact, but these return encounters always made her nervous. After all, she didn't know anyone on the island. Everyone who had been alive during her last visit had long since died. The Umae also bore such incredible expectations of Eve and her crewmates.

The Chronicler Hall was much more elaborate than the other structures. The frame of the main door was elegantly decorated in designs carved into the stone. Some of the designs showed faded remnants of color that, at one point, must have been striking. Along the top was a familiar set of symbols. At the far left was an empty square – "absent". In the center was a square with a single vertical line in the center, its ends equidistant from the top and bottom of the square – "alone". On the right was a square identical to the one in the center, except a horizontal line had been added that crossed the vertical line at its center – "not alone". The symbol on the right brought Eve some measure of comfort. Despite the fact that she was not familiar with any of the individuals currently living on the island, she was with her people. She was different, and a stranger. But she was also an Umae. She was not alone.

As Eve approached the main door to the Hall, two Guards stepped into her path. They said nothing, their huge forms barring her progress.

"I . . . . need to speak with Shu," she said uncertainly.

The men studied her for a moment. "You are a Journeyer," said one.

"Yes." She assumed he had asked a question. The men held their positions but said nothing. "Can I see her?" she asked meekly.

One of the men turned and went inside. The other took a step to the side so as to be directly between Eve and the doorway. "No one except Chroniclers and their staff may enter the Hall," he said. The man standing in front of her was enormous. Most of the inhabitants of the island were of similar size. While the males were slightly larger on average, the difference was minimal. Eve's head was level with the bottom of this Guard's breastbone.

"Is that man . . . . I'm sorry." She chuckled nervously. "I am Eve. Is that man getting Shu?"

The guard's expression didn't change. "Yes. I am Lod."

"Lod," echoed Eve. She looked away and tried to calm herself.

"Greetings Eve of Hap and Vil," came a familiar voice. Shu stood at the door with the other Guard. "You need to speak with me?"

"Yes." Eve felt relieved. The presence of the Guards made her uneasy. "Can we go somewhere?"

"Certainly. Why don't we walk?"

The water's edge was not far, so the women walked in that direction. Neither said a word until they reached the beach. A few water birds were scrambling back and forth, dodging the small waves that came in. In the distance they could see a group of people pulling a cart filled with newly harvested hemp.

"The Guards. They are so big."

"Yes," said Shu plainly. "Is that unusual?"

"Well, yes, it is. They haven't always been like that. They weren't like that the last time I was here."

Once again, Shu looked off into the distance. "Interesting. They have been that way since I can remember." Shu sat down on a large rock. "Sit." Eve obliged. "What did you need to speak about?"

Eve looked around. "We can speak openly here?"

"Yes. Our fellow citizens understand that when a Chronicler is in conversation, they must avoid overhearing what is said. They understand the same about a Journeyer. I can only imagine what they must be thinking now, with the two of us talking to one another." Shu smiled and appeared pleased at the concept.

Eve hadn't had an opportunity to sit down and speak with Shu face-to-face. She was surprised by her apparent youth. "You are awfully young," she noted finally. "For a Chief Chronicler, I mean."

Shu's cheeks flushed slightly. "I am," she admitted. "According to our records, I have fewer ellipses than any Chief in our history." Her last statement was tinted with embarrassment. Shu broke eye contact with Eve and looked out at the lake.

"Well, you must be very talented then," said Eve. "How long have you been Chief?"

"Over an ellipse," said Shu, still not choosing to look at Eve as she spoke. "It was shortly after the ground shook. The previous Chief, Earl, was a casualty. He had named me as his successor shortly before his death."

Eve remained silent, waiting for Shu to turn back towards her. Once she did, Eve spoke up again. "Were there many deaths? Someone had mentioned the shaking, but we don't have much information about it."

"His was the only one," she said. "He was alone in the Hall when it happened. Apparently, he either fell or something fell on him. He suffered a serious injury to his head. He had already died when Bal found him." She lowered her eyes.

"You were close?" asked Eve softly.

"Yes. He had been my teacher," said Shu. "I struggle each day attempting to preserve his legacy."

Eve reached out and gently placed her hand on Shu's shoulder. "He chose you for a reason, I'm sure. If you were a danger to his legacy, he would have chosen someone else."

Shu took a deep breath and forced a smile. "It was a surprise, being named Chief. We didn't find out until after he died. Everyone had assumed that Bal would be his successor."

"Why so?"

Shu wiped a hint of moisture away from her eye. "He had been Earl's Adjutant as well. It is traditional that the Adjutant becomes Chief when the Chief dies, although it is not required. I don't think Bal was pleased when he found out he would not become Chief."

"Did he say something?"

Shu remained silent for a moment, trying to determine the appropriate way to answer the question. "Bal is extremely skilled in the use of our panel. His ability to safely extract information from it is remarkable. Apparently Earl became concerned that Bal was spending too much time doing that. He suggested that Bal take charge of the Chronicler Guard, as a diversion. This, of course, was before my time."

"'Safely'?" asked Eve. "Is there some danger involved in the panel's use?"

Shu could see nothing inappropriate in Eve's question. "Yes. There is an enormous amount of information stored in the panel about almost every possible subject. We Chroniclers train for a very long time to enable our minds to only be open to discrete bits of information when we operate it. If we are unskilled, or if we seek to access information that is too complex or detailed, there is a risk that the information surge could overwhelm the operator's mind. The result would be....grave."

"'Complex or detailed'", continued Eve. "Like scientific data?"

Shu was near the edge of what she was comfortable disclosing. "No, it applies mainly to historical information. Some events are minor and have little if any long-lasting impact. They are harmless. Others are central to our history. They can be perilous if sought incorrectly or by the wrong person."

"We have studied the other ship. We know it launched from the Land Bridge settlement. It is called the *Aurora*. It seems the crew may have gained some potentially significant information about Haven's location."

"They found Haven?" asked Shu excitedly.

Eve looked about to see if anyone else had noted Shu's outburst. "We don't know," she said quietly. "The specific information was . . . .damaged. But we think there is a good likelihood that the information would still be at the Land Bridge community."

"From the tether signal," added Shu. "It's very possible. Is this community nearby?"

"It is about three rotations by water. We need to go there," said Eve. "It could be very important."

"Impossible," said Shu.

Eve was stunned. "But why? This is vital information."

"The Protocols prohibit a Journeyer from entering any settlement other than his own. Otherwise, it would render our exile laws meaningless as it applies to Journeyers. They could just go to another settlement."

"Journeyers can be exiled?" asked Eve.

"Anyone . . . .can be exiled," noted Shu coolly. "You will have to get the information some other way."

Eve's anger heated in response to Shu's formal tone. She collected herself and continued. "Can you tell me if there has there been any contact with any of the other settlements?"

"No. The Hek prohibit that. It is too dangerous. They are powerful, vicious brutes. They would kill us on sight."

"I remember the stories," said Eve. "So, how long has it been since you had any information about the other Umae?"

"I would have to research that to give you a specific answer. I would estimate that it has been several thousand ellipses at least."

Eve couldn't believe what she had heard. "So, you know nothing about what has happened on this planet, aside from this island, for the last several thousand ellipses?"

"Correct. Even the mere sight of the Hek is a basis for exile. Anyone, save a Chronicler, who encounters the Hek is subject to banishment. We have constantly educated our people about how deadly they are. That has served to keep them away from the mainland. The Directive keeps the Atlans safe and prevents us from needlessly losing citizens."

"Are you concerned about the size of the population on Atla?"

Sitting back Shu cleared her throat. "The general Protocol is that no one can enter our society without the approval of the Chroniclers. We are required to maintain our population as close to 2000 as we can."

"But I thought you said you don't have contact with any other communities?"

"We don't, but our own people still give birth. As you know, the babies born to mothers who did not obtain permission prior to conception are exiled as soon as they are weaned. They do nothing to maintain the population."

"What proportion of the newborns is exiled?" asked Eve. She had already begun making calculations in her head.

"Again, I'd have to check to give you specific figures. There are several each ellipse," she stated flatly. "Over the last thousand ellipses or so the frequency has gradually risen. This makes the prohibition against encountering the Hek even more crucial."

"But they are exiled to the mainland. Doesn't that increase the chances of encountering the Hek?"

Shu shrugged. "We use the gifts the Journeyers have given us and follow the protocols."

"Doesn't that violate the protocol against killing? Just leaving the babies there to die?"

Shu stared at Eve, unblinking for several moments. "We don't know that. Do we?"

"How can you not know?" demanded Eve. "Leaving an infant all alone like that?"

Shu managed to sustain her composure. "We are not responsible for what happens to it after it is left," she explained. "We have not killed it. The Protocols instruct us so."

Eve was not convinced by Shu's explanation. "But the probabilities are….."

"Stop!" said Shu. "There is a line in the Protocols between killing and permitting death," she said finally. "We have livestock that we use for leather and food, but we do not kill the animals. These goods are not harvested until after the animal dies. It is not your place to question the Protocols, or their purpose. They were given to us by the Directors, may they guide our way. It is your place to find Haven."

"I know my place," replied Eve quietly. "Your advice is appreciated."

CHAPTER 5

Kat watched uneasily as her crew began their preparations. Gull had effectively been the Technical Agent for some time now, ever since Gram's illness had made it unwise to remove her from repose too often. He had assisted Gram as she finished the last adjustments to the sensor array. Olm and Ath stood by at their panels, waiting to see if the creature could be moved to the shuttle bay.

"Sensors. . . . are ready," Gram said. Her voice had become more of a wheeze.

"Is the integrity of the seals on the bay doors compromised at all?" asked Kat firmly.

"No," said Gram after consulting her panel. "They are as tight as they can be."

Kat couldn't shake the nagging sensation that she was overlooking something. "All right. Open the exterior bay doors. We will go from there."

"Opening bay doors," repeated Gram. Gram manipulated her panel to input the command.

"Put the bay on the alpha display," said Kat.

Her display came to life. As the exterior doors opened, she could see what appeared to be a dark brown length of rope snaking its way inside. On its end was a tan sphere about the size of her head. The sphere waved back and forth a few times before attaching itself to an interior wall. Seconds later, a much larger sphere, easily twenty times the circumference of the first, drifted into the shuttle bay. It was attached to the other end of the rope-like tether opposite the smaller brown sphere. As it entered the bay, it towed dozens of smaller spheres along behind it, each attached to its own tether. Once the large sphere was completely inside the bay, all of the smaller spheres attached themselves to the walls as the first one had done. The creature vaguely resembled an enormous brown spider with a multitude of spindly legs protruding from its round body.

"Well, that didn't take long," said Kat.

"I suspect that it needed to shelter itself from something outside," offered Olm. "When it was provided with an opportunity, it didn't hesitate."

"Is it completely inside?" asked Kat.

Gram checked her display. "Yes. Should I close the bay doors?"

Kat thought for a moment. "No. If it is intelligent, it might see that as an attempt to capture it. Will our scans be compromised if we leave the doors open?"

Gram shook her head. "Impossible to say. We don't . . . .know for certain why we couldn't scan it in the first place."

"I see. Commence scans with the doors open. If there continue to be anomalies, we will talk about approaching it another way." Kat got up, motioned for Gull to follow her, and walked to Olm's panel. "Thoughts, Olm?"

Olm was studying the preliminary data from the sensors. "It was certainly eager to come inside the ship," he noted. "There could be any number of reasons for that. It could be trying to avoid something, like radiation of some sort. It could be looking for something."

"Like what?" asked Gull.

"Food. A new lair. A place to reproduce," replied Olm. "All the basic biological impulses. Or it could be trying to demonstrate a level of trust."

"Assuming it is intelligent," said Kat.

"Yes."

"How are the scans coming along?"

Olm ran his hands over the display. "It looks like a pretty standard bio scan to me. Gram, how do the scans........." The old woman was slumped over on her panel.

Olm quickly jumped out of his chair and hurried over to examine her, Gull and Kat in close pursuit.

"Gram?" said Kat softly. "Can you hear me?"

Olm consulted his scanner. "Her metabolic decay is accelerating. The strain since her last awakening has been too much. She is no longer fit for duty." Kat turned and scowled at her Life Agent. "You know I have to tell you that," said Olm in a low voice.

"What else can you tell me?" asked Kat. She gently stroked the gray hair on the back of Gram's head.

"I have never seen a case where the patient deteriorated so rapidly. I still think she has about 5 rotations," said Olm. "But her level of function will be very low. Her cellular respiration is highly compromised. I . . . ." Kat turned and looked at him, her eyes moistening. "I wish I had more to offer."

Kat stood up, straightening herself. "Take her to her quarters," she said quietly. "Make her comfortable. Give her whatever she wants." A pair of waist-high mechs rolled into view. With delicate precision, they extended their utility arms and gently lifted Gram from her seat before rolling away with her towards the back of the ship.

"I know she has taught you a lot," said Gull. "Why don't you sit with her? The scans will take a while to accumulate any significant data."

"No, I don't think you do know." Her tone was neither bitter nor accusatory. "But I will do as you suggest. The second the scans reveal anything useful, I want to know it." Kat walked off in the direction of the crew quarters.

"How long before your scans are complete?" asked Gull.

"Well, assuming they work at all," said Olm, "a quarter rotation at most. And that is only because of the degree of analysis that Kat requested. Half that time for preliminary data."

Gull rose and walked over to where Gram had been seated. "I'll monitor the scan from here," he told Olm. "I'll let you know when it is finished."

Eve returned to the Journeyers' pyramid. Min was awake and looked a bit stronger that he had previously. Jack and Sol sat talking to Bal.

Min slowly walked over to the table and sat down on a simple wooden stool. "Jack filled me in after I woke up. What did Shu have to say?"

"I don't think she understands the immediacy of the situation," she said, looking at Bal. "It seems that a Journeyer can't enter any settlement other than his own or face exile."

"That is correct," confirmed Bal.

Min sighed and rubbed at his eyes. "Fine." His voice was hoarse and he was developing circles under his eyes. "I guess I will have to go there, then."

Eve scowled at him. "You can't be serious. You can't go anywhere in your condition."

"I have to agree, Min," Sol interjected, "you are not well-suited for travel."

"Perhaps now that Eve has returned, I can share my information with you," said Bal.

"About what?" asked Min.

"A pair of Rearers just returned from the mainland with their Charges. I was the Chronicler who recorded the events surrounding the trip. It is rather disturbing."

"Go ahead," said Min. Bal had Min's full attention.

"They went on a routine ag maintenance trip," began Bal. "After they worked at the Garden for most of the rotation, they encountered a group of Hek."

"Hek? Is there any doubt about it?" asked Min.

"None," said Bal. "Short, muscular, covered in light hair. They gave chase but the group was able to escape in their canoe. In their haste, they left their barge behind." Bal paused to ascertain the reactions of the Journeyers to this last bit of news.

"But don't they use the resonance scanners? How can that have happened?" asked Min.

"If you mean the device that is supposed to provide notice of the Heks' presence, I can only assume that it didn't work. Cap, the male Rearer, reported that the device provided no such warning."

"Where is the scanner now?" asked Min. "I want to examine it."

"Chroniclers' Hall. Of course you may do that."

"Did they give you any other specifics?" asked Sol.

"Yes. They said the Hek were using torches for light."

"That . . . .can't be," protested Min. "They aren't advanced enough yet." He looked at Sol. "Possible?"

Sol shook his head. "They should not be developed enough intellectually to use fire for several thousand more ellipses. If that information is accurate......."

"Then the projections of the Directors concerning Critical Closure, may they guide our way, aren't accurate," said Eve. She looked over at Min who was already lost in thought.

"How long has it been since any sort of survey has been performed on the Hek?" asked Jack.

"I have never seen such a survey," said Sol.

"There aren't any," said Min. "We are prohibited. Doing even a routine scan is the same as an 'encounter' for purposes of the law," he added, looking at Bal.

"That is correct," said Bal. "The Hek are to be avoided in every conceivable way. Even if a Journeyer used your technology to encounter the Hek, the Journeyer would be subject to exile once his or her Journeycraft landed."

"And how would you know that?" demanded Jack.

Min turned and stared at his pupil, causing him to draw back slightly. "The tether beam. Every Journeycraft periodically transfers informational updates to its home Chronicler Hall through the beacon satellite."

"But . . . .why?" interjected Eve. "I can understand how the Atlans are served by that Protocol, because the Hek are a direct threat to them physically. Shu advised me that the purpose of the law was to prevent the Atlans from going ashore without authorization and potentially putting themselves at risk. We could gather all of the information we wanted about the Hek from space. There wouldn't be any danger to us at all."

Bal took a deep, controlled breath. "No one is above the Protocols," he said firmly. "Not even Journeyers. Such is the will of the Directors, may they guide our way."

"But......" began Eve. Bal raised his palm.

"No......'buts'," he said. "This is not a debate."

Min had closely observed the interaction between Bal and Eve. "Back to these torches. They are certain of what they saw?"

"I am only retelling what I have been told," he said defensively. "You may speak with the Rearers themselves."

"Where are they now?" asked Sol.

"The encounter with the Hek was a Protocol violation," said Bal. "The Rearers and their Charges will all be exiled eventually. Right now they are in quarantine."

"I would like to speak with the Rearers," said Min. "And I'd like to see the resonance scanner as well."

"It will be arranged," said Bal as he stood up to leave. "Immediately." Bal turned and departed.

Eve looked around at her fellows. "Suppose something is wrong. Suppose the Hek really were using fire. What then?"

"It isn't possible, trust me," said Sol. "There is another explanation. If it is true, it would accelerate the projected date of Critical Closure by thousands of ellipses."

Min rested his elbows on the table. His eyes briefly met Eve's. She was an expert in data analysis. She knew that if the Heks' development was that far ahead of the Directors' projections, the amount of time they had left to find Haven was significantly reduced. The less time they had to find Haven, the less likely it was that they could be together.

"I do trust you," said Min. "They must be mistaken about the torch light. Once we talk to them, I'm certain we will figure it all out."

"Well Shu didn't offer much," said Eve. "The Guards have been their present size for her entire life. And no one seems to know much about what is on the mainland."

"What else did she say?" asked Min. "I have never been able to question an individual Chronicler."

"Yes," noted Sol, "Hab always did that when we came back before. And he didn't share much with us about that."

"Despite my best efforts," said Min.

"No one on Atla has had any communication with any other Umae for several thousand ellipses," continued Eve. "The Hek made it too dangerous."

"That is.....odd," noted Sol.

"What do you mean, Sol?" asked Eve.

"Because there are over forty ship wrights on Atla. I counted them when I went to address their customary respiratory diseases. I don't ever remember there being more than three or four." He looked around at his crewmates. "For a community that severely restricts trips to the mainland by its citizens, what do you suppose they have been doing with all of those boats since we were last here?"

Min sat up and tried to stretch. "I need to talk to Shu." He noticed Eve averting her gaze. "We need to know more details about the Protocols as well as the Catalcysm. This may be our only chance."

———————

Once he was advised that the creature was in the shuttle bay, Ath eagerly set himself to analyzing the signals it was emitting. His technical title was Data Analyst. His training enabled him to study large quantities of information and sort through it to find orderly relationships. His specialty, and his favorite activity, was decoding. Languages were of particular interest to him. After all, the various methods organisms used to communicate were nothing more than codes requiring a cipher.

His panel was employing a set of analytical algorithms he had written himself. He had used them to understand birds, sheep, and even insects on Uma. The prospect of trying it out on something extra-planetary was almost more exciting than he could bear.

The signals from the creature were foreign, but not particularly complex. He programmed the sound emitters in the shuttle bay to return electromagnetic pulses similar in structure to those the creature was emitting, hoping the creature would respond. The responses could then be factored into the panel's calculations, effectively allowing the creature to teach the panel how to speak to it.

For the first twelfth of a rotation, the panel and the creature exchanged what sounded like random electromagnetic "noise". Kat appeared behind Ath, studying him for a moment before speaking.

"Any progress?" she asked.

Ath hadn't noticed her approach. His eyes were closed and he had his palms placed flat against the display. His mind was searching for an intelligible response. "Hmmm?" he replied absently. "Oh. The panel is analyzing the creature's patterns. It shouldn't be much longer."

"I was expecting something by now," said Kat, a hint of irritation in her voice. "Are you using those algorithms you have told us all so much about?"

Ath continued to focus on the screen. "Yes, yes," he replied offhandedly.

"Look," said Kat, her irritation growing, "we need information and we need it quickly. If your methods aren't doing the job, I want you to try something else. Understood?"

Ath turned in his chair and faced his Command Agent. "They . . .will . . .work," he groused. "I just need a little more time."

"You had better have something for me soon." Ath turned back to his display, rolling his eyes once he thought Kat couldn't see his face. "And lose the attitude," spat Kat. "I can appoint someone else to do what you do." With that, she walked over to Olm's display to check on how his scans were working.

"Oh? Who?" muttered Ath. Once again, he closed his eyes and pressed his hands against the display.

Yes.

That single word blossomed inside his mind.

Ath looked back on the data exchanged between the panel and the creature to see what the reply was connected to.

Can you understand this?

Ath smiled and looked over at Olm and Kat. They were both entirely focused on Olm's display. Ath's genius would soon become apparent.

I am Ath. He focused his reply back into the display.

He waited, practically bursting with excitement.

I am Frhsgetdfe.

Are you well?

Again, he had to wait. He tried to completely clear his mind.

Are you well? He repeated.

Ath, how are you able to communicate with me?

Ath rocked back and forth in his chair. Olm and Kat were still immersed in Olm's studies.

Algorithm conversion.

Of course. Brilliant. You are brilliant, Ath.

Thank you. Are you well?

Ath, are you the leader? You must be the leader.

Ath subconsciously clinched his teeth. *No. I am not the leader.*

The frustration of his response echoed inside his head.

What is this structure?

Ath assumed that it was referencing the ship. *It is a Journeycraft. It travels through space. This one is called the Aurora.*

Ath, can your leader speak with me as you can?

Ath smirked. *No. She cannot.*

Your leader is a female? The creature's reply had come almost instantly.

Yes. Her name is Kat.

I do not understand. If you can do that which she cannot, why is she the leader?

Again, Ath smiled. "Excellent question," he muttered aloud.

The creature continued. *Can she do things that you cannot?*

Ath groaned inwardly. *She can bear young.* It was the only thing that came to his mind. He almost laughed.

There was no immediate response. Ath looked over at Olm and Kat. Kat left Olm's display and walked off in the direction of Gram's quarters. Olm continued his work.

I must consider that. Ath frowned, puzzled by the reply.

What do you mean?

The display indicated a higher level of static coming from the creature. Ath adjusted his algorithm to compensate.

What do you mean?

Is bearing young a pre-requisite for leadership in your species?

No. We choose our own leaders based on merit.

Ath attempted to keep his mind empty so as to better understand the creature's replies. The void was filling with his frustration.

But you said that she cannot do anything that you cannot do. How is she more meritorious?

Ath wanted this being to know the truth.

Our prior leader believed that she merited the leadership position. I do not.

So your most able are not your leaders. Interesting.

Ath sat back in his seat. He repeated his previous question.

Are you well?

Ath thought that he had lost his connection. He became alarmed by the amount of time the creature needed to reply.

No, Ath. I am not. I need your help.

————————

Cap and May were led into the Journeyers' pyramid. Bal provided Min with the resonance scanner. He immediately began studying the device.

"Cap," began Bal, "please advise them about what you saw."

Cap nervously glanced at May. They were now in the presence of both a Chronicler and a group of Journeyers. "Why are we being restricted?" he asked anxiously. "We have done nothing wrong."

"I will explain that to you," said Bal coolly. "But for now, they would like to hear about what happened to you and your Charges."

Cap took a deep breath and studied the Journeyers for a moment. Min was examining the resonance scanner and didn't seem to be paying him any attention at all. Jack and Eve were obviously eager to hear what Cap had to say. Sol watched him with a more sympathetic expression. Cap sensed that he alone was aware of his unease.

"Well, we started out early on the ag maintenance trip," he began. "Once we got close enough to see the mainland, I checked the box, just like I am supposed to. It looked like it always looked, so we went ahead and went ashore. We proceeded to the Garden to do our work."

"Tell me about the Garden," said Sol.

Bal held up his hand to Cap before Cap could reply. The Chronicler then approached Jack and Sol.

"Your question is odd," said Bal in a hushed voice. "What are your intentions?"

"Why is it odd?" replied Sol quietly. "We are just trying to find out what happened."

"I can tell you about the Garden later," offered Min. "Tell me Cap, did you see anything strange before using the device for the first time that morning?" Bal gave Min a quizzical look. Cap waited to gauge Bal's reaction before answering.

"Yes, yes I did. In the sky, there was a very bright streak of light."

"Tell them what happened when you left the Garden," said Bal.

"We started walking back towards the boats from the Garden. That was when we saw the lights coming in our direction."

"The lights?" asked Jack.

"Yes. I saw them coming through the trees. They were lit torches. They were carrying them."

None of the Journeyers had an immediate question.

"What happened after that?" asked Bal.

"We ran," said Cap simply. "We ran back to the boat. We got in the boat and rowed out into the lake," said Cap. "They were close behind us, so we had to leave the barge behind."

"Thank you, Cap," said Bal. "Please return to the others. I will be by to talk with you later."

"Not just yet," interjected Min. "How long did it take you to get from Atla to the mainland?"

"It takes about a quarter of a rotation usually, with a crew of wards anyway," said Cap.

"A rotation of what?"

Cap leaned back slightly, nearly lost for words. "What do you mean?"

"You said a 'rotation'. What is rotating?"

The other Journeyers shared the same confused expression but remained quiet. Bal awaited Cap's answer.

"I……..don't know," admitted Cap. "It's just a word. Isn't it?"

Min smiled. "Indeed. Thank you Cap. We appreciate your meeting here with us." Cap backed away slowly. He and May were then escorted outside by a pair of Guards.

"Well?" asked Bal.

"The resonance scanner seems to be operating correctly," said Min "There is some possibility that Hab's re-entry interfered with its functions."

"The light in the sky?" asked Bal.

"Hab," said Jack. "Of course. But could that have generated enough energy to interfere?"

"It is the most likely explanation. We have more pressing issues, so we will have to be satisfied with that for now." Min stood up and handed the scanner back to Bal.

"If you need nothing else at the moment, I will take my leave," said Bal. He rose, and hearing no objection from the Journeyers, left the pyramid.

"What did you think of their story?" asked Min.

"They appear to have observed torches," said Sol. "That would seem to require a recalculation of the projections given us by the Directors, may they guide our way. But that might be impossible."

"Why so?" asked Jack. Min recalled his student's confident belief that any problem could be solved.

"Their projections about the Heks' development start at a specific point in time, but we know nothing of their history before that," said Sol. "And since we have no data concerning the Hek, I would wager that any new projections we might make would be highly inaccurate."

"I would agree," said Eve. "And the further we can study a trend going backwards, the more accurately we can predict it going forward," noted Eve. "From a standpoint of data analysis, it is rather odd that the Directors, may they guide our way, would handicap us like this. Particularly with what is at stake."

"Then we will have to assume the worst with every projection," said Min. "We must assume that Critical Closure will be at the earliest possible time based on the projections we were given." Eve turned slightly towards the wall before lowering her eyes.

"They were talking about a Garden," noted Jack. "You said you knew something about that?" he asked Min.

"It was something Hab told me about," began Min. "The island developed problems with soil quality. The law wouldn't let our people adjust their farming methods, so Hab and his crew constructed a large Garden on the mainland. It is surrounded by a huge stone wall. The resonance scanners were provided to prevent any encounters with the Hek. They were calibrated to detect the Heks' protein templates as they should be structured based on the projections by the Directors. Hab said they never detected any Hek at all either near the shore or closer to the Garden. That's why they determined the Garden to be safe."

"But this one didn't work," noted Sol. "You think Hab's return interfered with its functions? If that wasn't what happened......"

"I'm fairly comfortable with that explanation," he said. "A lot more comfortable than I am with the possibility that the projections about their proteins are that inaccurate. As you said before, the Heks' protein sequences are extremely static. There just isn't any plausible reason why the projections would be off by that much."

Sol thought for a moment. "The use of fire is related to intelligence, which is also related to their protein schematics. It isn't inconceivable that somewhere along the line, a Hek saw lightning strike a tree or . . . .something. We can attempt to quantify these things as much as we want, but some factors will always be random."

"So you are saying they could have just ....gotten lucky?" asked Eve.

"In a manner of speaking," said Sol.

"If that is the case, that gives us more time, not less," said Min. "This might be the only group of Hek on the planet using fire. If it was just . . . .luck . . . ." His voice trailed away.

"What now?" asked Jack. He was ready to act.

"Our primary task now is to recover that data from the Land Bridge Chronicler Hall," said Min. "We don't know for certain how accurate the Critical Closure projections are now. Eve, what is the current projection?"

"About 20,000 ellipses, within a margin of about 1,200."

"Assuming the Hek developed fire on their own somehow, can you determine what impact that would have on our timetable?"

Eve shook her head. "No, we don't have the actual computations. We only have the projections and a few minor variables to apply."

"And the development of fire is far more than a minor variable," noted Sol.

"Min?" began Eve. "Why did you ask Cap about what a 'rotation' is? You knew the answer to that already. The poor man had no idea what you were talking about."

"I wasn't asking him," said Min. "At least not directly. I was asking Bal. Bal got rather defensive when you asked about the Garden, Sol. There was information there that Bal has that he didn't want Cap to share with you. But when I asked about what Cap thought a 'rotation' was, Bal stayed silent. I think that is because Bal doesn't know either and therefore didn't have any reason to think the question was off limits."

"I'm not following," said Jack. He was a bit distressed at having to make such an admission to his mentor. However, it was apparent that Sol and Eve were confused as well.

"The Chroniclers state and enforce the Protocols and can even relate what the purpose of any particular Protocol is," answered Min. "Like Shu did when she explained the Exile Protocol to Eve. I always assumed the Chroniclers had a lot more understanding about science than the rest of the Umae. Now I'm not so sure. If they don't, then the purpose of any particular Protocol is something they recite by rote, not because they figured it out on their own."

"So maybe the real intent of the Protocols is something other than what we have been told?" offered Eve.

"It's a possibility. And one I don't think we should ignore," said Min. "I suspect they will send at least one

Chronicler with us on our trip. Hopefully, I can get that person to provide me with some useful information that will help with our calculations. But right now, we need to focus on getting that Haven data back from the Land Bridge."

"But......," Eve wanted to be sure her reasoning had really led to the conclusion she was weighing. "Why would the Directors, may they guide our way, mislead the Umae about the purposes of the Protocols?"

Min let that questions penetrate the thoughts of everyone in the room. "That's a question I hope we are able to answer. And soon."

———————

Ath watched as Olm stood up and walked to the interior doors of the forward shuttle bay. Olm waved his hand over a panel near the doors and they slid open. He disappeared into the bay.

Can you help me?

Ath closed his eyes again, reaching out towards the display.

Help you with what?

I didn't tell you. I am in terrible pain.

Pain? From what?

You are very compassionate, Ath. The energy wave in space. Do you know about it?

Ath sat back in his seat. Energy wave? Could it be talking about the beacon signal? *I know of an energy wave. I don't know if we are referencing the same one.*

The shuttle bay doors re-opened and Olm returned from the bay.

"Making any progress?" he asked Ath.

"Hmmm?" Ath looked up. He hadn't expected Olm to speak to him.

"Making . . . .any . . . . progress?" Now Olm was mocking him.

"Yes. Yes. I expect to have completed the informational analysis soon," he replied. "Very soon."

Olm turned and walked back in the direction of Gram's quarters. Again, Ath pressed his hands to the display.

I *was trapped in the energy wave. Badly hurt. Cannot continue unassisted.*

Ath's felt a tightening in his gut. *Are you dying?*

Dying? My metabolism is becoming very inefficient. Is that what you mean?

I don't know, thought Ath. And I'm sure not ready to ask Olm.

Maybe. What do you need?

Ath waited for a couple of moments, but there was no response. Olm came back, accompanied by Kat. Kat approached Ath's station. He quickly removed his conversation from the display.

"What do you have?" she asked, taking a look.

"It's . . . .close," muttered Ath as he nervously watched the display.

"Close?!?" snapped Kat. "There isn't anything on there at all! What have you been doing?"

Ath swallowed and looked at the display. "The panel is doing the processing off-display," he said. "Watching it doesn't help anything."

Kat leaned down and looked closely at Ath's face. "Are you all right? You look a little flushed."

Ath smiled, trying to look at ease. "I'm fine. I just don't get to decode alien languages every rotation."

Kat looked at the display again before standing up straight. "Okay. You have me there. The second you have anything, I want to know." She joined Olm at the doors to the shuttle bay. Gull was there now as well. Ath placed his palms on the display again and focused. The being was waiting for him.

I need to come inside. Inside away from the energy.

Ath shuddered anxiously. The plea bounded about inside his head.

I need to come inside. Please, Ath. Only you can help me.

A bead of sweat trickled down Ath's forehead, making its way to his cheek.

"Ath? Ath?" It was Kat.

"Y-yes?" he stammered. He entered a command sequence into the panel. Kat walked back to where he was seated.

"Are you sure . . . ." Ath cut her off by pointing to the display. It now showed a single word.

Please.

"Sweet moons," gasped Kat. "You are talking to it. You are . . .talking to it."

Ath swallowed and shook his head.

Kat looked back at Gull and Olm. "Ath has established communication. Should we tell it our plan?"

Gull and Olm looked at one another with astonishment. "You are certain?" Olm's voice dripped with incredulity. It was not lost on Ath.

"Yes," said Ath firmly. "I'm certain."

"Then, yes," said Olm. "Tell it."

"Tell it what?" asked Ath.

"Olm has been able to gather a great deal of data from the creature, but the signals from the scan are very complex. It will take a long time for him to make any sense of them, even with your help," Kat explained. "He wants to take the forward shuttle out and obtain a tissue sample."

"No!" protested Ath. "You can't do that!"

Kat stepped away from him, looking confused. "Wh . . .why not? Ath? Why not?"

Ath looked at his display.

Please.

He entered another command into his panel. Instantly, the doors to the shuttle bay slid open. A dozen of the creature's long brown tentacles snaked through. One fired a long, needle-like projectile, which impaled itself in Kat's stomach. Another struck Ath in the neck. Both of them immediately crumpled to the floor. Gull seized Olm by the collar and pulled him backwards into the forward shuttle bay just before the bay doors slid shut, sealing them inside. Olm tumbled to the floor near the shuttle. His body trembled with spasms.

Gull quickly entered a command into a small panel by the door. "Olm! What happened? What is wrong?"

Olm was breathing hard. He rubbed his face with his hands. "The shuttle. Come on!" He pulled himself off the floor and stumbled for the shuttle craft sitting in the bay.

"Wait!" yelled Gull. "We have to help them!"

Olm reached the base of the shuttle. The access ramp was already opened, allowing him to enter. Gull started after him. Inside, Olm was standing next to the command panel.

"What are you doing?" asked Gull angrily. Gull looked at Olm. The Life Agent was trembling again and was near panic. "We have to get out of here. We. . ." He grabbed his head in his hands and shut his eyes tight.

Gull's attention was drawn away by a banging sound coming from the far side of the shuttle bay doors. He could see Kat and Ath through the portal, beating on the doors with their fists.

"I don't understand," said Gull. Olm was now curled up on the floor of the shuttle. "Olm, what is wrong with you? I need for you to get up!" Gull attempted to pull Olm up by an arm and managed to get him on his feet. Olm's expression was distant and unfocused.

Kat and Ath continued to pound at the bay door.

Gull seized Olm's shoulders and shook him vigorously.

"Can you open the exterior doors to this bay?" Olm mumbled.

"Yes . . .but, why?"

"We need to go. We need to go before they get those doors open."

Gull looked at the doors and then back at Olm. "What are you talking about?"

"We need to go now!" screamed Olm. "Please!" He was near tears. "If I'm wrong, it won't matter. If I'm not, then . . . . ." Olm covered his face in his hands and sobbed. Kat and Ath were still on the far side of the door, throwing their bodies against it.

"All right. But you had better have a good explanation." Gull helped Olm stand up before dragging him to the front of the vessel. Gull sat down in the pilot's position and began entering directives into the ship's panel. The shuttle's engines whined as they came to life. The exterior doors opened and Gull expertly guided the shuttle out of the bay, into the cold darkness of space.

CHAPTER 6

Later in the afternoon, Shu appeared at the Journeyers' pyramid. Sol had been busy completing the examinations of his fellow crew members. Eve and Jack were in excellent health. Min was improving. His stamina was increasing and he was better able to move about the pyramid.

Upon seeing Shu, Min invited her inside. "Bal said you had questions concerning the Protocols?"

"Please. Sit." The five of them sat down around a low, oval table. Eve offered Shu a cup of water.

"How may I inform you?"

"It is my understanding that you will not permit us to go to the Land Bridge community," said Min. "It is imperative that you allow it."

Shu peeked briefly at Eve. "I have already had this discussion with her," she said off handedly. "And it is the law that does not permit it. I merely pronounce what the law is."

"I still don't think you understand," said Eve. Her tone reflected her frustration. "We believe they found Haven. That information may well be in the Chroniclers' Hall at the Land Bridge."

Shu remained unmoved. "It is you who does not understand. If a Journeyer enters any community other than his or her own, exile follows. It is clear."

"So, we CAN go," noted Min. "But we would be exiled for doing so."

Shu was suspicious of where Min's logic was leading. "I believe that to be correct."

Sol couldn't remain silent any longer. "So, assume we all go and the information about Haven's location is there. What then?"

Shu bought time by taking a slow sip from the cup in front of her. "You would still be exiled. Some other Journeyer group would have to use the information."

"But the entire reason we exist is to find Haven!" snapped Jack. His outburst drew a stare from Min, which eased the younger man back into his chair.

Shu was visibly shaken. "I do not make the law," she said slowly. "I pronounce the law. I enforce the law. That is all."

"My original plan makes sense then," said Min. "I'll go."

Min's proposition drew a chorus of protest from the other Journeyers. "No!" said Sol. "Your health won't allow it."

"I won't allow it either," said Eve. Min's eyes grew wide at her pronouncement.

"I'll be fine. And" he added, looking at Eve, "it is MY decision to make. Recall, I'm not flying any more anyway. Shu, suppose I asked you if I could just stay here on Atla until I died. What would you say?"

"Impossible," said Shu.

"Impossible?" echoed Sol incredulously. "Why? This is his home."

Shu moistened her lips before taking another drink. "Because the Chroniclers derive our authority from you, the Journeyers. If a Journeyer were here all the time….."

"So, he would be a threat to your authority," continued Sol with disgust.

Shu gathered her composure. "And the Atlans don't know that Journeyers die. What would we tell them when Min dies?"

Min turned towards the other Journeyers. "I suspected I wouldn't be allowed to stay, although I wasn't sure about the reasons why. I'm going to be effectively exiled anyway. It makes sense for me to go to the Land Bridge community."

"But if it is the Haven data that is the reason for the trip, shouldn't I go as well?" asked Eve. She had a point. After all, she was the Data Agent. It was a question Min had anticipated. He wasn't pleased about the response he had to give.

"Impossible," said Shu. "I cannot prohibit Min from going since it does not effectively change his status. But I will not simply allow Eve to elect exile. She is too valuable."

Min was inwardly relieved. He had a detailed explanation about why Eve should stay behind, but she would have seen through it eventually. What he needed was time, and distance, from her. It was the only way he could make an objective decision about whether she was leaving on the *Starshine* or going to the moon with him. Shu had bailed him out.

"I'll be fine," said Min. "I can find the data and bring it back. Then you can study it all you want."

"How do you plan on getting there?" asked Shu. "To the Land Bridge, I mean?"

"Boat," said Min. "Didn't you say that an entire crew of canoers was preparing for exile? They can take me."

Shu evaluated his suggestion. "But you can't stay on the water for three rotations. What of the Hek? You will have to go ashore at some point."

"We can avoid them," said Min confidently. "The resonance . . ." He noted Shu's confusion with that term. "……..the box will warn us if they are nearby."

"But it didn't before," said Jack. "What if the problem wasn't the e-m pulse?"

"Like what?" asked Min.

Jack lowered his head in thought. This exchange was much like those he had had with Min dozens of times during his training. "I don't know," he admitted finally.

"Besides," said Min, offering a smile to his student, "I know you checked that resonator yourself while I was asleep."

113

"But...... how?" asked Jack.

"Didn't you?" Jack returned his teacher's grin before nodding his head.

"I don't like this plan," said Sol. "But I know you are going to do it anyway."

"I know you don't, but you are right," said Min. He looked at Shu. "What do you think?"

Shu stood up and folded her arms as she slowly paced back and forth. "A Chronicler will need to go with you," she said. "The Umae at the Land Bridge don't know there are any other settlements. They believe they are the only ones, as do the Atlans. If a Chronicler goes, at least you will have a spokesperson that can address the Land Bridge Chroniclers."

"So what are we supposed to do while you are gone?" asked Jack.

"Be Journeyers," said Min. "Find out what the Atlans are having problems with and discretely fix them. We also need to start evaluations for the new Journeyer trainees. Shu, I assume you have some sort of data concerning the abilities of the adolescents of Atla?"

"Yes, and there is one group that is plainly superior to the others in terms of ability. In fact, a pair of them was being considered as future Chroniclers."

"'Were'?"

"Yes. I speak of the members of the crew who encountered the Hek."

Min looked down at the table. "The exiles."

"Yes. The exiles."

"They will be our trainees then," he announced. "Better space than . . . ."

"The Hek?" asked Sol.

"Exactly," said Min. "When can we meet them?"

"It will be arranged," said Shu. "The trip to the Land Bridge should not be delayed."

Eve lowered her eyes. She and Min were being pushed apart. Whether it was by circumstance or Min's own priorities, the hurt was the same.

———————

Kat and Ath watched passively as the shuttle bearing Olm and Gull left the bay. Kat turned to Ath and intently studied his face. Satisfied, she sat down at the nearest panel.

"We need to go and get them." Her voice was nearly void of intonation. "I wonder if there are any other crew members still aboard."

"Tech Agent Gram is in crew quarter seven." Kat looked around, attempting to discern the source of the robotic voice responding to her statement.

"What was that?" she asked.

"Alpha Panel voice input fully functional," replied the voice.

Kat turned towards the panel. "Oh yes. Who am I again?"

"Command Agent Kat," advised the panel.

"Kat . . . Kat," she muttered to herself. "That makes me the leader, does it not?"

"As Command Agent, you are at the apex of authoritative hierarchy on this vessel."

"I am in charge," she stated flatly. "Where is crew quarter seven?" The panel in front of her activated, displaying a schematic of the ship's interior. Highlighted was Kat's current position as well as Gram's quarters. Kat stood up and gestured to Ath. "Let us go."

Ath followed along just behind Kat as the two walked to Gram's quarters. Gram was lying down on her side, facing the door as they entered. She slowly lifted herself up and sat on the side of her bed.

"Wondered . . . . .when you'd come," she said weakly.

Kat watched Gram closely as she struggled to sit up. "Everything is under control now. But I need your help with something."

Gram attempted to stand. She grimaced before sitting back down. "Can't . . . . ."

"I can." Kat approached Gram and easily hoisted the elderly woman into her arms, cradle-style.

"W-hat..........?" began Gram.

"You are useless to me back here." Kat effortlessly hauled Gram back to the doors to the shuttle bay. She roughly tossed the elderly woman forward and Gram fell awkwardly to the floor. Gram's arm was caught underneath her as she hit the deck.

"My . . . .arm?!?" she moaned with confusion. She rolled over, cradling her injured limb. "Why did you . . .do that?" She stared up at Kat, her eyes welling.

"I said I needed you," said Kat plainly. "How do I operate this ship?"

Gram blinked hard, trying to clear her vision. "I don't know." She looked at Ath, hoping he might enlighten her as to the circumstances.

Kat knelt down next to Gram. "Now," she said quietly, "one more time. How do I operate this ship?"

Gram struggled to catch her breath. Kat was stone-faced. Ath stood by, equally without expression.

"I said......?" said Gram.

Kat shook her head. "No. Give me another answer."

Gram's arm was beginning to throb. Any slight movement amplified the pain, causing it to shoot upwards towards her shoulder. "Voice directive," she said quietly.

"Acceptable," said Kat as she stood back up. "Ship, open those doors."

"Environmental warning," came a voice from the panel. "Failure to close the exterior bay doors first would result in catastrophic depressurization......"

"Fine," replied Kat. "Do whatever needs to be done to get these shuttle bay doors opened safely."

Slowly, the exterior shuttle bay doors began to close. Once the bay was tightly sealed, the interior doors slid open. Kat stood stiffly, waiting for the process to be completed.

The remains of the creature were still in the bay. Its central globe was shrunken to nearly a tenth of its original size. Its appendages had stiffened and many had dropped off onto the floor. It was lifeless and unmoving. Kat studied it for a moment before nudging the form with her foot. It remained still.

"The Mistress has left us," she told Ath. "We need to locate the other shuttle."

"Where is . . . Olm?" muttered Gram. "My arm . . . .broken . . . .I think."

"They are gone," Kat said absently. "Gone. But we are going to get them. Well, not 'you', but 'we'. How can we fly that other shuttle?"

Gram tried to slide herself over to the wall so she could use it to sit up. Exhaustion and the pain from her arm limited her to a simple half roll to her side. "I don't know," she said, looking away. "Not . . . .a pilot."

Kat folded her arms and slowly shook her head. "Not . . . .good," she mumbled. Once more, she knelt down and lifted Gram up off the floor. Entering the shuttle bay, Kat stopped at the top of a ladder that led down to the bay's landing deck. She seized Gram's long white hair tightly in one hand dangling her beyond the edge of the ladder. "You are certain?"

Gram mewled timidly as she swung slowly back and forth. Kat released her and watched as she dropped to the shuttle bay floor, making an awkward 'thunk' upon landing. Gram hit the deck feet-first, but she was too weak to brace herself for the impact. She absorbed the brunt of the landing force on her right hip. Still cradling her arm, she writhed weakly next to the shuttle.

Kat easily leapt down, eschewing use of the ladder. She landed lightly next to Gram and sat down next to her. Gram's face was twisted in a combination of pain, fear, and disbelief. "I have a theory," said Kat quietly. "Voice directives for the shuttle too?" Gram shuddered but said nothing. Ath leapt down, landing softly next to Kat.

"Sit her up," ordered Kat. Ath roughly grabbed Gram by her shoulders and wrenched her into a seated position. Gram groaned in pain at this forced maneuver. Kat lightly caressed the old woman's cheek. "And to think, you are probably one of the smart ones."

She quickly seized Gram's upper left incisor between her thumb and index finger and gave it a sharp jerk. Gram screamed as blood flowed from the side of her mouth. Kat wiped the extracted tooth off with her other index finger. She regarded the wet, red fluid. "I think this is going to work very well," she said to no one in particular. She tried to flick the blood away from her finger but managed to only spatter the floor at the base of the ladder. The rest she wiped on to her pant leg. "Take her to the exterior doors," she said with a nod of her head. She popped the tooth into her mouth and swallowed it.

Ath dragged Gram by one leg to the far side of the shuttle bay, next to the exterior doors. Gram was now gasping quietly, fighting to draw breath. He left her there before joining Kat aboard the shuttle craft. Seconds later, the exterior bay doors opened again. The shuttle shot into space, slowly trailed by the remains of the creature and Gram's still-writhing body.

———————

Gull and Olm moved down the hall, away from the portal. None of the overhead illumination elements were functioning. Gull's suit's sensors advised that the air temperature was barely warmer than that on the moon's surface. The ceiling, floor, and walls were all made of the same gray metal. They were smooth without visible seams.

There was an intersecting hallway running from left to right. Gull pointed to the left and the two men walked in that direction. There was artificial gravity here and the men could feel the bulk of their suits pulling down on them. They saw a small machine next to the wall. It was about as long as the length of Gull's arm from his elbow to the tips of his fingers. It had tracks along its bottom and a pair of short metallic "arms" extending from its body.

"What's that?" asked Olm. Gull shined the light down the passage, revealing similar machines about every ten paces.

"It's a mech," said Gull. "Sort of like the ones we have on the ship. They perform routine maintenance and cleaning."

"Why isn't it doing anything?"

"No power," said Gull. "It needs a port to recharge, and none of the ports have enough energy. Mech maintenance is a low priority."

"Can we get it started?" asked Olm. "Or get them started, I guess," he added, noting the presence of the other small machines in the passage.

"We need to get to the energy panel before we do anything else," said Gull. Gull stopped in front of a small display. He entered a command and a dim light arose on its face. "It looks like someone has been here at some point." He directed his attention to the display itself instead of the information it offered.

"What is it?" asked Olm.

Gull continued his examination for another moment. "I upgraded this panel the last time I was here," he said finally. "Now it looks completely different. If I get time, I'd like to look it over and see what modifications were made. Based just on what I'm seeing here, I'd say whoever did this work was very, very skilled."

"When were they here?"

"No way to tell right now," said Gull. "I was here a little over 900 ellipses ago. There should have been a lot of visitors here since then."

"Every ship stops here?" asked Olm hesitantly.

Gull looked up from the panel. "No," he said finally. "Of course not. Just teacher-student pairs. Or any ship that needed particularly extensive repairs. You didn't know that?"

Olm stared ahead down the passage. "Is it always so dark?"

"Energy reserves are extremely low. Illumination is not a priority if no one is here," said Gull.

"So what do we do?"

"We can activate the solar array," said Gull. "It will take a while, but that system absorbs a lot more energy than it uses. Once we have stored enough, we can use the excess to ramp up the reactor. Then we will have more power than we could ever need."

Olm turned and looked down the hallway in front of them. Gull began entering more directives into the panel. "Do you think we are close to the other ship?" asked Olm.

Gull finished entering his last directive. "It can't be too far. I'd guess that we have covered about half of the Citadel on foot already."

"It is larger than it looks then," said Olm.

"A lot of it is actually underneath the surface of the moon. It is difficult to tell, but we have been walking on a gradually declining slope."

Olm looked down at the floor. "I hadn't noticed."

Gull took one final look at the panel. "Good. The solar array is in good shape. Let's check out the crash site."

"And then?"

"It depends on what we find. Hopefully, none of the Citadel's major systems were damaged. Once we get enough power restored, we can run a full diagnostic."

"I see," said Olm flatly.

"And you will want to look at the data we took from the creature," added Gull

"Creature?" queried Olm. "Oh yes. Of course."

Gull noted Olm's unease. "Any theories on what happened up there? You were pretty anxious to get away. I assume you had a reason."

Olm drew a deep breath. "I have a number of ideas," he said. "Come," he said, starting down the hallway. "The data I collected will allow me to narrow them down."

———————————

Min, Eve, and the rest of the crew sat at a large rectangular table in the center of a large pyramid. Shu, Bel and three other representatives from the Chroniclers' Hall had joined them. A group of Chronicler Guards led Cap, May, and their Wards in single file. None of them had been inside this pyramid before. The apex towered overhead. The table was made of sturdy wood and was easily the largest single piece of furniture any of them had ever seen.

The rowers, especially Dom, were quickly drawn to the Journeyers seated at the far side of the table. Shu bade them all to be seated opposite the Journeyers and the Chroniclers. The Guards stood silently by the doorway as the new arrivals sat down.

"You're from the ship!" gushed Dom. May shushed him as Min smiled uncomfortably.

"Yes," he replied. "My name is Min. What is your name?"

"You don't know?" exclaimed Dom. "You know everything!"

"Dom, quiet," said May.

"No, it's fine," said Min. "He was just answering my question." He looked back at Dom. "Now I know your name, Dom."

Dom beamed back at him but remained silent.

"Can we know why we are here?" asked Cap. He assessed the collection of individuals seated across from him and was fairly certain he wasn't going to like the answer to his question.

"Yes," offered Shu as she rose from her seat. "We have need of you and your rowers. Min and I have to go somewhere and we need for you and your crew to take us."

"You are going yourself?" Min asked Shu.

"Yes," she replied. "Bal and I discussed it. Either the Chief or the Adjutant should go. Bal suggested that I would be better able to endure the stress of the journey."

"Although it may not seem so compared to you," said Bal to Min, "I have a large number of ellipses myself."

"I don't understand," said Cap. "Why not use an adult team? It would be much faster."

The Journeyers and the Chronicler contingent remained silent for a moment. Cap looked over at May, his anxiety rising.

"It is my place to explain," said Shu finally. "Once you have heard what I am going to tell you, you will be constantly quarantined until rotation after next when you leave on this journey."

"But . . . . " started Cap.

THE PROTOCOLS OF UMA

"Silence," said Shu firmly. "You will understand soon." Dom was still staring at the Journeyers. The older rowers had all picked up on their Rearers' nervousness and were becoming uncomfortable themselves.

"I'm listening," said Cap.

"You are going to take us to a place called the Land Bridge. It is eveningside from here. It should take approximately three rotations to get there. When we arrive, we expect to meet with another group of Umae."

May took a moment to be sure she had heard Shu correctly. "Is it a rescue mission? Who?"

"No. Another community of Umae. They have lived there for as long as we have lived here. Now we have need of communication."

Cap slumped down in his chair. He was starting to see where all of this was going. "Cap?" asked May quietly as she placed her hand gently on his shoulder.

"This has something to do with what happened to us, doesn't it?" asked Cap without looking up from the table.

"Yes," said Shu plainly. She paused to swallow. "You have seen the Hek. That is a protocol violation that requires exile."

May screeched and the rowers erupted with gasps of disbelief.

"What does that mean?" yelled Dom. "'Exile'? What is that?"

"Calm. Please," said Shu raising her hands. "There is much more."

"How can you expect us to be calm!?!" thundered Cap as he rose from his seat.

Two of the Guards started towards Cap but Shu waved them away. "There is more. Please sit." Cap glared at her, but reluctantly sat back down.

"As you know, some rotations prior to the arrival of Min's Journeycraft, another Journeycraft arrived. Min has advised that it is empty. Therefore, it requires a crew."

May looked at Cap and absently squeezed his shoulder. "We are to become . . .Journeyers?"

"Not you," she said pointing to the rowers. "Them. You and Cap have too many ellipses. The rowers will be assigned to one of the Journeycraft and Min and his crew will train them." May shrank under the weight of this revelation.

"I'm going to be a Journeyer!" exclaimed Dom. "I'm going to fly!" He leapt out of his chair and began running around the chamber with his arms extended in simulated flight. It was all Bal could do to tolerate this explosion of excitement.

"Dom," said Min firmly. The boy was oblivious as he continued his flight.

"Dom!" blared Cap. "Sit!" Dom stopped abruptly and stared in shock at his Rearer. He then shrugged and hurried back to his seat. He could barely hold still.

"Dom," began Min in a quiet tone, "you don't have enough ellipses for Journeyer training. I'm . . . .sorry."

Dom's shoulders began to tremble as his face reddened. "Not enough?!? I DO have enough!" he screeched. "I DO! That's not fair!" He scrambled up on the table and lunged at Min. Min managed to get his hands up in front of him, so Dom grabbed one of Min's wrists. "You can't do that!" Dom screamed.

Cap stood up and seized Dom by the waist and tried to pull him back across the table. The boy refused to let go of Min's wrist. "Dom, stop this!" demanded Cap. "Let go!"

Dom began to sob. "But it's not fair! It's not . . . . fair!" Finally he let go of Min and Cap hauled him back to his seat.

"So what about the rest of us?" demanded Cap. "What about May and Dom and me?"

Shu waited for the disturbance to abate. Dom hid his face in Cap's chest. "Under the Protocols, there are no alternatives for the three of you."

Cap placed his hand on the back of Dom's head and pulled the boy to him. "So we all go on this trip, but May and Dom and I don't get to come back?"

"Yes," said Shu calmly.

The rowers grumbled in protest. "Why?" asked Lin tearfully. "Don't we even get to know that?"

Bal stood up next to Shu. "No. You don't. It is the result dictated by the Protocols. They are the counsel of the Directors, may they guide our way. Do your Rearers a service and accept the law. I'm sure you have been taught that."

May put her arms around the two Charges closest to her. She leaned down and kissed each on top of his head. "Rotation after next you said?" asked Cap.

"That's right." said Min.

Cap picked up Dom and the boy put his head on Cap's shoulder. "We will be ready," said Cap gruffly. With that, he and May led their Charges out of the pyramid under the escort of the Guards.

Shu and Bal returned to their seats. "There are two others who are going," said Bal.

"Oh?" asked Sol. "Who?"

"A mother, Pol, gave birth to an unauthorized child. That child has enough rotations to be weaned. Pol has elected to accept exile along with the child, as is her right."

"Are Pol and her baby going to the Land Bridge with us?" asked Min.

"It is your choice," said Shu. "The Protocols provide no such guidance. Your mission is paramount."

"Fine," said Min as he rose slowly from his seat. "I'd rather not think about that now. I'm going to get some rest."

Olm and Gull found one of the secondary panels. It was in good operating condition, albeit very low on power. The solar array was collecting radiant energy and directing it into the Citadel. It was a slow process. The systems within the structure were designed to focus first on restoring living conditions. They began attempting to increase the temperature and adjust the air's composition to match that found on Uma. Olm and Gull kept their suits on as they waited for the process to complete.

"It will be a while before I can activate this panel," said Gull. "Environmental controls are a priority. Why don't you share your thoughts about that creature while we wait?"

The two men sat on the floor as their suits provided too much bulk for them to fit into any of the chairs. They had been walking for quite a while and Gull noted how good it felt to finally sit down and rest. He was more fatigued than he had realized. "I haven't seen much of the data at all," said Olm. "But obviously its life functions focus on radiation. It feeds on it and needs a certain level for habitat."

"But Ath said he was communicating with it?"

"If it can communicate like that, even through an algorithmic buffer, it is exceptionally intelligent. The buffer essentially taught it Ath's language, which it mastered in a very short time."

"It looked sort of like a long-legged spider, I thought," said Gull. "Big central body with a lot of legs."

"No," said Olm. "It was a colony. The central structure is the 'executive' while the smaller, similar structures are drones. The organism is magnificent." Olm's face brightened as he explained his thoughts concerning the creature.

"You sound confident given your lack of data." Gull stood up to check the power levels.

"The data will bear me out."

"You were awfully afraid in the shuttle bay. Surely you hadn't figured all of those things out already?"

"It was imperative that we leave," said Olm plainly. "Kat and Ath had been hosted by the Executive."

"'Hosted'?"

"They became drones. They were going to try to kill us."

The display in front of the two men was monitoring both the energy accretion from the solar array as well as the climactic adjustments. "We still have quite a while before we can ignite the generators," said Gull. "The climate is static. I was afraid of that."

"What?"

"The collision must have compromised the exterior wall. We won't be able to restore the interior climate until the breech is repaired. We will be in these suits until that happens. The alpha panel isn't far from here. Let's see what sort of shape it is in."

The two men continued down the hallway, in the opposite direction from where they had come. The illumination panels glowed dimly but did not provide enough light to enable Gull to extinguish his wrist lamp. They walked past a number of smaller side corridors, favoring the main one.

"You have been here before," said Olm. "I'm not sure I understand what exactly it is used for."

"Yes. Actually before my training was completed. Every Tech Agent makes one trip here with a mentor as a part of his or her training. I was here with Gram." Gull had forgotten about her. She was not on the bridge when the creature entered. "Oh . . . . .moons," he muttered. Olm remained silent, waiting for Gull to continue. "The Citadel is designed to collect information from the Journeycraft. The precision of the data concerning the search for Haven is crucial, so it is transferred directly from the Journeycraft instead of solely through the tether beam. Since Journeycraft are unlikely to ever be in the same place at the same time, it provides a way to compound the data that is collected. Each Journeycraft has its own beacon satellite that it transfers general data to by way of its tether beam. The satellite then sends that data to its Chroniclers' Hall. When a Journeycraft returns to Uma, any data it has collected relating to Haven is sent to the beacon satellite by a high-powered, short-range transfer beam. That greatly reduces the chance the data will be corrupted. The satellite sends the information to the Citadel where it is analyzed and incorporated into all previously collected data."

"So no data about . . .'Haven', you said?"

Gull's eyes narrowed. "Yes. The name of our future home."

"Of course. No data about Haven is sent through the tether beam?"

"Not exclusively," said Gull. "The probability of the data being compromised is almost certain. Information that is relayed through the tether beam becomes somewhat corrupted because of the distance it has to travel. Other Journeycraft rely on Haven data to search very precise regions of space. Compromised data would result in some areas being searched multiple times while others aren't searched at all. Of course, our data was different. We tried transferring it every way we could."

"I see," said Olm. "How do you know where to look?"

"Probabilities," said Gull. "There is a greater concentration of suns in a specific orientation away from Uma. More stars mean more planets to look at. Every Journeycraft follows a path that is within about a three-dimensional 30-degree arc of every other Journeycraft. The orientations of the tether beams are adjusted according to the courses set by the Journeycraft."

Olm was rapt in his attention to Gull's explanation. "I had no idea."

"Apparently not," said Gull. "But I don't know much about life science, either." He stopped at a four-way intersection and looked around. "I don't think anyone has been here for a long, long time."

"Why not?"

"It would take at least a few hundred ellipses for the reactor to go off-line like that. The power levels here are far lower than they ever should be. Anyone who came here would have done something about it."

Olm looked down the three new passages. Each of them was as wide as the one they had been following. "How long can we stay here?"

"We can stay here for as long as we need to," offered Gull. "Once we get the power going, the Citadel can provide us with everything we need to live. And we might find ourselves in that position."

"Oh?" Olm turned back towards Gull.

"If our shuttle wasn't damaged by the collision, we could use it to get to Uma," said Gull. "It was far enough away that I think that will be the case. But if your theories are anywhere close to accurate about that alien, we may want to disable our shuttle as well. Then whatever was in the other shuttle can't reach Uma either, on the off chance it survived."

"They didn't," Olm responded promptly.

"That," said Gull, "is the only thing I hope you are right about."

———

Min spent all of the next day resting up for his trip. Even though he expected to spend much of the journey riding in a canoe, he anticipated a fair amount of walking once they reached the Land Bridge.

Eve entered just as he finished inspecting his pack.

He didn't say anything. She walked over to him and they embraced. He buried his face in her hair and let himself be filled by her scent. She wrapped her arms as far around him as she could, pulling him close.

"Hello," she said, pressing her nose to his. Min smiled.

"Hello. What have you been up to?"

Eve took a half step back but didn't let him go. "Sol and Jack were going to walk around and awe the Atlans," she said wryly. "It's in the Protocols, you know."

Min pulled her back towards him, closing the small space that she had opened a moment earlier. "Can we talk now?"

"That's why I'm here." She took Min by the hand and led him to a pile of nearby cushions where they both sat.

"Tell me what you think about my plan," he said. Eve stirred excitement within him, and that made him nervous.

"Which one?" she asked. "You have made a lot of them."

He couldn't sit there, looking at her, and even imagine sending her away. "About what happens when I get back from the Land Bridge," he said. "I think there is a good chance that you won't need to leave on the *Starshine* next time."

"Why, because I'll be on the *Aurora*?"

Min couldn't tell whether or not she was kidding. "Or the *Aurora*," he added. "If we have reasonably definitive data about Haven's location, I don't see why Jack and Sol can't do what needs to be done."

Eve held his face in her hands and looked into his eyes. "You had better not be teasing me," she said with a smile. Her eyes glistened. She drew back slightly. "What about Critical Closure? What if all the Hek have mastered fire?"

"We are likely a long ways from Critical Closure. I don't see how I can access any more data or reformulate a new projection. If the *Aurora* found Haven, it can't be more than four of five hundred light ellipses from here," said Min. "Even if our projections are way off, that would give them plenty of time to get there and back, even with a new crew. The ships' tutorials can do a lot of the training for them."

Eve threw her arms around his neck. He could feel her tears warming his cheek. "I have thought so much about how I could leave you," she said finally. "But I could never figure it out. I wouldn't be able to do it. I can't tell you how happy I am." They held each other without reserve, feeling one another draw breath.

"You may end up being lonely, you know," he said. "Sol says . . . ."

"I know what Sol said. Twenty ellipses, is that right? Well, I'll take that. I'll take all of them."

Min slowly released her. "But what will you do then? The Citadel is a big place, and you will be there all by yourself. You won't be able to return to Uma in a shuttle. The Chroniclers wouldn't permit it."

"Not grandiose enough.......I know," she said with huff. "But I'll worry about that later. For now," she said, pulling him in again, "I just want to focus on us and what we will do. Together."

CHAPTER 7

Min walked slowly from the Journeyer pyramid to the beach. Cap and May were helping their Charges ready the canoe for departure. This boat was slightly larger than the one they had taken on their last trip to the mainland. Shu and Bal met Min before he made it to the edge of the sand.

"How do you feel?" asked Shu.

"I'm still tired, but I think I am better than I was. Scl expects me to have good rotations and bad ones. He has given me a number of instructions to follow. I'll be fine."

Near the boat, Dom was shouting at an older Charge. He was saying something about where he planned to sit.

"He isn't bashful, is he?" asked Min.

Shu folded her arms and watched Dom gesture angrily at the older boy. "He is very bright," she said, perhaps a bit defensively. "His academic progress has been consistent. It is unfortunate that our community is losing him." Bal stood silently, shaking his head. "Bal?" quizzed Shu.

"You hold him in higher regard than I do," he said plainly. He glanced over at Min. "But any citizen lost is a loss to the community."

"He certainly was upset about not becoming a Journeyer," noted Min. "Maybe if he knew what it was really like . . . . ."

"You are revered," said Shu. "Most of our people never even see a Journeycraft. Many had even grown to doubt that Journeyers are real. For Dom to learn that he, among all of his class, is excluded from your position . . . well, I can see where he might be distraught."

Min saw Dom climb into the boat, precisely where he had told the other boy he planned to sit. "Particularly given his exile," he commented. "The boy hasn't had a very good rotation."

"You two should be going," said Bal. "That information is vital," he added. The other Charges began to board the boat, each testing the oar at his or her station. May was walking towards the bow and Cap and Dom were seated at the stern. Shu and Min walked across the beach towards the craft.

"Good morning," said Min to Cap. The Rearer looked up briefly but remained silent. Dom locked onto him with a scowl. "Where do you want us to sit?" asked Min uncomfortably.

Cap pointed to a vacant area just behind him and Dom. "There are your spots," he said gruffly. "I trust that you know where we are going?"

Min nearly winced at the question. *We are all going to the Land Bridge. Then, you and May and the boy*...... He looked around at the people in the boat.

"Where are our other passengers?" he asked Shu. Before she could reply, they saw a woman shuffling up the beach towards the boat. She was carrying a child that was partially concealed by her wrap. She stopped next to the boat but said nothing. Her face looked rather haggard and her eyes were red-rimmed and puffy. She stood with her head down and her shoulders slumped. Periodically, her eyes would peek upwards at Shu.

"Good morning Pol," said Shu. The woman's nod was nearly indiscernible. "Did you decide upon a name?"

"'Joba'," said the woman in a quiet voice. "His name is 'Joba'."

Murmurs rippled through the crew. Min turned and stared at Shu. "Two names?" he asked.

"No. One name. 'Joba'."

"But I don't . . . . ."

"I will explain later," said Shu as she moved over next to Pol. "May I help you board?" she asked. Joba peered about, taking in his surroundings.

Pol closed her eyes tightly for a moment. "No. I am fine," she said finally. Without asking where she was supposed to sit, she simply found an open spot and stepped aboard. She was careful to maintain her balance as she lowered herself down onto an empty bench. Once she was aboard, Min and Shu stepped into the boat and sat in their assigned positions. The Charges turned the nose of the boat towards the water before pushing it onto the lake. They then climbed in and awaited May's cadence.

The initial pace was slow and steady. Dom was still not rowing. He made no effort to avert his glare from Min. Shu turned and watched as Atla slowly faded in the distance.

The sky was its customary deep gray. The wind was almost non-existent. "Continue heart-side until we can see the mainland," said Shu. She wasn't entirely sure who was in charge of navigation. May set the pace, while Cap seemed content to simply sit in the stern of the boat and observe. "Then, we will follow the land eveningsidedly."

Min tapped Shu on the shoulder. "'Heart-side'?" he asked.

"I don't understand your question," she said.

"Why is a direction called 'heart-side'?"

Shu thought for a moment. Min's ignorance caught her off guard. "There is 'morningside' and 'eveningside'. But there are four basic directions. The other two are based on an individual facing morningside. One side is 'heart side', and the other is 'empty side'." Shu was surprised that the Journeyer wasn't familiar with this concept.

Min thought back to the discussions he had had with his crew about the state of technology on Atla. Magnetism was entirely unknown to them. Without even a basic compass, the boats that left the island had to stay within hearing range of the drums. They had terms based on the light in the sky and each end of a rotation, but nothing for the other two directions.

'Heart side' and 'empty side' were certainly crude. At least that approach provided a method that any Umae could use. He was glad that he had brought a few devices with him so his life didn't depend on the current navigational technology employed by his people. Interestingly, he didn't recall these terms being used during any of his earlier visits to the planet. Despite the Chroniclers' best efforts, the Umae had innovated.

Pol did not speak. She alternately peered down at Joba or stared blankly at the horizon. Soon, Joba began squawking fussily. Some of the rowers stole furtive glances at the mother and child before looking at their fellows to see who else was doing the same thing. Pol set Joba on the floor of the boat. She then opened her top baring her left breast. She picked up Joba and held him closely to her. His squawking ended abruptly, as did the glances of the rowers.

Min watched for a moment as Pol fed her son. She would soon have to provide for herself and her oddly named child without any assistance. He wondered if Cap and May would travel with them. He didn't have the stomach to ask. The Rearers appeared to be intelligent, healthy people. They could likely survive exile for quite a while. Pol and her child were another story. She didn't look well, and it would be many ellipses before Joba could provide any care for himself. They could potentially be subjected to any number of unpleasant deaths.

He watched as the Rowers pulled their oars in response to May's vocal pacing. How old had he been when he was chosen to be a Journeyer? None of these young people had been formally tested. The decision to take them into space was based primarily on Shu's advice about not only the Charges, but the Rearers who had taught them. There was an empty Journeycraft to crew. There was apparently nothing in the Protocols addressing that situation.

Shortly after a brief rest at noon, Cap announced the sighting of the shore. "Land," he noted. In the distance was the beach where they had seen the Hek. "How close do we need to be?" he asked.

"As long as we can see it, we are fine," said Min. "Let's make our turn now."

May changed her tone and directed the port rowers to stop while the starboard rowers brought the boat about. Soon the boat was traveling parallel to the beach, beyond which the strange people with the torches had chased them just a few rotations ago. She inspected the landscape closely, focusing on any indication that they might still be there. But the beach and the top of the rise were vacant. Beyond that, she couldn't say. Maybe they were all still waiting for them beyond the rise, or maybe they were far, far away. She couldn't see the barge on the beach. That made her wonder about what they had done with it. She tried to push those thoughts out of her head and focus on her cadence. Even if they were out there, they couldn't get to her. Not now. Of course, on the return trip, that would be different. Everything would change when she, Cap, Dom, Pol, and her baby had to set off and fend for themselves.

Gull and Olm stepped into a debris-filled chamber just off the main corridor. One metallic wall had clearly been compromised by the collision with the shuttle. A few of the illumination elements had fallen from the ceiling. Several spots along the damaged wall were still glowing white hot. There was a broad fissure where the exterior wall had been shoved inwards. At the right angle, Gull could see through it to the moon's surface. He studied the debris and his shoulders slumped.

"What is it?" asked Olm.

Gull kicked at a piece of metal on the floor. "Of all the places for the shuttle to hit," he said dejectedly. "This is . . . .was.... the alpha panel for this entire place," he said glumly. "We can't get much done without it."

Olm studied the panel. A large crack ran down its center. A number of its displays had fallen over. "Can it be repaired?"

Gull sighed. "Yes. Preferably by a team of technicians. Working by myself . . . .well, it might take ellipses to get it going again." He withdrew a small scanner from his belt and analyzed the damage. "Fortunately, most of the damage seems to be to the support structures," he said with obvious relief. "All of the directives within the panel appear to be uncompromised. But I'll still have to repair the operative structures. If the necessary equipment isn't around here somewhere, then I will have to fashion the required tools from scratch. And we can't fully restore life support until that hole in the wall is repaired." He leaned forward staring outside as best he could. From what he could see, the other shuttle was essentially demolished. It was what he would have expected to happen to a shuttle under the circumstances.

Olm looked at the debris on the floor. "Can I help? Maybe you can teach me how to do some of the work."

The question seemed absurd. Gull thought back to all the time he had spent training and studying Umae technology. Then again, how much could Olm learn in say, one ellipse? Would that enable him to provide enough assistance to shorten the entire job by more than an ellipse? If not, it would be an inefficient use of time.

"Have you had much technical training?"

"I'm afraid not. But I think you will find me to be a quick learner. And I'm interested. That should count for something. Are there any tutorials available to me here?"

Enthusiasm. Gull had that in abundance as a young student. It did matter. "There are, but we would need command authority to access them. We don't have that."

"How do we get it?"

It was an odd question. Olm seemed ignorant of the most basic Journeyer functions.

"We don't," said Gull finally. "We need someone who already has that authority. Kat does......."

"I don't think she can help," noted Olm.

Gull paused. Was that an attempt at humor? "Me neither. Let's take a look around and see if we can find any of the equipment that we will need," said Gull. "If we don't have the ability to do any quantum locking, then we will never be able to finish anyway."

"Quantum locking?"

Gull forced a smile. "That will be about lesson sixty-eight. Follow me."

The pair left the chamber and continued down the main hallway. A short ways farther down, Gull stopped at a doorway. He entered a directive into the panel adjacent to it and the doorway slid open. The illuminators on the ceiling were still dark. "This should be one of the main storerooms," said Gull. He increased the intensity of his wrist light.

Metal shelves lined all four walls. On the shelves sat a variety of different gadgets as well as boxes of various sizes. Gull went to the nearest shelf and began sorting through all of the equipment. "This is encouraging," he said, waving a wand-shape device at Olm. It was almost the length of his arm. "A quantum locker," he said enthusiastically. "Now we just need to find a few power packs."

"What should I do?" asked Olm eagerly.

Gull looked around at all of the shelves.

"Search these shelves and see if you can find any metallic boxes about this big," he said, indicating with his hands. "They will be rectangular-shaped and will have four or six small portal plugs in them."

"What's in those boxes?" asked Olm.

"Foodstuffs," replied Gull.

"There don't appear to be very many," he noted. "What if we run out of food?"

"We won't," said Gull. He pointed to a large device along the far wall. "That is a replicator. Once the power is on, we can use it to create more food or medicine or whatever other consumable we need, as long as we have a sample to copy."

Olm walked to the far side of the room and began looking for the power packs. Gull was a bit worried about some of the equipment he was finding. The technology was rather dated. This served to reconfirm his prior belief that no one had been to the Citadel for a long time. Either the Journeys were becoming much longer than anyone had anticipated, or a lot of the Journeycraft weren't making it back anymore. Neither possibility improved the prospects of finding a new planet for the Umae. That made it even more critical that he and Olm complete the repairs as soon as possible. Once the alpha panel was repaired, they had to transfer the information about the planet the *Aurora* had found to the beacon satellites. From there, it could be relayed to every Chronicler Hall on Uma. Any Journeycraft that returned would know what to do with it from there. Gull released a heavy sigh as he looked down at the collection of outdated technical utensils in front of him. The door on his race's survival was closing, and he had a lot of work to do.

———————

The boat followed the shoreline until it started to get dark. Min withdrew his resonator and noted its steady blue light.

"How do you know it is working?" asked Cap skeptically. "Ours didn't."

"I looked it over very carefully before we left," said Min. "And I increased the range dramatically. There isn't . . . .anything . . . .to detect within about a 2-rotation walk. It's fine. Can you ask May to have them take us in?"

Cap looked towards the bow of the boat. May immediately understood his meaning and directed the rowers to take the boat into shore. Once they reached waters that were shallow enough, the adolescents stepped out of the boat and pulled it up onto the land. The beach was rocky and provided a home to a variety of short, shrubby plants.

Dom jumped out of the boat and started splashing towards the sand.

"Dom! Wait." called Cap. "Where are you going?"

Dom stopped, the water reaching to just below his knees. "I want to go and look around," he said.

"Absolutely not. It will be dark soon. We need to get our camp ready."

Dom huffed before turning and slowly walking towards the rocky beach. "But Min said it was fine!" he pleaded.

"Come on everyone," implored May. "Let's set up the lean tos." The rowers complied by hauling several sets of fabric rolls off of the boat. They immediately set to the task of erecting their temporary shelters. They each had brought a small amount of dry wood with them. If they had time, they would try to find more wood along the beach that was passably flammable. Even if the wood was moist, they could oftentimes get it to burn by adding it to an already raging fire.

The dark gray of the sky was steadily transitioning to jet black. The day had brought no rain. Once the lean tos were ready, the rowers squinted in the darkness trying to locate material for a fire. Min had everything he needed to make one out of practically nothing, but he paused. Even though most of the young men and women on the boat were going to become Journeyers, he didn't know if he should expose them all to that technology just to brighten up camp a bit. It wasn't very cold...yet. He looked up at the darkening sky and wondered if he would regret his decision.

———————

The signal from the beacon satellite had been constant for over thirty thousand ellipses. Its signal, a high intensity electro-magnetic wave, had guided the travels of ten different Journeycraft.

The wave itself was designed to crest and trough at regular intervals. The pattern of the signal was relatively simple and repeated itself entirely several hundred times per rotation. Its organization allowed it to stand out against all of the other random energy waves weaving their way through space. The Journeycraft traveled within the wave as much as possible. This facilitated the relay of information to its home Chroniclers' Hall and helped prevent it from becoming lost.

The creature had found the wave quite by accident. It had been dormant since its birth. Encapsulated in a vacuum-defying protein suit, it drifted aimlessly through space. Then, there was the signal. It aroused the creature's consciousness. Instinctively, it began to draw energy from the signal, allowing its nervous system to completely develop. Once that occurred, the creature became ravenous. It continued to absorb as much of the energy as it could. But it wanted more, so it started following the signal to its source.

The origin of this signal would hold more food and, more crucially, the possibility of reproduction. Others of its kind might be following similar paths. If that were true, a nest must be readied for the next generation. These urges pushed the creature through the cold emptiness of space.

As its neural paths developed, so did its intelligence. Base instinct gave way to calculation. The pattern was not natural. It was the product of something intelligent. It would find this intelligence. It was the only way to extend its genetic legacy. The creature was determined to sire a new, superior generation.

The collision with the machine changed everything. The creature attached itself to the exterior of the machine and was initially taken back in the direction of its origin. Then, the machine reversed its course and brought the creature here. The creature had to make a choice. The machine had order, which meant it was connected to intelligence of some sort. But the machine had purposefully returned to this planet. The planet might harbor even greater intelligence. The new machine orbiting the planet was the source of the signal. The creature decided to detach itself from the old machine and study this source.

The creature studied the beacon satellite. It was simply a tool. It was not clear what the tool's purpose was, but that was now unimportant. The real prize was hidden on the planet's surface. The first machine was gone now, having vanished into the clouds. The creature had chosen poorly, but it was a mistake that could be corrected.

The creature's form was a simple, deep brown sphere. It allowed the planet's gravity to pull it away from the satellite. Then it began to fall. As it did, its protein armor began to burn away. Slowly, thousands of smaller brown globes drifted away from its central sphere, attached only by tiny filaments of highly durable proteins.

The faster it fell, the faster its protein coat burned off. The small globes drew their protein leashes taut as the central sphere began to slowly rotate. By the time the entire structure had almost reached the bottom of the cloud cover, it was spinning with incredible speed. As the last of the protein coating dropped away, the tethers snapped simultaneously, hurling the tiny globes away from the central sphere in every direction. The sphere itself plunged downward, hurtling towards the planet's surface.

The dark gray clouds above became saturated with water vapor. Heralded by the rolling rumble of thunder, the skies began to rain.

————————

Olm proved to be a remarkable student. Gull's instruction was mostly hands-on. He would give Olm a task, instruct him how to go about it, and then periodically check his work. Initially, Olm was limited to the most basic chores. Over time, he not only became capable of more complex tasks, but he asked questions of Gull that demonstrated a deeper understanding of the technology involved. Gull had certainly never thought of Olm as dim-witted. Now Olm's quick proficiency with physics, metallurgy and above all, mathematics, made Gull wonder how Olm had never been chosen to train as a Technical Agent.

The task of repairing the Citadel turned out to be much more involved than Gull had anticipated. They simply didn't have all of the tools they required, so the tools themselves had to be fashioned. They also lacked raw materials. The shuttlecraft's collision with the exterior wall of the Citadel had done considerable damage. Not only did the wall itself have to be restored, but the alpha panel was nearly damaged beyond repair. There were specialized coupling and quantification mechanisms that would need to be replaced. The Citadel did not store such supplies. There was only one place where they might be located – the shuttlecraft. The forward shuttle was essentially a utility craft. It was only used under extraordinary circumstances. The bow shuttle was much larger and more advanced. Any of the required mechanisms, if they survived the collision, would be there somewhere within the debris field.

Gull and Olm had sealed the breach at the alpha panel so it no longer compromised the atmosphere of the rest of the Citadel. That process required Gull to build a set of atomic recalibrators nearly from scratch. While this provided an opportunity for Olm to learn a lot about elemental transformation, it took almost a full quarter of an ellipse to complete the job. They both welcomed the day when they could finally remove their vacuum suits. While the suits kept them fed, hydrated, and surprisingly clean, they also slowed them down a great deal. The environmental controls had long been charged and online but had remained useless so long as there was a gaping hole leading to the airless surface outside.

Despite the availability of separate chambers, the men decided to share a large quarters designed for four people. They were the only living creatures on the entire moon. Privacy wasn't a very high priority.

Olm sat on the edge of his bed, rubbing his hands along his face and arms. "Odd isn't it? I rather like the feel of this skin." Gull was seated across from him, studying a schematic of the alpha panel. "Still looking over the schematic?"

"Afraid so. A lot of the parts we need aren't here."

"Can't we make them?"

"No. Not all of them. Some of the more delicate instruments have to be calibrated using a fusion generator. The only place I know that has one of those is a Journeycraft."

"Can't we build one?"

"This won't make a lot of sense. The only way to build a fusion generator is by using another fusion generator. The amount of energy to start and stabilize the necessary reactions is immense."

"But someone had to build the first one, right? How'd they do it?"

"All of the initial attempts were done in space," replied Gull. "And, according to what I have been taught, the first hundred or so ended up in spectacular failure. The uncertainties at the sub-atomic level are staggering. Eventually, one didn't blow up and we had fusion power."

"So, you are saying that the first successful ignition of a fusion generator was . . . . .luck?"

"'Luck' isn't a good technical term," said Gull. "I'm saying that the first success was the result of several dozen potentially disastrous processes simultaneously tracking through a series of rather narrow margins of error."

Olm stood up. "Not reproducible?"

"You want to give it a shot?"

"I guess not when you put it like that. So, what are our other choices?"

"The shuttlecraft, or whatever is left of it," said Gull. "It will have instruments that should be modifiable to serve in the alpha panel. Assuming they weren't destroyed," he added.

"When do you plan on going out?" asked Olm. "I'd like to go too."

"You were pretty shaken when all of that took place on the ship," said Gull. "You don't have to go if you don't want to."

"No," insisted Olm. "I'll be fine."

Gull drew the covers back on his bunk and slid underneath them. "When we wake up then," he said. "No sense waiting any longer."

————————

The fire at the campsite didn't last very long. Despite the lack of rain that day, the available deadfall was still damp from the showers the day prior. They had packed some dry wood on the boat but decided to conserve most of it for now. The wind was calm and the lean-tos would keep any rain that fell overnight off of the campers.

Min checked his resonator again to make sure it was functioning properly. If any Hek entered the scanned radius, he would receive a warning. The radius was large enough that they would have plenty of time to move back to the safety of the water. Cap and May had checked their Charges into their respective lean-tos. The Wards were very tired from rowing all day. Dom had been dashing about energetically, frequently asking if he could go off exploring. He did stop by Min periodically to gain reassurance that the stocky men from the rise wouldn't be making an appearance. Eventually, even Dom grew tired, leaving the five adults and Joba sitting around the nearly spent fire.

Pol sat quietly, holding Joba in her lap. She had said nothing during the entire day, except for when she sang private songs to her son. Min tried to revive the fire with a long stick.

"So, 'Joba', that is an interesting name," he said to no one in particular. Pol did not respond at all. Min looked over at Shu. "But confusing." Cap and May watched the Chronicler with interest.

"We knew this was going to happen," said Shu. "For some time, it had become increasingly more difficult to find unused names for newborns. The child born just prior to Joba, Yun, used the last available name. Since we cannot repeat, Joba became the first child with a two-syllable name."

"The child is special," said May in a low voice. "And you send him away?" Cap put his hand on hers.

Shu paused. "All of our people are special. That is why we do not share names. There will never be another 'May' or 'Cap'. When that name is referenced, it will only be connected to you."

May did not appear comforted. "Don't you see?" she said raising her voice. "The first child born to our people with such a name, and you are sending him away? There will be a price."

Pol's apparent disinterest continued, despite the topic. "Such has been the law for thousands of ellipses, May," said Shu. "You and Cap and Dom and all of the other members of our society are special because we limit our numbers very carefully. If we allowed our numbers to grow unchecked, then each subsequent child makes those who came before it less important. No single individual is above the law. Not even the first child with a name like Joba's."

May bit her lip and turned away. Min was intrigued. He had always assumed the purpose of the population limit was to minimize the need for innovation that would attend population growth. Shu's explanation offered no societal advantage at all that he could think of.

The wind picked up slightly, causing the dying flame to dance vigorously in the center of the group. "We should all get some rest," said Min. "Especially me." He stood up and arched his back. "We have another full day tomorrow."

Shu also stood up. She considered adding to her prior comments but thought better of it. "Sleep well," she said as she walked towards her lean-to. Cap and May stood, and May waved to Pol who walked off with them. Min doused the dying fire with sand before heading in the direction of his lean-to.

By the time the creature's central sphere reached the bottom of the cloud cover, it was roughly the size of a man's fist. The wind pushed it horizontally as gravity pulled it straight down. It reached the surface at a muddy bank next to a small creek. It plunged deeply into the mud, making a modest popping sound in the process.

All was calm next to the creek. The water was shallow and slow. A small owl hooted in the distance as it scanned the darkness for food. A group of bullfrogs called to one another along the bank. The owl suddenly took flight and the bullfrogs dove for cover into the water. The ground issued a low hum and the mud next to the creek was soon covered with earthworms. They practically burst from the ground by the dozens. They were all slithering through the grass as quickly as possible, away from the creek.

A bullfrog peeked out from just under the water's surface. Something had frightened it, but it could not locate any source of danger now. It quickly propelled itself back to the water's edge. Its keen eyes caught something moving in the grass next to the creek. The frog sat low in the water. Its primitive brain was trying to determine whether it should flee or attack.

A lone earthworm slithered out of the grass and onto the muddy bank. The frog remained perfectly still as the worm slowly made its way towards the water. Once it was close enough, the frog rose up slightly and expertly snagged the worm with its long, sticky tongue. In an instant, the earthworm was gone. The bullfrog, content for the moment, turned and dove back into the creek.

Min awoke to a tapping sound. He sat up slowly and tried to gain his bearings. The tapping had come from the top of his lean-to. As he listened, it became more frequent. It was still jet-black outside. As the tapping accelerated, he could hear it coming from all over the camp. He squinted into the darkness, hoping to gain some clue as to what was happening. He braced himself on one hand as he prepared to rise. As he did, he could feel that the ground was covered with small, cold pebbles. He stared closely at his hand and could barely make out a number of tiny white globes that were now stuck to him.

Ice. The globes were made of ice. They were falling from the sky.

"Min?" He could hear Shu call to him in the darkness. He could also hear commotion coming from the other members of the venture.

"Stay where you are," he called. "It's only ice."

Ice? Would they even know what that was? He guessed not. Ice falling from the sky was something he had never heard of here on Uma. Once it stopped and there was some light, he would investigate. Until then, he could only sit quietly in the darkness, listening closely to the ice balls pelting his shelter.

———————

With the first signs of light, the serpent stirred from its hole in search of food. It was solid black and as long as a man's arm. Its forked tongue tested the air. The serpent virtually disappeared into the grass as it easily winded its way towards the creek.

The bullfrog crawled out of the water and onto the mud. Its big eyes scanned the grass beyond the edge of the mud. Nothing seemed to be moving. With one powerful push from its hind legs, it launched itself to the top of the tiny rise beyond the mud, improving its vantage point.

The bullfrog saw the serpent crawling towards it. The frog let out a long, deep croak, puffing out its chest. The serpent, tongue flickering, reared its head a bit to better gauge the air. The frog began crawling slowly towards the snake. The movement in the grass caught the serpent's attention. It lowered its head and began to slowly slide through the grass in the frog's direction. The frog stopped and sat back on its broad haunches.

As the snake neared its quarry, it repeatedly licked at the air to confirm the frog's location. The frog was not moving, but it did not matter. The serpent had locked onto its position.

Once the snake was in striking distance, it coiled slightly. Its prey was simply sitting there, looking at it. A flicker of confusion washed across the neurons inside its head, causing the snake to hesitate. The frog took a pair of small, determined steps in the snake's direction. The serpent struck, seizing the frog in its jaws. It began to coil around its prey. Just as it started to do so, the serpent writhed wildly, releasing the frog. The frog lay on its side, twitching awkwardly. One of its thick hind legs kicked randomly in an effort to right its body.

The snake rolled and twisted across the top of the grass, its mouth wide open. It then closed its mouth and repeatedly flicked its tongue. Ignoring the frog twitching on the grass, the serpent slithered off, following the flow of the water in the creek.

CHAPTER 8

Gull and Olm retraced the long walk back to the portal they had used to enter the Citadel. They carried their vacuum suits. After being confined within them for half an ellipse, they decided to wait as long as possible before donning them again.

Gull manipulated the operations panel for the portal briefly before entering a number of directives. The portal slid open, revealing the barren lunar landscape outside the base.

After a brief, gliding jog, they reached the remains of the forward shuttle. The damage was impressive. As he compared the wreckage to the damage done to the exterior wall, Gull had a renewed appreciation for the structural soundness of the Citadel. The Citadel's exterior wall was compromised by the collision, but not so much that they had had to go outside in order to repair it. The damage to the shuttle, however, was extensive.

The shuttle's spherical shape was now nearly crushed flat like a saucer. The exterior wall of the Citadel had bowed significantly, but the actual breach in the metal, now repaired, had been relatively narrow. The entire craft sat amidst a tangle of twisted metal shards.

"It's unlikely anyone survived that," said Gull through the communicator in his helmet. "The shuttle fared even worse than I thought it would."

Olm studied the scene. "I agree. The amount of force involved would have been beyond what they could have endured."

They carefully approached the craft, picking their way through the debris field. The shell of the bridge was entirely compacted. The effective area within that part of the shuttle had been reduced by at least tenfold.

"I'd like to get a look down into the bridge area," said Gull. He pulled his pack from his back and began digging through it.

"What are you doing?" asked Olm.

"I'm going to use a remote imager," explained Gull. "There is no need for us to climb up and risk having the entire wreck shift underneath us." He removed a sphere about the size of his hand and manipulated a small panel on its exterior. He then reached out towards Olm.

"Give me your arm." He opened a cover on the exterior of Olm's suit and entered a brief series of directives. "This will enable you to see what the imager sees on the inside of your helmet." He then opened a similar cover on his own suit before tossing the imager into the air.

Once the imager reached the apex of Gull's toss, it stopped, hanging motionless. It then slowly propelled itself towards the shuttle until it was directly over it. Both men immediately saw images of the shuttle on their masks.

The seats in the bridge area were surprisingly intact, but there were no bodies in them. Gull had the imager review the entirety of the passenger area. "That doesn't make any sense," he muttered. "They should still be strapped in."

Olm looked at the image in front of him. "Could they have been in another part of the shuttle?"

"Well, someone had to be manually flying the shuttle. Otherwise the shuttle's automatic functions would have prevented it from crashing the way that it did." He took a couple of deep breaths and looked around. "The equipment we need, if it is here, will be just under the bridge."

"Wait," said Olm. "If someone were manually directing the shuttle, nothing within the shuttle would have prevented it from crashing?"

"Only the pilot," said Gull. "That's why we have pilot training. But even then, voice command is extremely simple. You tell it what to do, and it does it."

"So how did this happen?"

Gull thought for a moment. "Kat was an excellent pilot," he said. "She would have never had this accident. The directive that caused the collision with the Citadel would have had to have been extremely simple and short-sighted."

"Like what?"

"Like......I don't know......'follow them' or 'go where they do', something like that. A trained pilot would never have given such a directive for that very reason. When operated manually, the shuttle does exactly what you tell it to do." He sighed. "It sort of makes your theory about remote control a bit more plausible."

Gull searched for the remnants of the shuttle's alpha panel. He finally found it. Its exterior had been crushed. On Gull's command, the imager did a subsurface analysis of the interior of the panel.

"Any luck?"

"The best kind. I can't believe this, but it looks like the shell of the panel absorbed most of the impact. The internal portion is almost undamaged. I think we will be able to salvage everything we need."

"Excellent. What can I do?"

Gull directed the imager to maintain its position. "Just stick close. For now. I'm going to have to go up to remove the panel. You might step back a ways in case the shuttle shifts."

"You think it will?"

"Unlikely. The shuttle is pretty massive. The chances that the addition of my relatively small mass could cause it to move are slim. But still, I'd step back."

Olm complied. He continued to closely follow Gull's activities through the images on his helmet.

Gull carefully propelled himself upwards using some of the thruster power from his suit. He set himself down as gently as possible on the top of the shuttle's remains. The shuttle stayed put, as he was sure it would.

It didn't take long for him to finish his work. He freed the panel from the crushed metal surrounding it and removed a few of its internal components, storing them in a small metallic-colored bag on his belt. He then gestured to Olm before lowering himself back to the ground.

"We should look around," said Gull.

Olm's eyes swept the debris field. "Does it matter if we do at this point?"

Gull began to step gingerly though the pieces of metal. "Yes. We may end up needing to take some of this metal inside and use it for building material. I'd like to get an idea about how much of it is salvageable."

"I wonder where the bodies are."

Gull was wondering the same thing. "Why don't you stay here? This won't take very long."

He walked towards the center of the debris field. Most of the metal was so deranged that he couldn't even tell what part of the shuttle it had once belonged to. Some, however, was reasonably intact. There would be plenty to use for the remaining structural repairs inside. Just as he finished his review and started to walk back towards Olm, something caught his eye.

It was a foot.

Gull stopped. The foot was protruding from underneath a large sheet of metal from the shuttle's landing array. "Olm, I need you," Gull said over his communicator. He waved to him. Olm began to cross through the debris field.

Once he reached Gull's position, Gull pointed out the foot. Olm stared at it, his face blank. "What do you want to do?"

"We should look," said Gull finally. "I need to look."

The two men made their way over to the piece of metal atop the foot. The foot was still attached to a leg. The remains of . . . . .someone . . . .were underneath the metal.

"Can we move it?" asked Olm.

"Maybe. The gravity isn't very strong and our suits will do most of the work. Let's give it a try."

Each man grasped the same end of the piece of metal and pulled. Together they were able to slide it to one side. They found Kat and Ath. The trauma to their bodies was massive, but they could be distinguished by their clothing. Kat's Command Agent insignia was easily recognizable.

"Why do you suppose they are over here?" asked Gull. He had intended for his question to be rhetorical.

"Why not here?"

"They should have been strapped in," said Gull. "They should be up there, strapped to their seats on the bridge," he replied, pointing back to the remnants of the shuttle. He gauged the distance from the remains of the shuttle to the bodies, comparing it to the strength of the moon's gravity. "They must have been ejected along with some of this debris," he offered finally.

"We may never know."

Gull stepped back and let his section of the metal drop. Olm did likewise, reconcealing the two bodies. "Once we get the alpha panel fixed, we'll know," said Gull with a determined voice. "You will be able to process all of that stored data about that creature, and then we will know. They will keep out here. Maybe you can do a full analysis later."

"Of course," said Olm. "I hope you are right."

Gull started walking back towards the Citadel. Olm looked down at the metal sheet for a moment before starting off after him.

———————

Once the sound of the ice pelting his shelter subsided, Min poked his head out and looked around. In the near-perfect darkness, he could vaguely make out the faces of others who were also looking out from their lean-tos.

"Min?" called a voice. It was Shu.

"A moment," he replied. He slipped on his shoes and stepped outside. Pea-sized balls of ice were strewn about the camping area. He could see Shu carefully working her way towards him. He went to meet her.

"What is . . . .are . . . these?" she asked looking about. "I am unaware of any record of this happening before."

Min knelt down and picked up a couple of pieces of ice. "It is frozen water," he began. He looked about to see if anyone else was listening. Almost everyone was looking warily around at the ground, discussing the small whitish globes amongst themselves. "When water gets cold enough, it turns into this. It is called 'ice'."

Shu also knelt down and cautiously touched a piece. "Why does this happen? I have never heard of such a thing."

Min looked up at the sky. "I'm not sure it ever has," he said. "Not around here. It never gets cold enough. There must have been some unusual atmospheric flux that caused a large variance in ambient temperature." Shu looked at him impatiently. "Something . . . .I don't know what . . . caused a lot of the energy in the air to concentrate in one relatively small area. The area that was left without as much energy got very cold and the water that was there froze. Just a theory."

Shu dropped the ice and stood back up. "You have seen this somewhere else?"

"Some planets have a lot of ice on them. Uma's moon has ice underneath its surface." He noticed that many of the campers were gravitating towards them.

"Is everyone all right?" Shu asked. A number of murmured responses assured her that no one was hurt, although everyone seemed distressed by the experience.

"You still don't see, do you?" asked May accusatorily. "Yet another sign. But you refuse to see." Shu folded her arms and stared at May, stone-faced.

"Dom?" said Cap looking around. "Where's Dom?"

Lin stepped forward. "He kept talking about going and looking around last night," she said sheepishly. "But he fell asleep before I did."

Cap grimaced. "I'll bet he did. Moons!" He jogged back towards his shelter. "We have got to find him." May gave Shu one final hard glare before heading off after Cap. The Wards all retreated to their shelters to dress and get ready to search.

"Can I.....?" began Min, turning towards Shu. "I'm not strong enough to go on a search mission," he said, gritting his teeth. "If that is all the help I am allowed to offer."

"I understand. I will go with them. May is angry and is directing her anger at me. If I don't go. . . . . "

"Yes, you should go," agreed Min. "He can't be far, I'm sure."

"Indeed. When I get back, I would know more of this 'ice'".

"Yes. I'll tell you all about it. Now go."

———————

Dom walked along the side of the creek, occasionally stopping to toss a stick or a small pebble into its calm surface. He listened to the croak of bullfrogs coming from alongside the bank, only to hear the frogs splash into the safety of the water as he approached too closely. Several of them dove in almost simultaneously, and then the creek was silent.

He waited for a while, but the sounds of the frogs did not return. Curious, he went down to the edge of the water and perched on a wide log to keep his feet out of the mud. Still, no sounds.

Up above, he heard a faint whining sound. It was well up the creek from where he was now. He thought he saw a brief flash of light in the distance, followed by a popping sound. Min had said that none of the Hek could be close enough to find them. It had to be something else. Something like the streak of light in the sky he had seen before. He was determined to find out just what.

He hopped off the log and back onto the grass. He moved as quickly as he dared in the near darkness. Something hit him on the cheek, and then the hand. Soon, a fury of tiny white balls was pelting him from above. Whimpering, he tried to protect his head with his arms as he scrambled towards the cover of some nearby trees. He crouched on a root of a huge tree, its canopy shielding him from the pellets. Before long, the bombardment stopped. The ground was covered with them. Dom was unwilling to touch the strange objects. He leaned against the tree and waited to see if they would start to fall again.

He must have dozed. The morningside sky hinted at the coming rotation. Dom stood up and stretched. While the tree had made a good shelter, it did not make the softest bed. He hurried off, following the creek in the direction he had seen the light in the sky.

———

The serpent carefully moved along the side of the creek. It chose not to dare the water. An undetected predator could divert it from its task. It attempted to scan the sky above for danger, but its eyesight was poor. So, it clung to the ground in the tallest grass, hoping to remain unseen.

The water's surface abruptly broke in the center of the creek. The serpent froze and flicked at the air with its tongue. Something was amiss. Then the surface broke again. An odd noise came to it from farther downstream.

Dom still had no idea what had caused the light. He had found a number of good, smooth stones and decided to take a break and toss them into the creek. He tried to hit the same spot each time. *Plop! Plop!*

The coal black snake watched the creature tossing the rocks. It was amusing itself. The snake slithered soundlessly through the grass, trying to get closer. The creature seemed completely distracted by its game. The snake reached the edge of the tall grass and then stopped. It could get no closer without revealing itself.

The last rock landed almost exactly in the same spot as the others. Dom congratulated himself for his marksmanship and continued his walk up the creek. He was getting tired. It couldn't be that much farther.

The scent of the creature filled the snake's mouth. It was rather large, although its hide appeared to be somewhat thin. The serpent was a constrictor. Its teeth were made for grasping, not penetration. It would have to bite *hard*. It coiled slightly and waited in the grass.

The mud at the edge of the creek gave way to a stand of tall grass. Dom's feet were caked with mud. He stopped for a moment and tried to wipe them off on the ground, but it was too wet. Dom stepped through the mud as best he could. He knelt down next to the water and washed his hands. Some of the pebbles in the mud sparkled slightly. They were yellow brown, but none were big enough to make good throwing stones. He had never seen any rocks like that on Atla.

The serpent was directly behind him now. It edged its way forward, onto the mud. Dom was splashing around in the water in front of it. The serpent waited for him to stand up and then struck.

The snake locked its jaws onto the back of Dom's leg just above his heel. Dom let out a wail of surprise before stumbling forward into the creek. He was down on all fours, screaming with panic. The serpent coiled around his lower leg, biting down with every bit of strength it could summon.

When Dom saw the snake, his panic took on a maniacal fury. He kicked and swatted at the snake as he attempted to simultaneously crawl back to the bank. The snake resisted his attacks. Dom dragged himself out of the creek, bawling furiously. He picked up a rock next to his hand and tried to hammer at the snake. His blows were mostly off the mark. Then, Dom's body stiffened and the rock dropped to the ground. His eyes rolled back into his head. The snake went limp and hung loosely from his leg. Dom keeled over on his side, his body wracked by spasms for a moment before growing still.

The morning birds had long fled. The crickets in the grass did not make a sound. Dom sat up slowly and unwrapped the serpent from around his leg. He calmly tossed it to the ground. The snake writhed aimlessly, coiling about itself. Glancing down, Dom knelt and wiped at the trickles of blood oozing from a line of scratches on the back of his leg. With one more look at the contorting serpent, he began walking along the creek, drawn by voices in the distance.

———

Gull was easily able to modify the components from the shuttle for use in the alpha panel. The metal casing around the panel itself was badly bent in some places. Gull showed Olm how to use an electron arranger to return the metal back to its original form. As had become customary, Olm wanted to understand how the device actually worked. Once Gull gave an explanation, Olm again insightfully related it to the other technical lessons Gull had provided. His assistance was having a profound impact on the speed with which the repairs were being completed.

"Have you always been a Life Agent?" Gull asked as the two worked on the Citadel's alpha panel.

"Of course, why?"

"You have such an aptitude for technology. I wonder why no one noticed and put you on that course."

"I wasn't interested," replied Olm.

"So?" replied Gull. "Since when did that matter? My interest was in data analysis. It isn't like we had a choice."

Olm returned his attention to the alpha panel. It had taken several rotations, but the majority of the critical systems had been restored. Now it was a matter of initiating the function routines that made it work. The entire repair process had taken just over half an ellipse.

"How long do you think it will take you to get your data on the creature analyzed?" asked Gull.

Olm stopped working and turned towards him. "You are rather anxious about that aren't you?"

"Aren't you?" responded Gull curiously. "It is a previously unknown life form. It did do something bizarre to our crewmates. Don't you want to know what it is?"

"Of course," said Olm quietly. "It shouldn't take long. Then I'll tell you all about it." He looked over the expanse of the alpha panel. "I'm guessing this panel is much more powerful than the one on the ship?"

"By a factor of thousands."

"Then, after everything is done, less than a rotation I'd say. Then we will know."

"Terrific. If all goes well, we can have this ready by tomorrow. Then, you can be done by the following day."

"Then what?" That was the question that had hung over the two of them since they reached the Citadel.

"Well, we need to see what data has been uploaded by the other Journeycraft. Then we can generate a space grid to see what sectors have been covered. Most importantly, we need to add the information we have about our new planet. Then we will have to go into repose."

"Repose?" Olm was aghast. "Why?"

"Because it is going to be a long time before any Journeycraft make it back here. Besides, we don't have anywhere else to go. We can't very well arrive home in a shuttle craft. Can you imagine what the Chroniclers would do?"

Olm thought for a moment. "It has been a long time," he said finally. "But our work together should be done soon." Gull was still deeply focused on his task. Olm's darkening scowl was lost to him.

———————

The two men worked the rest of the day on the function routines. The next day was much of the same, with Gull running a series of detailed analyses to assure the routines were synchronized properly. By all indications, they were. The men went to sleep that night ready to initiate the panel the next morning.

The initiation proceeded flawlessly. Gull opined that the panel probably worked better than it ever had as they had improved upon some of its previous technology. Gull began to input the data on the new planet.

While Gull worked, Olm analyzed the data about the creature that had been collected onboard the *Aurora*. Gull seemed much more interested in Olm's work than he was his own.   Olm sat stone-faced as he manipulated the various processes required to find meaning in the stream of information being fed into the panel. By mid-day, Gull was done entering his directives.   Olm was still working intently.

"Coming along well?" asked Gull as he looked at Olm's display.

"Oh yes," said Olm. "Very well."

"Good.   I'll go get us some food.   Maybe you'll have something to share when I get back."   Gull started off down the corridor towards the provision chamber.

Food was one thing the men didn't want for at the Citadel. The provision chamber was fully stocked with foodstuffs that would remain edible indefinitely. Gull sorted through the shelves and prepared a collection of fruits, vegetables, mushrooms, and nuts for their lunch. He also took a couple of small containers of grape juice. He stacked all of the food on a tray and headed back to the alpha panel.

Olm was still at work, engrossed in the display. Gull set the tray on a small table next to the panel. He wasn't sure if Olm had even noticed his return.

"Here you go......" he began.

"Remarkable," said Olm.

Gull paused. "What is?"

"The creature."

Gull picked up a handful of nuts and popped a few into his mouth. "What did you find out?" He looked at Olm's display. It was blank.

"It is actually multiple organisms. There is a central executive connected to hundreds of sub-agents by protein filaments. The filaments create a quantum connection between the executive and the sub-agents that continues even after the filaments are severed."

"Connection?"

"The sub-agents serve the executive absolutely. The executive's sole goal is to find or create a suitable environment for reproduction. The one on the *Aurora* was a female."

"The panel is functioning properly then. Excellent. But why did you take all of the results off the display?"

"It requires a sheltered environment with a rather high degree of radiant energy. If the environment it is in doesn't have that quality, the creature manufactures it."

"You mean it is capable of generating its own radiant energy?" asked Gull with disbelief. "Like a star?"

"It, along with its sub-agents, is capable of manipulating other life forms through parasitic attachment. These hosts then bring about the environment for the creature."

"A parasite?" echoed Gull. "That explains the black projectiles, and the behavior of the others on the ship. You were exactly right. Do you think it was following the beacon signal because of its energy level?"

"Its order. The energy had order. Where there is order, there is intelligence. Where there is intelligence, there are adequate host candidates."

"Sweet moons," muttered Gull. "Unbelievable. And you were able to determine all of that from the relatively brief scan?"

"It is intelligent. It is cunning. And" he added after a brief pause. "It has a sense of humor."

Gull stared at Olm. "The data tells you that? I'd love to know . . . . ."

"And it calls itself *Frhsgetdfes*." Olm confidently articulated the name, holding the second "s" a bit longer than seemed necessary.

Gull froze. His eyes wide, he began to step back. Olm swiftly seized him by the collar. Gull tried to pry himself loose, but Olm's grip was immoveable. "Let.....me..."

"If this accursed body had been female, this would have been so much easier," he hissed. "But it is rather difficult to differentiate genders with your species. At least, at first sight." Gull struggled harder to free himself from Olm's grip, but to no avail. "Developing the required technology won't take long at all," said Olm with a smile. "You brought me right to it. And to accelerate the process, my sub-agents destroyed part of your building. You see," he said drawing Gull's face close to his. "If you repair something practically from scratch, you have to understand how it was put together in the first place. My agents, fortuitously, couldn't have hit a better spot."

Gull brought his legs up and tried to push himself away from Olm. It was useless. Olm's body was as rigid as the wall Gull was being pressed up against. "What ...are....you..."

"What am I going to do?" finished Olm. "How about what I'm not going to do?" He drove his index finger into Gull's forehead. Gull twitched and weakly mumbled as Olm swirled his finger around the inside of his skull. "No repose, that's for sure. I don't need it to wait that long. And you," he said as he allowed Gull's body to drop to the floor. "You just don't need it at all." Olm shut down the panel in front of him. "Oh," he said, looking down at Gull's lifeless body. "I should thank you for the science lessons. They will serve me well as I establish my domination of your planet."

———————

Cap and May each led a pair of their Charges in different directions. Shu went with Cap and his group. No one seemed to expect Min to leave the camp area, and no one said anything when he stayed near his lean-to.

Cap spotted some footprints in the sand. He jogged along, following their trail. While his Charges could match his pace, Shu struggled.

Soon, they saw a creek that emptied into the lake. The banks of the creek were muddy. Beyond the mud were patches of grass of varying heights. Unfortunately, Dom had demonstrated some uncommon good sense and stayed clear of the mud. Still, there was little doubt where he had gone.

"We'll find him up the creek," said Cap confidently. "He's probably throwing rocks or something."

Shu was winded. "C-can we . . . .stop for a moment?"

"No. You can stay here. If I happen to be wrong, he may come back this way along the beach. Someone needs to stay. It may as well be you."

Shu signaled her agreement by sitting on a fallen log. Cap and his Charges were quickly out of her sight as they headed upstream.

The stream was broad, but rather shallow and slow. Bullfrogs stopped their croaking calls and sought shelter in the water as Cap's group approached. Beyond the muddy banks, the grassy area allowed them to make good time. An early morning fog limited their range of vision.

"Dom?!?" called Cap. He cupped his hands around his mouth. "Where are you?" There was no response.

"What do you think he was looking for?" asked Lin.

"Nothing," said Cap. "Nothing in particular anyway. Just looking." Cap stared into the low fog, as if he could will it away. They continued moving. Cap stopped occasionally to search the mud for more tracks.

"Would he have left the creek?" asked Lin.

Cap stopped and looked off into the distance, away from the creek. "I doubt it," he said uncertainly. "The creek at least gives him something to focus his curiosity on. But there is no way of knowing what he might have been able to see before this fog set up."

"I don't think he could have seen much," Lin offered. "It would have still been dark then anyway. He probably would have been scared to wander away from the creek without knowing what was ahead."

"Maybe. But he wasn't afraid to leave the camp, was he? But I suspect you are right about not being able to see anything." Cap stopped and regarded Lin for a moment. She had been one of his Charges since she was a toddler. Now she was practically a grown woman, and an exceptionally bright one at that. She had frequently impressed him with her reasoning skills. Now Cap was torn. He would miss all of his Charges, certainly. But the thought that they would all be Journeyers made him very proud. All except Dom. Right now, Dom was simply irritating him.

"Dom!?!" he called again.

"Dom," echoed a quiet voice. Cap, despite his distress, couldn't help but smile. Dom emerged from the fog, slogging his way through the mud towards the group.

Cap hurried over to the young man, hugging him. "I know you have a good explanation for this," said Cap. "Do not do anything like this again." Dom stiffly tolerated Cap's embrace.

"Explanation," he said once Cap released him.

"You scared all of us," scolded Cap. "Didn't you even think how we might feel about your decision to run off?"

Dom looked around at the others before refocusing on Cap. "Decision....didn't good." He then continued walking downstream along the creek.

Cap started to reply but thought better of it. There would be time later for scolding. Dom, Cap, and the others walked back along the creek until they reached Shu. She was still seated on the fallen log. She rose as they approached.

Dom walked up to her and stopped. Shu knelt before inquiring of the youngest Charge. "Are you all right?"

Dom hesitated. "Are you all right?" he repeated.

Shu cocked her head to one side. "Yes. I suppose. Where did you go?"

Dom cocked his head as well. "Yes. All right."

"Are you sure he is all right, Cap?" she asked the Rearer.

"He is just being silly now," offered Cap. "Shu, are you ready to go?"

Dom stared up at her, noting the symbol of her robe. "Are we running off now?"

"I'm fine, Cap," she replied. "Maybe I need to get more exercise." She watched Dom closely.

"Take up rowing," Cap said flatly.

Cap and Shu walked back up the beach towards the camp with the Charges following along behind. They all had questions for Dom about what he had seen. His responses were deliberate and empty. "Nothing. Just a creek. That's all."

Soon they made it back to the camp. May and her group were already there. She ran to embrace Dom, squeezing him much more forcefully than Cap had. "I made a bad decision," said Dom at once. "I did not think how you might feel."

May put Dom down and tussled his hair. "Well, someone has already set you straight about that, huh?" she said with a grin. She took Dom by the hand and led him into the center of the camp.

"None the worse for wear?" said Min. He was seated next to his lean-to.

"I made a bad decision," said Dom. He waited to see how Min would react.

"Understanding that is what is important now," said Cap.

"Let's eat and move on," Min said. "We have a ways to go yet before we reach the Land Bridge." The Charges went to their respective shelters and began preparing meals.

"Dom, what do you want to eat?" asked Lin. "Help me unpack some of our food." He walked off after her, glancing back at Cap, May, and Min.

Cap was the largest, he must be the leader. May must be a mate. Shu was different somehow. He needed more information to know what she was about. The small man who had been in camp alone, he was weak and of no consequence. He would be disregarded. For now.

CHAPTER 9

Sol had offered to help Jack inspect the *Aurora* to see if they could find any more clues about the fate of crew. It was still very early in the day and few Umae were up and about. The two men walked up the access ramp of the *Aurora*, raising it behind them. Jack had been so eager to report his prior findings to Min that he had neglected to check out the living quarters.

The first living quarters was extremely tidy. A residual genetic scan revealed that it belonged to a relatively young woman. The uniforms in a storage compartment revealed her to be the Command Agent.

"Hmmmm……. she must have been very talented," said Jack. "A Command Agent at such a young age? It sort of makes you feel inferior, doesn't it?"

"Not me," said Sol soberly. "But maybe some." Sol thought back to his earlier conversation with Min. For his age and experience, Jack was as talented as could be expected. But was he ready for command authority? Eve certainly was. Sol didn't envy Min's dilemma.

The second chamber was less well-kept. Reading displays and clothes were strewn about and the bed was unmade. Jack activated one of the reading displays and looked it over. "A tech journal." He looked at a second one. "This one too."

Sol searched through some of the clothing. "Tech Agent," he said, holding up the insignia. "A female. But you techs are usually neater than this."

Sol had a point. Technical Agent candidates were selected for having a variety of characteristics. Intelligence and curiosity were priorities, but so was organization. "Maybe she couldn't clean up for some reason," he offered.

"An illness," said Sol.

"Or an injury."

They proceeded to the other quarters. None of them were remarkable in any way. The last one was plainly that of the ship's Life Agent. It contained health records of the various crew members. Jack and Sol sat down at the panel and began to read through them.

"Nothing too unusual here," said Jack. "Wait, it looks like the Tech Agent had some sort of cellular decomposition going on."

"The same condition Min suffers from. That would help explain the mess," said Sol. "And . . . . . here is something. The Data Agent apparently was showing advanced symptoms of DSM."

"DSM?"

"Deep Space Megalomania," said Sol. "Basically, its development is the result of being shut up in a Journeycraft with the same small group of people for a long time. One begins to focus on all of the things he doesn't like about the others while subjectively exaggerating one's own accomplishments. It is rather rare and not really serious, at least not in the early stages. I can see how it could become detrimental to a crew's integrity."

"I'll bet," agreed Jack. He terminated access to the records. "You know, they seem to be a lot like us."

"Who?"

"The crew of the *Aurora*."

"Much more alike than different," Sol said quietly.

Jack stopped at the door as they left, turning around for one last look. Having read through their records and searched their clothes and belongings, he felt like he knew them. He was more determined than ever to figure out what had happened.

The campers had a quick morning meal and then restowed their gear onto the boat. None of the Charges said anything to Dom about his disappearance. He picked at his food but ate very little. He stayed close to Shu, listening carefully to anything she had to say. In fact, they had sat by themselves, away from the rest of the group, obviously engrossed in conversation for most of the morning.

Before boarding the boat, Shu approached Cap and May. "I have decided to train Dom as a Chronicler." Dom stood next to her, obviously pleased.

"But . . . ." Cap and May looked at one another, unable to articulate a reply.

"He is plainly very intelligent," continued Shu. "He will do very well, I'm confident."

May wiped a growing tear from her eye. She would part with Dom, and soon. But at least now he wouldn't be exiled. He had a chance at a life now, possibly a very good one. She looked down at him and smiled.

"You will do well, won't you?" she asked him. Dom edged closer to Shu but said nothing.

"He will," said Cap assuredly. Cap was having problems believing what he had just heard. He had caught May wiping away her tear. He knew exactly what she was thinking right now.

Dom vacated his customary spot in the boat next to Cap and sat next to Shu instead. As the Charges began to row in compliance with the tempo of May's call, the beach where they had camped slowly faded from view. The morning fog was almost entirely gone. The land steadily rose from the sandy beach, forming a low cliff that faced the water. A number of boulders peeked out of the lake at the foot of the cliff. Various water birds roosted in the crags of the cliff's face.

"Dom," began Shu finally, "if you are to become a Chronicler, you must learn not to be so impulsive. In fact, you must be resolute and consistent in your actions. Impulsiveness is practically the last trait a Chronicler needs."

"What will I do?" asked Dom calmly.

"Do? When?"

"When I'm a Chronicler."

Shu found his sober attentiveness unsettling. "Well, **if** you become a Chronicler," she said, emphasizing the contingent nature of his fate, "you will be one of us who records events for the residents of the island. It is important that we keep track of everyday occurrences so we can make sense of things later. But you will not be a Chronicler until you have completed your training."

"Records of what?"

"Like . . . . the success of the gardens. We would collect information about what was grown, how much was produced, that sort of thing."

"So we can figure out how to grow more next time?"

"No," said Shu.

"Why wouldn't we do that?"

That was a difficult question. "We are also in charge of declaring the law. Our people come to us sometimes and want to know what the law is. Our laws were created by a sacred group known as the Directors, may they guide our way, for very specific purposes to benefit our people. The laws are very old and were designed to give us the best chance of survival."

The boy brightened considerably. "That sounds . . . . interesting. When do we start?"

Shu was pleased by his new enthusiasm. Cap had feared that Dom would never adjust to the realization that he wasn't going into space with the other Charges. "Not until we get back.

But if you have questions along the way, you may ask them. I may not be able to answer, but I'll try."

"You wouldn't answer my questions?"

"It may be that I know the answer, but just can't tell you," she said quietly. "Some of the training you will receive is secret. You will understand once you start."

"I am eager," he said, rubbing his hands together.

"Good," said Shu. "I am glad."

———————

The boat traveled eveningsidedly for most of the morning. May let the Charges rest and refresh themselves periodically. When the time arrived for the noon meal, the cliffs did not offer any place safe to land the boat. Instead, the group simply floated along as they ate.

"Any ideas about how far this cliff extends?" Cap asked Min.

"No. But it would be nice to have a place to land the canoe."

"If we don't find one, I guess we will just sleep out here."

Min wondered if he would be able to sleep at all. During his life, he had logged a lot more time in repose sleep than he had otherwise. Normal sleep was a skill that one learned like any other, and Min hadn't had much practice. It wasn't as if he weren't already tired.

He took a deep breath. In the back of his mind, he had initially intended to defy Sol's diagnosis. Min thought he was going to be up and about in a few rotations and be as good as new. Now he realized that wasn't going to happen. While his energy had risen a bit once he got used to being on the surface, his body was still heavy with constant fatigue. He had found that he needed to focus intensely on any sort of mental exercise. In a few more rotations, he would be on the moon. Sol had said that being there would help. Min still hadn't decided if Eve would be there with him.

After the mid-day break, May called on the Charges to move the boat ahead. The cliff face extended as far as they could see. The possibility of spending the night on the water was becoming more and more likely. As the daylight began to wane, May called the Charges to halt.

"I think they have done enough for one day," she called up to Cap. Cap stood up and gestured. The Charges all released their oars and sat back on their benches to rest before the evening meal.

Cap tossed the anchor over the side of the boat and made sure it was firmly attached. The tether still had slack in it when the anchor stopped sinking. "Not very deep here," Cap noted. "Maybe four or five bodies."

May negotiated her way past her crew until she was next to Cap. "Well, we don't have to worry about drifting then." She withdrew a poncho and wrapped it around her shoulders. The dark sky was starting to rumble. The Charges were also preparing themselves for a night in the rain. Min began looking through his pack for his own covering.

"It's dark and it's wet," called Cap to his Wards. "But we are all in good company, so things could be worse, right?"

Min studied his resonator. The warning light was a steady blue. The Hek were far, far away. Min slipped it back into his sack.

"What is it?" asked Cap nervously. The Charges were now silently focused on Min and his device.

"Nothing," said Min confidently. "All clear."

Cap was relieved. "Good. We all need our rest. I suspect the hard work is still ahead of us." With that, Cap slumped down on the bottom of the boat and closed his eyes.

Min pulled his poncho more tightly around him. He wasn't quite sure how to best position himself for sleep. After glancing around at the Wards as they settled in, he turned towards the cliff face, eyeing it warily in the last light of day.

Prior to exploring the living quarters, Jack and Sol had directed the *Aurora*'s alpha panel to analyze the barb Jack had found by the shuttle bay doors during his previous visit to the ship. The panel was just completing its analysis as they returned to the ship's life lab.

"It doesn't appear to be all that unusual actually," said Sol. "I haven't seen these exact structures before, but the replication strategies are familiar."

"Where?" asked Jack. As always, his curiosity was nearly insatiable.

Sol froze the display and pointed to a mass of colored structures. "Magnify." The display complied, dramatically increasing the size and detail of the structures. "These bands indicate that whatever produced these protein chains reproduces sexually."

"So, they have boys and girls?"

"Try 'male' and 'female'," said Sol. "And yes, in a sense. At least genetically. With this data, there is no way to determine anatomy, so how they combine their protein codes is beyond me. It doesn't look like we have an entire genome for the organism, or I would just have the panel reproduce one for us on the display."

"What else are you able to determine?"

Sol highlighted a different set of data on the display. "What do you make of these bonds in the protein templates?"

"I would say that they are very stable. It would take a fair amount of energy to break them."

"How much?"

"Something on the order of 10,000 mils."

"10,000? Really? Interesting."

"Why so?"

"Well, the bonds in Umae protein templates, relatively speaking, are very stable compared to other life forms. That is one reason why the mutation rate in our species is so low. But those bonds can be broken with far less than 10,000 mils. When we reproduce, there are very specific catalytic enzymes, which lower the energy required. Without them, our genetic markers would never unfurl and present themselves to the genetic markers of the other mating member."

"So," said Jack, leaning back, "do you think this species does something similar?"

"Maybe," began Sol slowly. "But . . . . .one moment." He manipulated the panel and the display shifted to a pattern of fast-moving colors and shapes. "No. There isn't any hint of that sort of enzyme here," he said finally. "And there would be if this species utilized such an approach."

"So, how do those bonds get broken?"

"The energy has to come from somewhere in the environment."

"Energy......" mused Jack. He abruptly leapt from his chair. "Stars, Sol. That's it! The beacon signal! That had to be it."

"What do you mean?" asked Sol anxiously.

"The beacon signal is nothing but a high energy beam of electro-magnetic radiation. If that is what this creature needs to reproduce, maybe it was drawn to the beam."

"Yes, it makes sense. How wide is the beacon signal?"

"It is approximately twice the width of a typical Journeycraft," said Jack. "It has to be substantial enough for an errant craft to find it again, but if it is too big it would require too much energy to maintain it."

Sol stood up now as well. "The creature happens upon the beam and begins following it. The Journeycraft is following the beam as well and the two literally collide. That must have been how the two came together."

"But how did it get in?" he asked quietly. "I checked the exterior integrity of this ship thoroughly. It wasn't compromised in the slightest."

Sol folded his arms and looked down at the display. "So, the crew let it in? Why would they do that with a completely unknown life form?"

"Maybe it asked?" Sol scowled at Jack.

"Well, none of them are here now," noted Sol. "The entire crew is gone as well as the organism. So are two shuttles."

"But two shuttles weren't necessary," said Jack. "The entire crew could have fit into one."

"Are you suggesting they took the organism with them in the other shuttle?"

"I'm not suggesting anything," sighed Jack. "I'm speculating out loud. Why else would they have taken two shuttles?"

"Maybe to . . . .escape?" offered Sol. "At least the first shuttle. The second . . .I can't explain."

"Pursuit?"

"Pursuit of what? The creature?"

Jack closed his eyes for a moment and thought hard before responding. "The first shuttle. Maybe the second shuttle was pursuing the first."

Sol started to object, but he had little to offer that contradicted Jack's theory. "I hope you are wrong."

"So do I, and I probably am." He checked his equipment bag and made sure he had everything he had brought onboard. "Can you think of anything else we need to look at?"

The Life Agent shook his head. "Not now. I just wish we had a more complete picture of this creature's genetic markings. That would tell us a lot."

Jack started walking towards the egress ramp. "Maybe we will think of something later. Come on. Let's go have some of that delicious 'bread'."

Sol rolled his eyes. "Chroniclers or not," he said half seriously, "I'm teaching these people about fermentation before I leave again."

Min had finally found enough comfort to doze off. The rain was relatively kind. It was very light – almost a heavy mist. The sound it made as it met the lake's surface was actually rather soothing. The Journeyer had sat down on the bottom of the boat, leaned back, and managed to fall sleep.

As his mind returned from a troubled sleep, Min grimaced at a tight pain in the small of his back. The morningside sky was just beginning to lighten. Min withdrew his black box. The light was still steady and blue. He turned his attention towards the cliffs. They were barely visible in the darkness.

"All right everyone," called May from the bow of the boat. "A quick bite and then let's get going. We don't want to have a settling later do we?"

The Charges responded with a half-groan, half chuckle.

"A . . . . .'settling'?" asked Min.

"Yes," said Cap. "If we get stuck in the boat for too long, we have a settling to relieve ourselves. Basically, we all take our clothes off and jump in the water. We swim a short ways away from the boat and do what we need to do. We settle in and everything settles to the bottom."

Min frowned. "What if you can't swim?"

Cap turned and stared at Min. "You can't swim?"

Min shook his head. "I doubt it."

"How can you not know how to swim?"

"Well, we actually have an exercise area on our ship that allows us to simulate swimming. And I did go swimming when I was a Charge, but that doesn't mean I could do it now. I suspect that I would tire rather quickly. I haven't been able to really exercise for quite some time."

Cap was slightly irritated. "Let's hope you don't fall in."

May and the Charges soon had the boat moving briskly across the top of the water. The rain stopped entirely, and visibility was excellent. The cliff face seemed to move with them as they traveled parallel to the shoreline. Looking into the distance eveningsidedly, the elevated cliff extended as far as they could see.

The Charges clearly needed a break. They had not relieved themselves since well before stopping for the night prior. May made her way to the stern of the boat and sat down next to Cap.

"I was joking about the settling," she said quietly, "but now . . . . ."

The Charges were anxiously watching their Rearers, fully understanding what their conversation was about. "Let's take the boat in a bit closer," Cap suggested. "We can see the shoreline better and the water won't be as deep."

"Take it in towards the shore, slowly!" May called to her crew.

The Charges turned the boat and began driving it towards the cliff face. Slowly, the cliff rose as they neared the shore.

"Look there!" said Cap pointing. There was a slender stretch of beach at the base of the cliff. It became visible once they had made it about halfway in. He cautiously surveyed the water ahead of the boat. He wanted to be sure there weren't any submerged rocks waiting to capsize the canoe. "Looks clear," he said, still watching carefully. "No settling today, I guess."

The boat soon reached the beach. The sandy area was just deep enough for the Charges to pull the entire craft ashore. With the approval of Cap and May, they all spread out quickly to relieve themselves. The adults did likewise.

Pol carried Joba to the base of the cliff and sat down. She checked her child's wrapping and then began to nurse. Shu sat down a short distance away. Joba was burying his face into his mother's chest. "He's beautiful," said Shu. "It may not matter," she continued, "but I'm .... sorry. I understand how you must feel."

Pol's lips curled back slightly. "Understand? How can you possibly understand? You see how beautiful he is, but you send him away? You understand nothing!" She quickly rose and stalked off along the base of the cliff clutching her child. Shu hugged her knees.

"Shu?" It was Min. She wasn't sure how long he had been standing there.

"Yes, sit," she said, trying to seem welcoming.

"I think we will be there sometime tomorrow," offered Min. "As I understand it, we are going to talk to them about the information they might have about that ship. Do you think it would help if I went with you to ask?"

Shu remained silently, carefully searching for her response.

"Remember, once you enter the settlement, your exile will be immediate. Perhaps I should see if there is any reason for you to do that first?"

"My health has already exiled me as a practical matter," he noted.

"So you say, but I'd thought you'd want to leave your options open as long as possible."

Options. Min felt as if he had very few left. The only one he cared about was the one where he and Eve stayed together.

"Say what?" It was Dom. He had managed to approach Shu and Min without their notice.

"Dom, where'd you come from?" asked Min.

"We are going to visit the Chroniclers' Hall at the other community," said Shu. "Maybe you will be able to go inside."

The boy smiled enthusiastically. "I'd like that very much."

Something struck Min lightly on the top of the head. A small pebble bounced away from him into the sand. On the beach, the Charges were scrambling in a near-frenzy.

"Boat!" yelled Cap. "Boat!"

Min, Shu, and Dom quickly rose and headed towards the boat. May was helping Pol and her child as they hurried along the water's edge. Min turned and stared up at the top of the cliff.

There were four of them. Each one was short and thickly muscled. Two of them carried long spears. Next to them were two medium-sized dogs that began barking frantically.

Min stood and stared at them while everyone else boarded. "Min, come on!" implored Cap. *My health has already exiled me.......* He removed the resonator from his bag and began manipulating the display on its face. It had been simple enough for him to modify it before the trip began to provide it with a scanning capacity. It was a change he hadn't mentioned to Shu. The four figures atop the cliff stood calmly while the dogs dashed back and forth, anxious to come down.

Once he was satisfied that the resonator had had ample time to record the data he wanted, Min calmly boarded the boat and took his seat. The four Charges pushed the boat into the water before stepping in themselves. May didn't need to call a cadence as the Charges simply rowed as fast as they could.

Dom sat, stone-faced, watching the figures and their dogs. He turned to look at the panicked reaction the figures provoked in each member of the crew. The expressions on their faces fascinated him.

May only allowed the Charges to take the canoe far enough out so that the cliff face was no longer visible. Once the boat was stopped, Cap tossed the anchor overboard.

He sat down across from Min. "Well Journeyer," he huffed. "What are we going to do now?"

Just after the evening meal, Eve walked down to the docks. Her dinner was surprisingly good, despite what they had been served earlier in their pyramid. Fresh fruit, vegetables, mushrooms, and fresh water – she didn't see any of the flat, crusty squares that were passed for bread.

The docks were abandoned. Several boats were moored, gently tapping against their berths with each wave of water. It had not rained since noon. The eveningside sky was a half-lit orange red.

She wondered where Min was, and what he was doing. The information from the *Aurora* was vital. If her crew had strong data indicating the location of Haven...... Once he came back, she knew he would tell her his decision. As much as she admired Jack's abilities, she knew he wasn't yet ready to command a Journeycraft. She felt sure that Min knew that as well.

The Hek had fire. Their development had somehow bolted forward at a rate no one had ever anticipated. Min seemed to think that Critical Closure was still a long, long ways away. Her own studies of the projections told her he was right. But the price for an error in that respect would be terminal for the Umae.

Min had mentioned that it was a three-day trip by boat to the Land Bridge. She wasn't sure how he reached that conclusion, but his logic and calculations were typically flawless. If he was right, he and the others would reach the Land Bridge late tomorrow. The information they gathered there would set the course moving ahead, for all of them.

She turned at the sound of approaching footfalls. It was Bal, accompanied by three hulking Chronicler Guards. The Chronicler waved a greeting and bade the Guards to remain some distance away.

"Eve, what brings you here?" he asked.

"I was finished early and thought I would take a walk. I sort of just . . .ended up here."

"It has been rather dry today," he noted flatly. "I wonder if Min and his group are making good progress."

Eve looked over at the Guards. They stood up perfectly straight. They looked almost identical. "I'm sure they are." she said finally. "Min is quite capable. I'm sure Cap and May and their Charges are as well."

"Cap and May are our finest Rearers," said Bal. "The Charges who finish with them are among our most well-rounded citizens. They will make fine Journeyers I think."

Eve had almost forgotten about the empty Journeycraft and the plan to train the Charges as its new crew. "I'm certain they will. Sol and Jack will make excellent teachers."

Despite the calm evening air, Bal pulled the hood of his red garment up over his head. "Who will be Command Agent now that Min will be gone?" His cowl concealed all of his face save for a contented smile.

"I don't know," confessed Eve. "Min will make that decision."

"He has not done so yet?" asked Bal.

It was a strange question. Eve could not remember ever having to replace an officer that was still alive. She didn't know, offhand, what the Protocols required for such a situation. "No, not yet. He wanted to go to the Land Bridge first."

Bal turned and looked back at the three Guards. They stood there, impassively staring out at the darkening sky over the lake. "There has been a misunderstanding," said Bal.

"How so?"

Bal walked closer to Eve. "Because once Min returns, his exile will have already begun. You won't be permitted to speak with him."

"What? Why not?" Her voice quivered.

"The simple act of mooring the boat at the Land Bridge will suffice. Once exile begins, no one may speak with that citizen. I thought you knew that."

"What are you talking about?" The Guards remained still.

Bal sighed. "That is all I can say. Perhaps it was not my place to tell you."

"So . . . .we won't be able to talk to him . . . .at all?" Her eyes were beginning to tear.

"Not without a Chronicler intermediary. He will remain solitary until his transport to the moon," he said coolly. "I suppose you could contact him after that, but that would also be a violation......."

"But what of the Wards?" she asked, trying to belie her crumbling will. "How can they be Journeyers if they are subject to exile?"

"An odd choice Min made, granted," noted Bal casually. "But it was his to make."

"Shu knows about this?" Eve asked incredulously.

"Of course. After all," he added in a lower tone, "she is our leader. We can do nothing without her approval." He leaned in a little closer to her, making little note of the tears streaming down her cheeks. "But such are the Protocols, and they have their purpose. If he were to speak directly with you, you would be exiled as well."

Bal waited for a moment, waiting to see if Eve had a reply. She didn't. She turned away from him and tried to focus on the water. It was as if Bal knew exactly what she had been thinking about. Bal turned without another word and left taking the Guards with him, leaving Eve alone on the empty, darkening beach.

CHAPTER 10

Min, Shu, Cap, and May huddled in the stern of the boat. The Charges whispered nervously back and forth to each other, staring uselessly into the darkness. Pol sat quietly, rocking Joba, trying to get him to settle in. Despite Min's best efforts, no one had been able to fall asleep.

"We aren't in any danger," said Min.

"How can you say that?" protested May. "They might be looking for us right now."

"They aren't. They don't come out on the water," offered Min. "Besides . . . . ."

"Besides what? I'm not very comfortable with what you think you know about them," said Cap. "Your devices have failed twice now."

"Yes, Min," said Shu. "What has happened?" Dom peered around her shoulder, clutching her arm. She seemed not to even notice his presence.

Min studied the resonator in his hand. There had been no obvious electromagnetic burst this time. There had to be another explanation.

"It must be . . . .them," he said finally. "The device is functioning normally. It should work without error. If the device is as it should be, then the only possible answer is that they are not."

Cap and May looked at one another, bewildered. Cap was beginning to get angry. Shu was struggling to understand.

"Can you explain more?" asked Shu.

Min looked at Cap and May. "Is that . . . .permitted?"

Shu shook her head. "They are already going into exile and you will be . . . ." She paused and wetted her lips. "You are going to the moon. Maybe if you explain, together we can determine what to do next."

Cap and May waited impatiently. Lin had moved up behind her Rearers and was listening quietly.

"The device is called a resonance protein detector. Here is how it works. It sends out a signal that resonates with a very specific protein pattern. If that protein pattern is within a certain range, the detector will notify us."

"Resonates? Proteins?" said May waving her hands. "What do you mean?"

"Resonance is sort of like . . . . . an echo," said Min. "But the device doesn't cause an echo with just anything. Every living thing is made out of proteins. This detector is made to echo when it interacts with the proteins of . . . . .them. That is how we know if they are nearby."

Cap frowned and stared hard at Min. He was angry with the Journeyer but wasn't sure exactly why. "Um.......Min?" It was Lin. She peeked over Cam's shoulder and addressed Min meekly. "How do you know what their . . . . proteins? . . . . . are like? Have you . . . . .resonated . . .them before?"

Cap had said Lin was exceptionally bright. Min would have felt free to appreciate her insight a lot more if her question hadn't just opened a fissure of discord in the group. Shu and Cap hadn't caught up with her yet, but they soon would.

"You . . .know . . .them?" asked Cap.

"We have some information on them," admitted Min. Shu's eyes widened.

"But you are saying that your box can't tell us where they are now, right?" asked Cap.

Min stared at him for a long moment. "No, it can't," he admitted. "Until I know specifically what the problem is, I can't tell you how reliably it will work."

"So, they could be at the Land Bridge when we get there." Cap's tone was accusatory.

"No," said Shu. "The Land Bridge community is sealed. It is in the middle of a narrow strip of land. Water is on two sides. The two sides that are on land have very large walls that will keep them out. The only approaches to the community are by water."

Cap took a long, slow breath. "You've been there," he said, trying to remain composed.

Shu hesitated. "No. I have not. But I am not obligated to share everything I know with you."

May clenched her jaw. "We should have been told," she spat. "You should have told us. You led us to believe that we were the only ones."

"I couldn't. The Protocols forbade it."

"The Protocols?" May spat into the water. She tried to gauge Shu's reaction, but the Chronicler maintained her composure.

Cap rubbed his hand through his hair. "What about those animals that were with them?"

Min shook his head. "They must have domesticated them. I would need to speak with Sol when we get back. I need to speak with him about the resonator as well." Domestication of animals. Min wondered what that might do to their Critical Closure projections.

Shu lowered her eyes slightly, continuing to avoid Min. He had now seen the Hek. Undoubtedly he would understand that his exile had become a certainty.

"So, we stay here until morning?" offered Cap. "Then we continue on?"

"Yes, there is no reason to stop now," she said firmly. "We need to get to the Land Bridge."

May made a half turn away from the others and muttered something under her breath.

"All right everyone," Cap said to the Charges. "We sleep in the boat again tonight." The Charges responded with a smattering of groans. "We are going to make good time tomorrow."

"Cap," said May, "join me in the bow. I would like to talk to you. Lin, please help Dom get settled." Cap rose and the Rearers began working their way in that direction. Lin had to practically pry Dom away from Shu's side. Min began searching for his poncho.

"I hope I haven't said too much," said Shu.

Min shrugged. "I don't think it matters at this point." He leaned in closer. "Shu, I need information about the Cataclysm and the Directors," he said as he pulled his poncho on over his head. "Were the Hek involved somehow? Their ability to avoid my scans has me rather concerned. I need all of the information about them that I can get."

"Impossible," said Shu. She was suddenly very anxious.

"Impossible? How so?" asked Min. "It's very, very important." It was important. The Heks' development was the central factor in the Critical Closure projections. They had already demonstrated that their technological development was far ahead of schedule. Min needed to know how that had happened. Apparently, their protein templates had changed as well. Either that or the original data about the nature of those templates had been wrong all along. "Are there recent records of any Atlans encountering the Hek?"

Shu was more at ease with that question. "None, at least not since the Garden was built. Before that, no one had been ashore for a very, very long time. Your box had never indicated their presence on any trips to the Garden, and no Hek had ever been seen. We assumed the box was working like the Journeyers told us it would."

Min tried to piece it together. The Atlans hadn't had any encounters with the Hek for thousands of ellipses. They never left their island and the Hek never left the shore. Then, when the use of the Garden became necessary, the Atlans were provided with a resonator that could detect the Heks' protein templates as they had existed for millennia. Based on Sol's explanation, these templates would evolve very, very slowly. The detector should still be finding them, but it wasn't. From what Shu had told him, he couldn't say for certain that the resonator had ever worked at all. Either the original information about the nature of those templates was wrong, or the Hek had undergone rapid evolution in the past few thousand ellipses. That was impossible. Nothing evolved that fast.

"The Hek are aggressive?" Min asked.

"Very," she said. "We avoid them because they are extremely violent."

Min was growing fatigued. "We are missing something," he said wearily. "But I'm not going to figure it out now. Particularly if you aren't going to tell me anything else."

"I cannot provide you with any information about the Directors or the Cataclysm," said Shu. By now she had rotated her body completely away from him. She was hiding.

"You can't or you won't?" demanded Min.

"That isn't relevant," said Shu. Now she turned to face him. She was trying to muster the strength to glare defiantly, but she was wavering.

Min could feel the heat rising in his cheeks. "Fine," he grunted, trying to make himself comfortable. He'd find a way to get it himself.

————————

Jack and Sol entered the Sustenance Hall for the evening meal. They immediately drew the attention of most of the other occupants. They made their way through the line, inspecting the food being offered by the Preparers. It consisted mostly of fresh fruits and vegetables. There were also nuts, mushrooms, and what Sol could identify as a form of freshwater kelp. Neither of them was excited to see the flatbread that was available as well. They both walked past it without adding any to their meal.

They sat near the end of a long table, some distance from everyone else. A few red-clad Chroniclers were spread throughout the Hall, as well as perhaps a half dozen members of the Chronicler Guard.

Jack thoughtfully chewed a mushroom. "How do you suppose they get so big?" he asked with a nod towards one of the Guards.

"There are a lot of ways it could be done," said Sol. "A better question is how the Chroniclers manage it given how little they seem to understand technology."

"Right. And unless they are breaking their own laws and doing some kind of research......"

Sol studied one of the nearby Guards. "Based on where they are now, it would take hundreds of ellipses before they had that technology. And that was assuming everyone in society was free to push the technological ceiling. But those Guards, they are all so . . . . .emotionless. Have you noticed that? They just seem to stand around, stone-faced, looking menacing. But the residents of the island don't seem to notice them that much."

"No, that's true. I wonder if they actually do anything."

"Like work of some sort?" Sol shrugged. "My guess is that they just walk around and look grim."

"So, what's your best guess?" asked Jack as he sampled some of the kelp.

Sol paused. "If they are selected at an early age, it is most likely some sort of hormone therapy. Protein management would work too, but hormones would be easier. Then there is always castration."

Jack swallowed his kelp and frowned. "Seriously?"

"Seriously," said Sol. "It wouldn't have a huge impact, unless it was combined with the right mix of hormones. But the procedure is fairly simple and I'm sure even Bal could manage it."

Jack stifled a laugh. "Where would the hormones come from?"

"They could be produced on any Journeycraft But here?" Sol leaned back. "Even if the Chroniclers knew the process, they would still need all of the processors. I doubt they have them stashed away somewhere. With their current technology, I honestly don't have a guess."

"Journeyers!" It was Bal, flanked by a pair of Guards. "Tell me, how does the food here compare to what you have…..up there," he said, pointing towards the ceiling.

Sol tried to lock eyes with one of the Guards. The huge Umae's eyes were static, unblinking. Both Guards stood in identical positions on either side of Bal. Sol was hard pressed to find any obvious differences in their appearances.

"This is better," said Jack. "Fresher. We try to fool ourselves into believing that the food on board is as good, but it isn't."

Bal exuded satisfaction. "Excellent. Our Preparers work diligently to provide healthy, delicious meals. I am pleased that you approve."

Sol offered the nearest Guard a piece of fruit. "Want some?" The Guard didn't react.

"No, no," interjected Bal. "He has already eaten. Please, enjoy that yourself."

Sol kept his eyes on the Guard. "He can talk, right?" He attempted to sound as diplomatic as he could.

"Yes," replied the Guard in a deep voice. "I am not hungry." His expression did not change.

"It really is very good." Sol took a bite of the fruit and winked at the Guard.

"So, what are your plans?" asked Bal.

"Plans?" said Jack.

"Yes. Until Shu and the others return. What are you going to do with your time?"

Jack and Sol looked at one another. "We don't really have any special plans," said Sol. "Do our people have an immediate need?"

"No. I was simply curious. Perhaps you could tour the farms on the island? I think you will be impressed. I will even serve as your guide."

Sol shook his head enthusiastically. "Yes. That sounds great. Can we do it tomorrow, just after dawn?" Jack watched Sol closely.

Bal took a deep breath. "Well . . .yes, I don't see why not. Shall we meet just outside the Sustenance Hall? It is a short walk."

"Fine," said Sol.

"Very well then, enjoy the rest of your meal." With that, Bal and the Guards walked off.

"You really want to see the farms?" asked Jack quietly.

Sol leaned in towards his crewmate. "No, but I want to get some readings on one of those Guards. The tour will give us an excuse to stay in proximity to one long enough for me to do that. Bal always has Guards with him."

Jack looked about anxiously. "Do you know what they might do if you get caught?" Sol shook his head. "Me neither, but it won't be good."

"Don't worry. We won't get caught. I want to know how they are producing these Guards."

Jack sat back, confident that no one was listening. "Sol, what if they are violating the Protocols?"

"I don't know. But we need to do something productive until Min gets back. If they are, we will talk to him about it."

"That's fine. Min will know what to do."

"Let's hope," said Sol. "He does seem to have a knack for that, doesn't he?"

"He is Command Agent for a reason." Yes, thought Sol, Command Agent by merit. Sometimes circumstances forced other choices

"Come on," said Sol, rising from the table. "We have an early start tomorrow."

———————

Min awakened with a start. Cap loomed over him. "We are getting ready to go," he said flatly. Min sat up. It was already fairly light. Once again, the lake was fog-free. He could see the cliff face in the distance. The figures from the night before were gone.

The Charges were already in position to start rowing. Min must have been a lot more fatigued than he had thought. Everyone else had apparently been awake for some time and had made preparations to go.

Min lifted himself up on a bench next to Shu. "You sleep soundly," she noted.

His back and neck were rather stiff. "Not always," he replied.

"Your device, how effective is it now?"

Min withdrew it from his pocket and studied its small display. The blue light still prevailed. "Hard to say since I'm not entirely sure why it isn't working like it should. They are still out there somewhere, but I can't tell you how far away."

"No matter," said Shu calmly.

"No matter? What if we have to go ashore again before we reach the Land Bridge?"

Shu was unconcerned. "Cap believes we can get there by the end of the day."

"But Cap doesn't even know where it is," noted Min.

Shu turned and locked eyes with Min. "I gave him some sense of the distance. It will be fine. Speaking of such things only serves to disturb the Charges," she said quietly. "We can't have that right now."

Min returned her gaze for a moment. May began her cadence call and the boat slid forward in the water.

"Pull! Come on now, we have work to do today! Pull!" she called from her perch in the canoe's bow.

Quickly, the Charges had the boat moving at its customary speed. Min stayed focused on the shoreline. The cliff face maintained a consistent elevation above the water's edge. For as far as he could see into the distance, it showed no sign of descent.

"Min, I want to talk to you about what we will do when we arrive," said Shu. "I assume they will see us approaching and that a group of Chroniclers will be there to greet us. I will go ashore first as I will need to explain why we are there. They may want to take steps to advise their people about why this strange group of Umae has suddenly appeared in their community."

"Do you think they are unaware of any other settlements?"

"I can guarantee that," she said confidently. "It could cause a great deal of uproar. Every community is led to believe that it is the only one remaining."

"I would think they would be pleased," offered Min. "Wouldn't you?"

"The Chroniclers or the people?" responded Shu. Min was taken aback by her answer.

"The . . . .? Well, both," he stammered.

Shu continued. "Once I have explained to them why we have come, I will ask for information about the Journeycraft that has been at our island. Do you think they will have any record of communication from them?"

"It depends on the condition of their Chronicler Hall," he explained. "The crew of the other ship would have included whatever Haven data they had in the tether beam. The data would have gone through the beacon satellite and down to their Hall. Hopefully, they were able to receive and record it and it wasn't too corrupted during the process. But if that type of data arrived in the tether, wouldn't they do something in response?"

She sat up straight and took a deep breath. "In all likelihood, they wouldn't know it had arrived," she said finally.

"They don't monitor the tether?" asked Min.

Shu again paused, searching for the right answer. "It is difficult. The tether typically is devoid of information for long periods of time. Then, when it does provide something, it is usually very detailed and beyond our understanding."

"So the information could be there without them even knowing it," concluded Min.

Shu decided to bypass all of the commentary swirling in her head. "If there is some problem with the technology there, as you indicated before, I must convince them to allow you into their Hall. Under the circumstances, I don't think that will be a problem. However, I don't know if they will permit everyone else on the boat to enter their community."

"So most of the people with us have come all this way and won't even leave the dock?"

"Exactly. It might be unavoidable." Min looked back at the Charges and the efforts they were making to propel the boat. "Our stay will be as brief as possible," she continued. "Then, on the way back, we will leave Cap, May, Pol, and her baby at a spot along the shoreline of their choosing. I will assume they won't want to be left at the foot of the cliff."

"Cap is a smart man," said Min. "I'd say you are right about that."

"Then, back to Atla."

Min's encounter with the Hek provided him with the luxury of knowing that his exile to the moon would happen sooner, not later. Shu hadn't mentioned that he was now an official exile, rather than a practical one, but Min was certain she wouldn't miss that consequence. "Does any of that bother you?" he asked finally. "Leaving them?"

Shu's back stiffened. "It is required by the Protocols."

"You said that already," said Min. "But that doesn't answer my question."

"Your question is irrelevant. I do what the Protocols require."

Min stretched backwards on his bench, trying to loosen his muscles. "You've made that clear."

———————

May gave the Charges a brief rest around noon before pressing on. The cliff still dominated the shoreline. The resonator continued to provide the same negative readings. It was well into the evening before they saw anything new. "Look!" said May. She was pointing straight ahead. A towering cliff was coming into view directly ahead of them. It extended perpendicularly to the boat as far as anyone could see.

"We are here," said Shu, obviously relieved. "The Land Bridge. The community is atop that cliff," said Shu. "But where…..?

"There," noted Cap. He pointed towards a flight of stone stairs that climbed up the side of the cliff face. A dozen or so thick stone poles projected out of the base of the cliff just above the surface of the water.

Shu smiled. "Cap, have them take us in to where the stairs and the mooring poles are. I don't want to wait until tomorrow before announcing our arrival."

Cap signaled to May and she directed the Charges to take them in towards the shore. There was a narrow walkway in between the water and the smaller cliff face that led to the steps. The stairs steadily rose to reach the top of the higher cliff ahead of them. The Charges brought the boat to a stop adjacent to the walkway and tied it off on one of the large mooring poles. Most of the poles were badly cracked and several had broken off at some unknown time in the past and fallen into the lake below.

Shu stepped from the boat. "I will return as soon as I am able," she said.

"What are you talking about?" demanded Cap. "You are going alone?"

"Yes," she said firmly, "you are to remain here until I return. I don't think it will be long."

"But . . ." protested Cap. He noted that Min was examining his resonator. "It isn't safe!"

"It is," said Shu, a hint of irritation entering her tone. "Now listen to me and stay here."

Cap grumbled and sat down. May glowered at Shu as the Chronicler started down the walkway. She began a quick ascent of the stairway. Everyone watched until they could barely see her reach the top before disappearing from view. She never looked back.

———————

Sol and Jack reached the Sustenance Hall very early, well before dawn. It was empty except for a couple of workers who were preparing the Hall for the day. The two Journeyers sat down at the same table they had sat at the night before.

"So," said Sol, "how much time will the device you put together need to get me the readings I want?" He kept his hand in his side pocket.

"The longer you take readings, the more detailed your analysis can be," said Jack. "Given the limitations on the device's size and the fact that it will have to remain concealed, it has its limitations."

"I understand," said Sol, "but I don't want to spend any more time at the farms than I have to. I can only imagine what their level of agriculture is like."

One of the workers hesitantly approached their table. "Excuse me?" she said nervously. "It is still very early. Do you want me to look and see if the Preparers have anything ready?" She was a young adult with high cheek bones. The bangs of her sand-colored hair stopped just above her pale eyebrows.

Sol smiled. "No, you don't need to do that. I am Sol. How are you called?"

A hint of color washed over her cheeks. "I am Yed."

"Well, Yed, I think Jack and I are fine. We are waiting for Bal, the Chronicler. Do you know him?"

"I know of him. I have not spoken with him. He comes in most mornings with his Guards for breakfast."

"Oh?" replied Sol curiously. "Do they all eat together?"

She shook her head. "Not really. Bal does. The Guards just stand there."

"What do the Guards eat?" asked Sol.

"I don't know," she said, a hint of embarrassment in her tone. "I don't remember ever seeing them eat."

"Interesting," mused Sol.

"Excuse me?"

"Oh, nothing. Just thinking out loud."

Yed glanced at Jack before frowning at Sol. "I need to get back to work. Let me know if you need anything."

Jack smiled as Yed returned to her duties.

"I'm guessing food," said Sol. "Did you see Bal's face when I offered the Guard some fruit last night?"

"Yes," said Jack. "You may as well have offered him a spider."

"Exactly. Hopefully, he will have more than one Guard with him. Multiple specimens are always better."

"'Specimens'?" echoed Jack.

"Sorry. My mind is in lab mode right now."

"Journeyers!" It was Bal. This time, his greeting rang through the otherwise empty Hall. Jack and Sol stood up. Bal was accompanied by three Guards.

"Perfect," muttered Sol.

"Are you ready to go to the farms?"

"I thought we might eat together first," said Sol. "It is early, have you eaten?"

"Well . . . .yes," said Bal finally. "I ate a bit at the Chroniclers' Hall."

"How about you?" said Sol to one of the Guards.

"He did as well," said Bal.

"I thought only Chroniclers were allowed inside the Hall?" said Jack matter-of-factly.

"And the Guards," replied Bal coolly. "Now, would you like to eat something before we depart?"

Jack clapped his hands. "You know, I am rather eager to see these farms. I assume they will have food there? We can wait and eat something after we arrive."

"Yes, that seems reasonable," added Sol. He reached into his pocket and activated Jack's device. "How long will it take for us to get there?"

"Not long," said Bal. "We won't need to rest on the way, but since you two have just recently arrived......."

Sol shook his head emphatically. "No, no, we are fine. Besides, we are in no hurry. If we leave now, we can make it a more leisurely trip."

Bal smiled. "Excellent!" He began walking towards the exit. "You've seen the shipbuilders already. Perhaps on the way back we can visit the Infirmary Hall."

Jack flashed Sol a worried look. "How did you know where we have already been?" asked Jack.

Bal's smile quickly faded, replaced by an expression of cold indifference. "I am a Chronicler. There is very little that happens on this island that I'm not aware of."

Sol ran his hand over the device in his pocket. How much **do** you know? The walk to the farms was going to be interesting indeed.

Bal led the group along a path leading away from the Sustenance Hall. They walked past a relatively large pyramid that served as the island's Infirmary Hall. They turned a corner and were confronted with a large contingent of Guards jogging in their direction. There were fifteen of them, and each was armed with a long spear that was easily taller than they were. Bal held his hands out, stopping Sol and the others. "Stay here!" he barked.

He marched forward towards the approaching group of Guards. Once they saw him, they came to a stop. Bal pointed to one of the Guards in the front of the group and he stepped forward. The others stood rigidly, staring straight ahead. Bal was waving his finger angrily in the huge Guard's face. Although he was too far away for Jack and Sol to understand what he was saying, he was clearly irate.

"What is wrong?" asked Sol of one of the Guards next to him. The Guard looked down at him before returning his attention towards Bal. He offered no reply.

Bal continued to berate the Guard for another moment before that entire contingent turned and jogged away in the opposite direction. Bal watched them go before turning about and stalking back towards Sol and Jack. His face was ablaze.

"Problem?" asked Sol.

Bal took a long breath. "No," he huffed. "Let us continue. I don't have much time."

Bal led them down the path. Soon, the various pyramids gave way to a wide, flat plain. They stopped atop a low rise overlooking the plain. Beyond was the lake.

"Morningsidedly, there is wheat and various fruits," explained Bal. "Eveningsidedly there are nuts, hemp and potatoes. Spread out within the fields are patches where mushrooms are raised."

"'Eveningsidedly'?" echoed Jack. His question was met only by Bal's blank silence.

"Never mind, Jack," said Sol. "Tell us more." His apparent enthusiasm was plainly inauthentic, but only to the one person present who knew him well.

They walked down the gradual slope until they reached the wheat fields. The plants were set out in neat rows. Workers were busily inspecting the plants for signs of blight or parasites. Beyond that were the hemp fields. None of the plants were as tall, or as robust in appearance, as Sol would have expected. Adjacent to that, mushrooms grew in a grassy area.

"How many people does this feed?" asked Sol spreading his arms. "I assume there is a deficit or you wouldn't have the Garden on the mainland."

"We have had the Garden for many, many ellipses," said Bal. "And until recently, there has been no risk associated with its maintenance. I may discontinue its use."

None of the workers were anywhere near as large as the Guards, although all of them were larger than Jack and Sol. All of the tools they used were made of wood. Some employed small carts to move the produce, but all of them were powered by Umae.

"No horses?" asked Sol.

"Horses?" Bal replied slowly.

"You know what a horse is, right?"

Bal's lips tightened. "Now is not the time," he said firmly. He looked at the three Guards. "We should move along."

Beyond the hemp fields was an orchard with a variety of different trees. Sol quickly identified apple trees, pear trees, as well as towering oaks. They were spread about with no apparent planning. At the edge of the orchard, another gradual slope led down to the lake. There was a short drop from the bottom of the slope directly into the water. There was no beach. Jack and Sol stood atop the rise, looking off into the distance.

"I have matters to attend to," said Bal. He clapped his hands and the Guards appeared at his side. "You said you wanted to see the Infirmary Hall. They will escort you."

"We went right by it," said Sol. "I'm certain we can find it."

"Please," said Bal. "It would be rather troublesome if something were to happen to one of you before you leave." He leaned in slightly towards them. "Indulge me," he said quietly.

Sol shrugged. "Sure." He turned towards Jack. "Ready?"

"I think we've seen enough," Jack said, trying to prevent himself from peeking at Sol's pocket.

"Excellent," said Bal flatly. "I'm sure we will see each other later."

"Can't wait," said Sol under his breath.

Sol and Jack started back in the direction of the hospital, accompanied by their three hulking escorts. Sol slipped his hand into his pocket, surreptitiously adjusting the settings on Jack's device. Now it was simply a matter of time.

———

After affixing the boat securely to the mooring pole, the Charges sat down on the walkway. Pol leaned back against the cliff face and nursed Joba. Min sat nearby, his eyes half-closed with fatigue. Cap paced back and forth, stopping periodically to stare at the staircase until the darkness precluded him from doing so.

"How long do we wait?" said Cap. "She has had plenty of time to reach the top of the stairs. What if something has happened?"

"We need to stay here," said Min wearily as he rubbed his face with his hands. "She needs to talk to whoever is up there so our arrival doesn't stir things up."

"How do you know all of this?" asked May accusatorily.

Min sighed. "What would you think if a boatload of strangers suddenly showed up on the beach of our island? Wouldn't that make you uneasy?"

"Yes! It would!" spat May. "All of this does! For all of this time we were told that there were no other Umae, that we were the only ones. Now, we are told there is an entire settlement of them." Her eyes narrowed as she glared at Min. "How many others *are* there, Journeyer? How many settlements?"

The Charges monitored the exchange between Min and their Rearer. Cap remained silent, defiantly folding his arms while awaiting Min's response.

"I . . . . .don't know," said Min finally. "I really don't. There are other places. I can tell you that. Perhaps Shu will explain more when she comes back, since . . . ."

"Since we are exiled?" snapped May. "So no one on Atla can find out?" She gritted her teeth and tore her eyes away from Min. "What else have we been lied to about?"

"May," began Min calmly, "I don't know everything that the Chroniclers know. You have to remember, I have only spent a total of about ten ellipses on this planet in my entire life. But the Protocols have a purpose." Min was being honest, just not complete. The Protocols DID have a purpose. He just wasn't entirely certain what it was anymore.

"You can't be serious!" interjected Cap. "Why should we believe anything the Chroniclers have told us?"

"Cap?" said May. "Look!"

High above them, a light swayed back and forth atop the plateau. The light itself was of an indefinite shape and appeared to bend slightly in the breeze. It was a torch.

The Charges started becoming anxious, muttering to one another. "What do you think it is?" asked Lin nervously.

"Min?" asked Cap. Min was a bit surprised that Cap would seek his opinion. However, although he could be stubborn, Cap was a practical man. Min was in a better position to interpret what was happening.

"The Land Bridge is sealed," said Min. "So, whatever is holding the torch has to be Umae. The fact that there is only one supports the conclusion that it is Shu."

"So how do we know the Hek aren't up there?" asked May. She looked up and watched the light go back and forth.

"Because they have no way to get up there," said Min. "At least not based on what Shu said."

"That doesn't make me feel any better," said May.

"Well, we could just stay here until morning," offered Min.

"No," said Cap firmly. "We will go. You, and me, and Lin. May can stay here with the others."

"You realize that it will take me quite a while to climb those stairs?" advised Min.

"I'll carry you if necessary. You came along for a reason. You should go now."

Min stood up and stretched. "I suppose I will have to get up there eventually."

"Lin, please gather up a couple of torches and some flint. I'll walk in front. You follow up behind Min." Lin headed back to the boat to gather the requested equipment. "The rest of you, stay here until we send for you." He walked over to May and took her hand. "Use your best judgment," he said quietly enough so that only she could hear. "If you think there is danger, leave us."

May stared into his pale, pink eyes. "If that happens, we will come back. Don't doubt that."

"I never would," Cap replied quietly.

"Here you go," said Lin. She was lugging a pair of torches. She had also slung her pack over her narrow shoulders. Cap took one of the torches and set it on the ground. A couple of quick strikes with the flint and the torch burst into flames. Lin held hers out so Cap could light it as well.

"We won't be gone long," said Cap trying to sound assured. "Come on."

He turned and strode off towards the steps. Min did the best he could to keep up while Lin trailed along behind. Soon, May and the others could only see the twin fires of the torches as they slowly rose up towards the plateau above them. The light at the top of the plateau was gone.

May sat back down and leaned against the cliff face. She couldn't shake the memory of the Hek looming over them at the beach, waving their torches and howling. Now she had to place her trust in the words of a Chronicler and the judgment of a Journeyer. She rested her chin on her knees and began to wait.

CHAPTER 11

Jack and Sol walked back through the fields towards the pyramids. The three Guards followed along closely behind them. "How are we doing for time?" said Sol as he returned his hand to his pocket.

Jack looked back uneasily at their stoic companions. "I think we will have plenty," he replied. "After we stop at the Mending Hall."

"Of course." Sol stopped and knelt down on the pretext of adjusting his shoe. "So, how do you men entertain yourselves?"

The three Guards stopped but remained silent.

"I mean, you do have to have fun sometimes, right?"

"Fun?" echoed one of the Guards.

The second Guard seemed interested in Sol's question.

Sol pointed to him. "How about you? What do you do?"

This Guard had a small spear-shaped insignia on the breast of his shirt the others lacked. "My name is Max. I grow plants," said the man. "And flowers."

Sol nearly lost his balance. "Flowers?" He stood up slowly. "Why?"

The Guard seemed lost for words. "I plant them. Take care of them."

"No, no," said Sol, "after that. Once they are grown. What do you do with them?"

Max shrugged. "I . . . . . look at them. I give them away to others."

"I'd like to see your flowers sometime."

"You like flowers?" asked Max. He was unable to conceal his own surprise, a fact not lost of Sol.

"Very much," said Sol. "I have studied them in great detail."

Max grinned. The other two Guards remained as unexpressive as they had been all day. "Certainly, you may see them," said Max.

The five of them resumed walking in the direction of the Mending Hall. The building was a medium-sized structure heavily covered with ivy on one side. As soon as they arrived, the three Guards headed off without another word leaving Jack and Sol standing outside.

"Well, quite an informative morning, wouldn't you say?" said Sol in a hushed voice.

"Yes, and as soon as we can get a look at my scanner, it should prove even more so."

"These people have no understanding of even basic genetics," offered Sol.

"Oh?"

Sol leaned against the exterior of the Hall. "For one, I would guarantee that inbreeding took out their horse stock. I can remember being here when the number of horses used in labor was substantial. They probably just penned them all together and let them breed at will. When their genetic markers became too similar, some common virus swept in and wiped them out. If we could get a Chronicler to be honest with us, there will be a record of the event, I'm sure of it."

"I don't get the sense that that is likely," said Jack. "I don't understand why they use that type of cart."

"You could hitch a horse to one of those if you had one," explained Sol. "You don't remember horses at all, do you? It looks like they continued making their carts the same way, even after the horses disappeared. This was the first time in several returns that I went to the fields. The horses probably died off a long time before you were born."

"That makes as much sense as the way they make boats, I suppose," noted Jack. "What did you make of the Guards' leisure activities?"

Sol took a deep breath. "Not at all what I'd expected."

"Imagine one of those emotionless men tending flowers for fun," said Jack.

"You mean Max," said Sol. "He was not nearly as unemotional as the other two. Didn't you see how pleased he was when he was talking about his flowers?"

"Now that you mention it…..," said Jack. "And did he seem less imposing to you than the other two?" He looked around the immediate vicinity, realizing he had dropped his guard a bit.

"He wasn't nearly as large as the others," Sol noted. "But certainly not small. And the insignia on his shirt. A spear? I wonder if he has some authority over the other Guards."

"He may be an officer of some sort," replied Jack. "As for the other questions, I'm sure the data we gathered will give us some answers."

"I hope so," said Sol and he started towards the entrance to the Mending Hall. "I have some patients to see."

"Do you have any more miracles left?" asked Jack.

Sol smiled warmly. "It's what I do."

———————

The ascent up the stairs quickly took a toll on Min. Once they could no longer see the group on the walkway, he sat down on a step, struggling to breathe.

"Are you all right?" asked Lin.

"At this rate, this will take all night," noted Cap. "And I'm not ready to carry you yet."

Min focused on taking slow, deep breaths. "Sorry," he croaked. "Trying."

Lin took a moment to study the steps. Despite a certain degree of weathering, their craftsmanship was obvious. Their lines were still sharp and the height of each one was uniform.

"Were the people who made these steps the same ones who made the wall around the Garden?"

Min was starting to breathe easier. He feigned difficulty to buy time so he could provide Lin with an adequate answer.

"Not the same," he said slowly. "But . . . . .related. You have a keen eye."

"Related?" echoed Lin. She beamed in response to the Journeyer's compliment. "How?"

"How do you know this?" asked Cap.

Min took a few more slow breaths. "I have almost 900 ellipses."

Cap was confused by Min's answer. So many questions swirled in his head that he couldn't decide which to ask, so he remained silent. Lin was entirely dissatisfied with Min's reply but deferred additional questioning in light of her Rearer's silence.

Continuing on, the three of them looked ahead periodically, searching for the torchlight at the top. They saw no sign of it. There was nothing ahead or behind them now, except darkness. The cliff face was to their empty-side and heartside, no doubt far, far below them, was the lake.

Although he didn't make it as far as he had on the first leg, Min was surprised by the progress he had made on the second before he needed another break. They stopped at a short landing and sat down. The stairs were wide enough for them to sit three abreast. They set the torches down on the landing and sat on the fourth step above it. Min was still breathing hard and his back and thighs were throbbing.

Lin found a small stone and tossed it over the edge. Between the sound of the breeze and the size of the stone, she had no expectation of hearing it hit the water. She listened, nonetheless. Cap sat up straight, annoyed at the lost time. Min lay back on the stairs, focusing on his breathing.

"Will we ever come back?" asked Lin.

"Back here?" asked Min.

"No, back to this planet."

I won't, thought Min. "I'm sure you will. You are young. I have been back several times. You will do the same."

"But I won't know anyone when I come back, will I?"

Min shook his head. "No. Just the members of your crew.

Lin seemed displeased by that prospect. "And you are going to a moon?"

"Yes, that's right. There is one that orbits Uma."

Lin looked up at the featureless black sky. "Have you been there before?"

"A long, long time ago," said Min. "All of the Journeyer Technical Agents go there with their mentor."

"Why?"

"Part of it is tradition," said Min. "But part of it is practical. It is part of the education every Technical Agent undergoes."

"I thought you were the Command Agent?" asked Lin.

"I am," said Min, "but only after our prior Command Agent died. Before that, I was the Technical Agent."

Lin tried to fit all of these pieces together in her head. "I'd like to learn about the ships," she said smiling.

Min sensed a deep curiosity about her. "Technical matters may be perfect for you."

"Are we ready?" said Cap as he stood up on the step.

Min stood up as well. "As ever," he grumbled.

Lin gathered herself and handed Cap's torch to him. The three continued their trek upwards. Min was growing accustomed to the ache in his back and legs. They were constant, but he was able to focus beyond the pain to some degree. His breathing problems made concentrating difficult. As he walked, he kept one hand on the step two ahead of his feet to assist him with balance. He was sure to stay as close to the cliff face as he could so he wouldn't fall.

Min lasted only a short time on the third leg, quickly exhausting himself. Just as he was ready to stop again, Cap raised his torch high and stared ahead.

"I heard something," he said, motioning for Min and Lin to stay back. With a bound, he quickly climbed ahead, taking two steps at once. Once he had cleared about twenty steps, he stopped. "Come on," he called. "I am at the top."

Min took a deep breath and pushed on. Lin gave him constant encouragement as she followed along behind him. Once he reached the top, he sat down and looked to see what, if anything, the torchlight would reveal.

Everything on the plateau was dark except for the two torches. There were two small pyramids directly in front of them. From the shadows between the two structures came a squeaking, gasping sound. Cap pulled Min up and threw Min's arm over his shoulder.

"Come on," he urged. He mostly dragged Min forward as Lin followed. Once they rounded the corner of the nearest pyramid, Cap held up his torch as high as he could.

Shu was sitting against the base of the pyramid. Her torch was on the ground next to her, extinguished. She was sobbing uncontrollably.

Cap eased Min to the ground. He got to Shu just after Lin did. "Shu?" he asked.

Shu shook her head and tried to speak but was unable.

"What is it?" asked Lin quietly. "What did you see?"

Shu gasped and tried to compose herself. "N-n-nothing . . . . ." Sobs shook her entire body. "G-g-gone. All . . . .g-g-gone."

Lin knelt down and put her arms around the Chronicler. Cap took a quick look around the alleyway between the buildings before returning to Min.

"What now?" he asked.

Min's brain was swirling with fatigue. He took another deep breath to clear his thoughts. He then felt the first few drops spatter against his check.

It began to rain.

The Mending Hall was little more than a single large room with a number of long, thin cushions spread out on the floor. Against the far wall, Jack and Sol could see three people seated next to one another on a bench, talking. They appeared to be the only "patients" currently in the room.

Sol closed his eyes, a broad smile warming his face.

"What is it?" asked Jack.

"The remedy. It worked." He looked about the mostly empty chamber. "No plague patients."

Jack patted his companion on the shoulder. "Life science must be very rewarding," he noted.

"It has its moments," Sol replied.

A man entered the room from a door in the near side and stopped to look over Jack and Sol. Apparently satisfied, he walked over to the three people seated by the wall. There were two men and one woman, all obviously possessing more ellipses than Sol. The woman had a strip of cloth tied tightly around her eyes. She sat in the middle of the two men who were engaged in a conversation that apparently didn't include her. The attendant said something to the woman before reaching behind her head and removing the cloth.

She was facing Jack and Sol but didn't appear to be aware of their presence. Although her eyes remained open constantly, she turned her head stiffly to focus on any sounds that were around her. The attendant leaned down and looked closely at her eyes.

"Any better?"

The woman shook her head. "No, nothing," she said, cocking her head in the direction of his voice.

"Nothing at all?" he asked dejectedly.

"No different than yesterday." The attendant grumbled something and began to replace the cloth around her head.

"A moment," said Sol moving forward. "Please."

The woman raised her head when Sol spoke, but her eyes remained unfocused. "Who is that Yar?"

The attendant held on to the cloth. "He is one of the Journeyers, Roz" he said in a hushed tone. The two older men grew wide-eyed.

Roz brightened. "A Journeyer? Well, aren't you going to tell me your name?" she asked finally.

Sol cleared his throat. "Of course. My name is Sol. My friend's name is Jack."

"Friend?" said Roz. She slowly turned her head back and forth and then frowned. "He's awfully quiet. Are you lost?"

"No," said Sol grinning. "We are just out looking around. It has been a long time since we have been home."

"You live here?" she asked.

"Sometimes, yes. Not often."

"I have never met a Journeyer before," said one of the men. "I'm Tra. This," he added, pointing to the other man, "is Nan."

"Tra and Nan are getting ready to take their walk," explained Yar. "I'm going with them. Are you two going to be staying here long?"

"Yes," said Roz, "I need someone to watch me." Her voice was saturated with sarcasm. Tra and Nan both chuckled to themselves.

"Certainly, we will stay as long as you like," said Sol.

Yar helped Tra and Nan to their feet. "We won't be long." Yar's patients moved slowly and stiffly towards the exit. They both maintained a hand on Yar's shoulder to help steady themselves.

Sol sat down next to Roz. "So, you have some sort of problem with your vision?"

Roz snickered. "Just that I don't have any."

"Well there isn't anything wrong with your sense of humor," said Jack.

Roz smiled again. About half of her teeth were missing. "I have slowly been losing my sight for a while. Now I can't see anything."

"Do you mind if I look?" asked Sol.

"How would I even know?" noted Roz. Sol leaned down and gently put his hands on the sides of her head. He stared into her eyes. Not satisfied, he produced a small, metallic cylinder from his pocket. He held one end up to her left eye and a narrow beam of light emitted from the end of the cylinder.

"Anything?" he asked.

"No, why?"

One again, Sol took a long look into each eye with his light. He shut the light off and returned the cylinder into his pocket.

"Roz, how would you like to see again?"

"Is that a serious question?"

Sol leaned back and rubbed his face. "One moment," he replied quietly. He turned around and looked at Jack.

"What are you thinking about?" asked Jack. "The Protocols say we can't expose them to any of our technology." Sol took Jack by the elbow and led him a ways away from Roz.

"What do you suppose 'expose' means?" Sol mused.

"I don't think I like where you are heading with this."

"Almost ready, Roz, I need to talk to my friend for a bit."

"Take your time," she said. "I can't go anywhere without you." Her answer struck Sol right in the gut.

"Jack, this is an easy fix," said Sol quietly. "She won't even know I did anything."

"Sol . . . ." said Jack hesitantly, "I don't know. What if they find out?"

"What could they do? We are leaving soon anyway."

"But" said Jack, "what about *her.* She would be exiled."

"They won't find out," said Sol finally. "If we hurry. Go watch the door they went out."

"There are two doors," Jack reminded him.

"And the odds are better if you are watching one of them."

Jack hesitantly walked back to the door they had entered. Sol went back over to Roz and sat down.

"So, what is wrong with your friends?" he asked.

"They are old, like me," she said. "You sound like a young fellow."

"Well, age is all relative, right?" He withdrew his light tube as well as another tiny ring-shaped piece of metal. He screwed the ring onto the end of the cylinder. "Can I look one more time?"

"I don't see why not." Roz was pleased with her attempt at humor.

"Hold still," said Sol. Once again, he shone the light in her eye. This time, a tiny line of particles traveled along the beam of light from the cylinder to her eye. He then did the same thing to her other eye. Jack began coughing. Sol looked up before quickly returning the cylinder to his pocket.

"I guess your friends are back," said Sol as he began to walk towards the door.

"Are you going to come and see me again, young man?" asked Roz.

Sol stopped and turned back towards her. "Hopefully," he said in a hushed voice, "you can come and see me next time." He brushed her cheek lightly with his lips.

Roz smiled. "That's not funny."

Yar entered with Nan and Tra. Despite their short walk, both of the older men looked rather weary. Yar assisted them over to the area with the cushions. Sol and Jack took their leave.

Once they were outside, Jack placed a hand on Sol's shoulder. "What did you do?"

"I just inserted some micro-surgs into her eyes. They will break down the tissue growths covering her corneas and then proceed directly to her kidneys. She will be able to see again in the next day or so. No one will be the wiser."

"I'll bet she will tell everyone about her visit with you." said Jack.

"Then I've done my job," said Sol.

"I hope she doesn't have any idea about what you did." said Jack earnestly. "She wouldn't fare very well on the mainland and I think she is too old for Journeyer training."

"Well, she isn't too old to see," he said, a hint of disgust in his voice. "I hope these Protocols we have are worth it."

Jack stopped. "You have doubts?"

"Min does," said Sol. "And he has an uncanny habit for being right."

"Hopefully, we can find out for sure."

Sol looked at Jack square in the eyes. "I think that will end up being a job for you younger folks," he said earnestly. "Let's get out of here."

———————

The lightless sky erupted with fury. In the darkness, the storm clouds had gathered overhead undetected. The initial gentle sprinkle almost instantly evolved into a torrent without warning. The rain battered the stone ground, creating a near-deafening roar. Cap emerged from the alleyway and began gathering everyone together.

"We have to find shelter!" He was practically screaming. He seized Shu and Lin by their collars. Lin reached out and took Min by the hand. Between the darkness and the sheets of rain, it was impossible to see anything. Cap backed up to where he thought the exterior of the closest pyramid was. Once he bumped into it, he maintained contact as he dragged the others along with him.

By the time they made it to the pyramid's corner, their clothes were completely soaked. Rainwater streamed along at their feet, riding the slope away from the base of the pyramid. Cap continued along the pyramid's exterior wall. After another two dozen steps or so, it gave way to an opening. He pulled everyone inside. The interior of the pyramid was utterly lightless, but dry. The four stumbled inside and sat down on the stone floor.

"Don't remember one quite like that," noted Cap. He tried to wipe the water off of his face.

"Should we try to find something to light?" asked Lin.

"I have a flint," said Shu. She reached out in the darkness, searching for Lin. "Lin, see if you can find something." She could feel Lin's hand removing the flint.

"But don't go back outside!" commanded Cap needlessly.

"I won't. I still have some kindling in my pack. Hopefully, some of it is still dry."

Min considered the removal of his poncho. His clothes were just as wet, but he decided to remove it anyway. He peeled it off and tossed it onto the floor.

"What about the others?" asked Shu. The roar outside continued unabated.

"May will keep them together," said Cap confidently. "They will just have to stay on the walkway until it passes."

"But the baby . . . ." said Shu quietly.

Cap could feel a fever of blood rise in his neck. "The baby?!?" he screeched. "Since when do you care about the baby?"

"Cap . . . ." said Shu firmly.

"Don't give me your speech about the Protocols," he snarled. "That baby is stuck in a driving rainstorm unlike any we have ever seen because of you and your Protocols. Don't try to tell me that you care."

"Here . . . ." came Lin's voice from the distant darkness. The three of them could see a series of faint sparks as she was apparently working the flint.

Cap stood up and started in her direction.

"Shu . . .are you all right?" asked Min. He was starting to shiver.

"We should see what Lin has found," she replied, barely audible.

"Fine," said Min, as he struggled to his feet. He reached out and found Shu's hand. The two of them walked slowly towards the sparks, taking care not to run into anything. One spark didn't flicker out, but instead grew slowly into a steady glow. They could hear the familiar crackle of dry wood burning. Once the flame grew enough, they could see a fire barrel with Lin and Cap standing next to it. The fire in the barrel was giving off a dense smoke.

"Excellent, Lin," said Min. He sat down close to the fire barrel and tried to squeeze some more water from his clothes.

He coughed a bit as the smoke irritated his throat. "What did you light?"

Lin feared his disapproval. "There was some wood in the barrel already, but I couldn't get it to light. Once I set my kindling underneath, the wood in the barrel burned too."

Min coughed again. "It's probably old, full of moisture and who knows what else. It should burn off quickly. I wonder what this building was used for."

Within range of the firelight, they could see the remnants of an assortment of cushions and a simple wooden table. The cushions were badly rotted and rather moldy. There were also stacks of wood against the wall.

"I think this is a building their Chroniclers used to interview those returning from the lake," said Shu.

Min slumped down onto his knees before lying down on the floor. "Are you all right?" asked Lin.

"Very . . .tired," he said weakly.

"We need to try and warm him up," said Lin. "Those wet clothes aren't helping." She removed her poncho and squeezed as much of the water from its fabric as she could. She then placed it under Min's head.

"We could all stand to dry out a bit," said Cap. "Maybe if we get those other barrels going, we can use them to dry our clothes. We can stick close to this one to stay warm until that happens."

"Can you help me move them over here?"

"Yes. Shu, see if you can get the rest of Min's clothes off. And get him as close to the barrel as you can." Cap had no problems directing his Chief Chronicler is this difficult environment. Shu had no problems accepting his direction.

"Very well," said Shu. She knelt down next to Min and began helping him remove his wet garments. Cap and Lin were able to roll a couple of the stone fire barrels over to their makeshift camping area. The wood inside those barrels was also

THE PROTOCOLS OF UMA

well-rotted and resistant to the fire. Lin lit the wood inside those barrels as well, exhausting her supply of kindling, before returning the flint to Shu. Thick smoke billowed from the barrels, stinging their eyes. Min was now completely nude and was huddled as close to the barrel as he could bear. Cap and Lin spread Min's wet clothes on the floor near one of the barrels. Cap, Lin, and Shu then removed their own clothes and spread them out as well. The three of them gathered around one of the barrels and sat down, waiting for the rain to relent.

———————

Jack and Sol entered their quarters, finding Eve seated on one of the cushions. She was intently operating a small, handheld device. She looked up as her crewmates walked in. Her eyes were rimmed in red.

"Eve?" said Sol as he quickly moved towards her. What's wrong?"

Eve remembered her official priorities. "Were you able to find out anything?" she asked hoarsely.

Jack and Sol each took a seat next to her. "We have some readings," said Jack. "I think it would be best if we did the study onboard the ship. We would get our results a lot more quickly, and in greater detail."

"May I see?" asked Eve. Jack handed her his scanning device. She activated it and studied the small screen. "Hmm . . . .yes, I would agree. This device is better-suited for gathering data than it is for ordering it." Her voice was a thick rasp.

"And you would know," said Sol. "What have you been up to?"

"Worrying . . . .mostly," she admitted.

Jack tried to sound positive. "I'm sure they are fine. He will be back soon."

Eve lowered her eyes.

"Eve? What is it?" asked Sol.

"We aren't going to be able to see him again after he returns." Her voice cracked as she recalled her conversation with Bal.

"What makes you think so?" asked Jack.

"Bal told me," she answered. "Min will be quarantined until he returns to the moon. Apparently they are afraid that he will share some forbidden information. Bal said Shu entered that directive before they left."

Jack pulled his knees up to his chest. "That will be a trick. Someone will have to go up with him to launch his shuttle. At least, we can tell them that."

Eve looked up. "Are you suggesting that we lie to them?"

"Look," said Jack, "we are pretty sure based on some of the things we saw today that they have been lying to us. If I have to return the favor just to say goodbye to Min, I will."

"And what are they going to do, make us stay?" asked Sol. "Based on what I've gathered about the law, we *have* to leave."

"And if they exile us to the mainland," said Jack, "they are going to have a pair of Journeycraft sitting in the middle of the island indefinitely."

Their words made sense and their logic brought Eve a measure of solace. "I have some things I need to tell him. Before he decides . . . . ."

"We have some time yet," said Sol. "They aren't expected back for a while. Maybe we should do our analysis while we wait?"

"Before he decides what?" asked Jack.

His question swung like a silent pendulum between Sol and Eve. Sol chose to speak. "We will need a new Command

Agent when we leave. I'm not interested. There is some likelihood he will be taking Eve with him to the moon."

"While he gives me the tour of the Citadel?" asked Jack. "If he is exiled, I don't think that can happen," he added dejectedly.

Sol made sure he still had jack's attention. "It can't. It would just be him and Eve." Jack immediately saw the implications of Sol's answer. The Life Agent put a calming hand on his shoulder. "We all know you can do it if necessary Jack. I'll be right there with you. But it hasn't happened yet."

Jack was reeling. Command Agent? He only had one journey. Did Min have that much confidence in him......or? He looked over at Eve. Jack had seen her and Min together. "I don't......know....," he stammered.

"I know you don't," said Sol. "So don't. We aren't done here yet."

The three rose and headed towards the *Starshine.* They moved quickly along the path through the maze of buildings towards the center of the island where the Journeycraft were. At the base of each craft was a trio of Guards. Jack approached the *Starshine*, stepped around them and reached out to activate the egress ramp. One of the Guards seized him by the wrist before he could succeed.

"Ahhh!" Jack's face twisted with discomfort. "What are you doing?" The other two Guards nearby positioned themselves in between Sol, Eve and the Journeycraft.

"No one is authorized to enter," said the Guard holding Jack's wrist. Jack twisted and pried at the Guard's fingers but could not affect his escape.

"You're . . . .hurting me . . . ." he groused. The Guard released him.

"Who said we couldn't enter the ships?" asked Sol. "We have work we need to do."

"It is by the order of Chief Chronicler Bal," said the Guard.

"Why? For what purpose?" demanded Sol. The Guard remained silent, locking onto Jack with an unwavering stare.

Sol took a quick look at Jack's wrist. "Where is Bal now?" asked Eve. "We need to speak with him." His eyes narrowed. "You said 'Chief Chronicler'?"

"I do not know," said the Guard. "He may be at the Hall."

"He was by the fields the last time we saw him," said Jack. The Guard did not respond.

"Maybe we should go to the Hall," said Eve. "There must be some sort of misunderstanding."

"Yes, I hope you are right," said Jack, flexing his wrist. "I'm sure you are."

The Journeyers started walking in the direction of the Chroniclers' Hall. None of the Guards seemed to watch them as they left. Once they rounded the corner of the nearest pyramid, they stopped.

"What do you suppose that was all about?" said Sol.

"What benefit could they have from keeping us from our ship?" asked Eve. "It doesn't make any sense."

"Particularly since we were just there yesterday," noted Sol.

"Maybe the difference is in who is in charge?" offered Eve.

"Bal seems to have a new title," noted Sol.

"Well," said Jack, "if that is the case, I'll be happy to see Shu again. I never imagined I'd say that."

"But when Shu returns, Min returns," said Eve. "We need to figure out how we are going to be able to speak with him."

"Yes, but let's go talk to Bal first. We likely won't change his mind, but it might be interesting to hear what he has to say."

CHAPTER 12

The Chroniclers of the Land Bridge had kept their chamber well-stocked with dry wood. Much of that wood was now badly rotted. The cords stored inside the fire barrels had fared somewhat better than the wood stacked on the floor. Lin rose periodically to refuel the fire barrels while the others slept. The rain still fell, but it was no longer the raging tempest it had been earlier. Occasionally, a flicker of lightning would briefly illuminate the area just beyond the entryway and she could see the water pooling on the stone outside. Keeping a torch lit outside was impossible, thus making a descent down the stone staircase a fool's errand. The group inside the pyramid trusted May to keep her group on the walkway together until circumstances allowed everyone to reunite.

Lin checked the clothes they had arranged on the floor. By morning, she expected them to be mostly dry. She looked down at Min. He was curled up on the floor very close to a barrel. He made wheezing sounds when he breathed. The stone floor couldn't have been very comfortable, but they had little alternative. The moldy cushions offered no practical option. It appeared that they hadn't been useable for quite a long time.

Lin was still apprehensive about becoming a Journeyer. The island was all she had ever known. Yet, she was curious. The Journeycraft were magnificent, and she knew that the other Journeyers would teach her and show her many incredible things. She could not have one without losing the other. Cap and May had often spoken of choices. This one was made for her by others. While she didn't necessarily disagree with her path, it was unsettling to have it thrust upon her so.

She sat down and leaned back against the wall, listening to the faint rumbles of thunder and the soft sizzle of falling rain. Eventually, the exhaustion of the day overcame her uncomfortable surroundings and she fell asleep.

—————

Lin awoke to the sounds of activity around her. Cap and Shu were inspecting their clothes. Min was awake but was still lying on the floor. The rain had stopped and light was coming in through the entryway.

"You kept the barrels going for quite some time," noted Cap. He was still completely naked.

Lin sat up. "How are our clothes?"

Cap handed her her clothing and poncho. They were dry and still warm from the fire. She stood up and began to dress.

"We need to go to the Chroniclers' Hall," said Shu as she gathered her clothes. "Hopefully, it is functioning," she added, looking down at Min.

"How are you Min?" asked Lin.

Min sat up slowly. "I wish I could say that I remember feeling worse," he said quietly. "But I can't."

"Will you be able to work on the Hall if necessary?" asked Shu. Her tone was fouled with apprehension.

Min took a deep breath and rose. "Depends on what needs to be done," he said. "Maybe someone can help me."

"Out of the question. Only Chroniclers may enter. I will assist as I can, but I am the only one."

Cap handed Min a wad of clothing. Min began to dress. "We need to go and see about the others," said Cap. "They will listen to May but staying on that walkway all night in the storm had to be unsettling. I hope no one panicked."

"What should I do?" asked Lin.

"Min will require assistance in reaching the Hall," said Shu. "We should be able to accomplish that together."

Min sat down on one of the chairs. He leaned forward resting his hands on his thighs. Raspy wheezes escaped from his mouth.

"Shu?" Everyone turned to look at the entryway. It was Dom. His clothes and hair were soaked.

"Dom!" cried Cap as he hurried to the door. "Why are you here?"

Dom looked blankly at Cap. "There were some problems on the walkway, so I came to find you," he said flatly.

"Problems?" said Cap. "What sort of problems?"

Dom turned towards Shu. "A lot of them were afraid of the storm. I think they wanted to try the stairway. Now I think they just want to get in the boat and leave."

"Impossible. Not yet. Cap, you have to go and talk to them."

"I'll get there as soon as I can. Should I have them come up here?"

She thought for a moment. "Yes, we can't leave them down there indefinitely. There is ample shelter."

"All right," he said turning for the door. "I'll get them up here as soon as I can." With that, he exited the pyramid.

"Dom, aren't you cold?" asked Lin.

"Not really . . . ."

Lin gave him a good once-over. "Well, if you change your mind, tell me. We can get the fire going again."

"The Hall will be near the center of the settlement," said Shu. "It should look much like our Hall. I will go ahead and begin inspecting it. Lin, help bring Min along. Dom should come with you."

"Come on Min," said Lin, trying to sound encouraging. "It can't be too far." She moved over next to him. He stood up and put an arm around her shoulder. Despite the age and gender differences, they were roughly the same height. She helped him back to the doorway. The three began the slow walk through the settlement.

Shu was already out of sight by the time they got outside and identified what had to be the Chroniclers' Hall. It was the tallest structure and had a long, thin metal splinter projecting upwards from its apex, just like the Hall on Atla. As they walked, they saw no signs of recent inhabitance. Fire barrels stood unbroken at the corners of most of the pyramids. Unattended clay pots sat upright and full of rain.

"I think they just . . . .left," said Lin. Min paused to rest.

"Why . . .so?" he asked.

Lin looked around a little bit more. "Well, it doesn't look like they abandoned any unfinished projects. And there doesn't seem to be any tools or anything lying around. They didn't leave in a hurry."

"Well analyzed," he said weakly. "Come on."

Eventually, they made it to the Chroniclers' Hall. Shu was waiting for them outside. She did not appear happy.

"Repairs will be required," she said grimly. "I hope you are up to it," she told Min.

"You will help?"

"As I can. Lin, you and Dom should remain out here. Don't leave. We will check with you periodically. Once Min has an estimate as to how long the repairs will take, we will tell you. Then one of you can relay that information to Cap. Understood?"

Dom stood passively, watching Min.

"Something wrong, Dom?" asked Min.

Dom shook his head. *No, Min. Nothing is wrong. Nothing at all.*

The entrance to the Chroniclers' Hall was barred by four burly Guards. They did not react as Jack, Sol and Eve approached. "We need to see Bal," said Sol. "Now." Slowly, one of the Guards took a step towards him. "He is not here," said the Guard in a deep voice.

"When do you expect him back?"

"We have no expectations. It is not our place."

"Not your . . . . ?" Sol stepped away, muttering under his breath.

"We need to speak to him," pleaded Eve. "It is of utmost importance."

The Guard was unmoved. "It does not matter why you wish to see him. He is not here. I do not know when he will return."

"Well, who else can we speak with?" demanded Sol. "There has to be **someone** here that can address our situation."

"There is not. You may only deal with Bal."

"Why is that?" asked Sol.

The Guard hesitated. "That is our charge. Now, move away."

Sol stood, staring up at the Guard. He was a physical marvel. The muscles in his neck bowed into broad, thick shoulders. Sol was eager to process his data so he could know how that had been accomplished. "Very well," he said dejectedly. "Tell Bal we need to speak with him when he returns, can you at least do that?"

The Guard grunted a rough affirmation. Sol turned and took Jack's arm, towing him away. Sol wouldn't put it past Jack to make an ill-advised attempt at the door risking countless possible consequences, all of them bad.

As they entered their own pyramid, Jack booted one of the smaller cushions across the floor. "Can you believe that? We can only talk to Bal now, and he is gone."

"We can still process the data, though," said Sol. "Right?"

"Yes", said Eve, "but we will have to be far more selective about what sort of information we are seeking. What should we be looking for?"

Sol sat down on one of the chairs. "It has to be either protein template manipulation or some sort of nutritional additive," he offered. "And I have a hard time believing they are manipulating protein templates. If it is nutritional, they could get by with knowing how to make something without understanding how it works."

"That seems reasonable," said Jack.

Sol withdrew the device in his pocket and handed it to Eve. "Try checking for patterns involving unusual concentrations of nutrients. If we can identify those, we can move on towards deciphering the actual compositions."

Eve took the device and activated it. She looked over its small display at the various readings Sol had managed to collect. She nodded her head subconsciously as she was wont to do when she was working. "You already have established a baseline one would expect in a control?" she asked.

"Yes," said Sol. "Courtesy of a pretty young girl who works at the Sustenance Hall."

"Will gender make a difference?" asked Eve. "We aren't the same you know."

"It should be statistically meaningless for our purposes," said Sol.

"All right . . . . . ." Eve began entering directives into the device. "I'll start with a routine levels analysis."

Eve placed her fingers on the small display and closed her eyes. Her forehead tensed and a light layer of perspiration began to form on her brow.

"Hmmm…" she said, double-checking the device.

"What?" said Sol as he made his way over to see.

"Gold?" asked Eve. "Can that be right?"

Sol took the device from her and looked over the readings on the display. "No……" he muttered with disbelief. "Surely not . . . .Eve, do a supplemental analysis for the following compounds." He read off a series of chemical formulae, which Eve converted into search patterns. Again she directed her focus into the tiny display.

"All elevated," she said. "And in precise ratios. Lucky guess?"

Sol took the device and looked long and hard at the display. He closed his eyes and his head slumped forward. "I can't believe this," he said finally. "It is a nutritional additive. It is based on gold's unique transitional energies. The signature ratios match."

"I have never heard of such a thing. Are you familiar with it?" asked Jack.

"Very familiar," said Sol with a sigh of disgust. "I invented it."

Eve looked at Jack, then back again to Sol. "You invented it? What is it?"

Sol was busy rechecking the ratios. "I have been working on a treatment for Repose Dormancy Termination Syndrome for a long time," he explained.

"For Min," said Eve.

"Yes. And for the most part, this formula was successful."

"'For the most part'?" echoed Eve.

"It does augment growth and physical development, allowing the body to better endure the rigors of repeated repose cycles. But it has a couple of side effects."

"Like what?" asked Jack.

"Flattened affect," said Sol. "It is also cycli-toxic."

"Explain what that means."

"Gold is a central ingredient but it is not an element that Umae require beyond the minutest amounts for metabolism," he explained. "The product results in an elevated level of gold in the subject's system. It also results in the production of certain compounds that prevent the gold from acting as a toxin within the body."

"I don't understand," said Eve. "Why doesn't anyone use it if it works so well?"

"Because once you start taking it, you can't stop. Once you do, the protective compounds are eliminated faster than the gold is. And it essentially flattens the subject's mood. No happiness. No sadness. No curiosity."

"And if you do stop taking it . . . . .?"

"Gradually, the protective compounds are eliminated, but the gold is not. Transition occurs within about five ellipses, depending on the dosage. Because of the irregularities of repose travel, I determined it was a failure and stopped my research."

"And all of this research was done onboard our Journeycraft," said Eve. "And the formula was uploaded to the beacon satellite along with all the other information uploads through the tether beam."

"Right down to the Chroniclers' Hall," commented Sol. "And the formula is simple. If the Chroniclers managed to find it amongst all the other data we beamed back, and if they had enough gold, they could probably manage to manufacture the stuff." He lowered his eyes. "Another gift from the Journeyers," he said disgustedly. "Moons! I wonder how many Guard prospects they killed before figuring out how to do it correctly."

"The boats," said Jack. "You said there were too many shipwrights, Sol. That's what Bal is using the boats for. I doubt there is much gold at all on Atla. He's sending someone to the mainland to look for it."

"Sending the Guards, no doubt," spat Sol. "To collect gold to.....make more Guards."

"Shu mentioned that Bal is rather skilled at retrieving data contributed to the panel by the tether beam," said Eve. "It makes perfect sense. He is, after all, in charge of the Guards."

"And now it appears he is in charge of everything," noted Sol.

"But the Guards are so obedient," noted Jack. "Is that a side effect too?"

Sol thought for a moment. "I suspected that could be an issue, but I didn't test it because that occurred to me after I had already decided to scrap the project. Obedience is basically the result of a lack of creativity and curiosity. One simply has no desire to question an order."

"So maybe we can tell them what to do," said Jack.

"Doubtful," said Sol. "By this point they have been conditioned to only obey the ones who have been giving them orders. In this case, Shu and Bal."

"And Bal seems to give more than his share of the orders around here," said Eve.

"Shu may not realize it," replied Sol, "but she isn't really the authority here. Bal may have let her think so. He's up to something."

———————

Shu did her best to support Min as the pair went inside the Hall. Even his slight frame was a burden for her. Just inside the door was a wall running perpendicular to the entrance. It served as an added layer of confidentiality. It was impossible to see directly into the Hall from outside.

They stumbled in the dark for a few steps and then stopped.

"I need to try and light a torch," said Shu. "There should be fire barrels inside." She began to rummage through a small bag that hung around her neck. Min turned and looked back at the door. He couldn't see Dom or Lin from where he was standing. He withdrew a short cylinder from his bag and ran his hand over one end. It began to glow with a greenish light that easily illuminated the hallway around them. Shu scowled as she took him by the elbow and began dragging him deeper into the Hall.

At the end of the corridor a door opened into a much larger chamber. Once they were inside, Min amplified the intensity of the light. In the center of the room was a long, bare, rectangular table with a dozen chairs next to it. At the opposite end of the room was a gigantic display that reached almost halfway to the apex. A number of doors lined the wall adjacent to the display. A pair of stone figures carved into a nearby wall drew Min's attention.

One was slightly taller than the other. Both were thin and dressed in long robes. Some type of elaborate trim lined their collars and the bottoms of the sleeves. Atop their heads were what appeared to be ornate circlets, adorned with strange-looking leaves. Their arms were folded across their chests, their hands concealed in their sleeves. Min stepped closer to the wall for a better look.

"Who are they?" he asked Shu.

"They are two of the Directors, may they guide our way," she said reverently. "Architects of the Protocols."

Min noted that their plan apparently included badly flawed projections about the Heks' technical development. "Do you know their names?"

"They are figurative. We do not know the names of the Directors. We also do not know with certainty how many of them there were. It was a long time ago, after all." She was growing anxious. "Please, do your work." The phrase "while you still can" hung unspoken, but Min gathered her meaning, nonetheless.

Min looked up at the darkened display. "Impressive." He then broke out into a fit of coughing that caused him to double over. Shu put her hand on his back, not knowing how else to help him.

"Are you going to be able to do this?" Her tone suggested a concern about the completion of the task at hand more than about Min's health.

"Eventually," gasped Min. He stayed doubled over, with his hands on his knees, until he was able to breathe more easily. "All right. Let's try."

He walked over to the display. "Do you have one of these on Atla?" he asked. Shu stared at him in silence. "I'll take that as a 'yes'". He reached out and touched the display. Shu lurched forward. His action had taken her off guard. Nothing happened. Min noted her sudden reaction. "You will need to tell me exactly how this is supposed to work, or I won't be able to fix it," he said.

Shu looked up apprehensively at the display. "Very well," she said finally. "It processes and stores historical information. It accepts both first-hand accounts from Chroniclers as well as narratives given by others but compiled by Chroniclers."

"That doesn't sound very complex," said Min. The hint of disappointment in his voice wasn't lost on Shu. "How do you input the data?"

"The first-hand accounts are taken directly from the memories of the Chronicler," she said. "I'm not sure how it works. We simply think of the event, touch the display, and it is recorded. The narratives are stored in a similar way. We read the narrative, touch the display, and it is recorded."

"It's called a neuron-tactile interface," said Min. "I'm very familiar with the technology. But, what if your perceptions are wrong, or you subjectively misinterpret what you saw or read? Doesn't that corrupt the record?"

He looked awful. His enthusiasm for this technical puzzle was propping him up, but Shu could tell that he would soon reach the limits of his endurance.

"No," she said, shaking her head. "Chroniclers undergo special training to sharpen the way we process our perceptions. We are conditioned to be objective. If anyone else was providing the data, there would be more problems."

Min took a couple of deep breaths. "What does the display do with the information?"

"It comprises a history," said Shu. "With the proper mental disciplines, a Chronicler can access almost any sort of information about past events."

"Any past event?" asked Min. "Could I, say, watch myself being born?"

"Achieving that degree of specificity would be impossible. Every display contains a history of that settlement from the Cataclysm forward."

"I thought you said you didn't have any information about the Cataclysm?" asked Min.

Shu stood silent for a moment, staring at him. "I believe I told you I couldn't provide you with any such information."

Min stared back at the display again. "And I assume the power source is this settlement's beacon satellite. This display isn't getting any power, so I have to guess that the problem is either in the connection to the satellite or in the satellite itself." He began coughing again. This time, the spasms wracked his body so hard that his face turned a dark red and he slid down to his knees. Shu knelt down next to him, watching anxiously.

"If you need for me to do some of the work, you will have to tell me what to do," she said.

Min wiped his mouth off with his sleeve. "It would take me too long to explain," he said weakly. "I should have brought Jack."

"Impossible."

"You don't make many concessions, do you?" Shu stood back up, remaining silent. Min slowly rose as well. "All right. Let's check the connection first. If the satellite is the problem, we may not be able to fix it from here."

"We must! Otherwise, we won't be able to find out where any of these people are!"

"And we probably won't know where their Journeyers went either," noted Min. Shu hadn't demonstrated any concern about the Haven data. He made his way to the side of the display. He removed a number of small implements from his bag and set them down in a row on a small shelf. He tracked the physical connection between the display and the apex of the pyramid. It was a thick, metallic tube that exited the back of the display before scaling the interior wall of the pyramid. The joint between the tube and the display appeared to be intact. He used a bonding inhibitor to disconnect them.

The tube easily slid away from the back of the display. Inside the tube was a clear metallic core. The central portion of the core was solid quartz. He scanned the interior of the tube and determined that it was structurally intact. There were several electron anomalies within the metal core of the quartz itself. That explained why the *Aurora* had landed on Atla instead of here, its home. There wasn't any connection between this Chronicler Hall and the Land Bridge's beacon satellite. The *Aurora*'s navbrain correctly interpreted this to mean that the Land Bridge settlement no longer existed and guided the ship to the next available settlement.

"Good news," he said to Shu. "I think it is the connection and not the satellite."

Shu was heartened by his statement. "You can fix it?"

"A moment." He doubled over again and began to cough. This attack was the worst one yet. He was quickly on all fours, struggling for air. Shu circled around him anxiously, unable to help. After several moments, he was able to regain his breath.

"How much time will you need?" asked Shu.

"If you send Dom and Lin to help Cap, I should be done before they get back."

Shu was plainly relieved. "What is wrong with it?"

He pointed at the ceiling. "Power surge, probably lightning. It happened quite a while ago."

"How can you tell?"

"The core is designed to reinsulate itself with regular use. That is why yours doesn't break down every time it is hit by lightning. This one is completely uninsulated. That would take a minimum of about one hundred ellipses."

"One hundred? They have been gone for that long?"

"I can't tell you how long they have been gone. But this panel hasn't been used for at least one hundred ellipses."

"I see," said Shu, striving to manifest composure. "I will tell Dom and Lin to go." She turned and walked back towards the entryway to the pyramid.

Min watched her to make sure she was gone. His act had gotten him right where he wanted to be. While he was rather ill, he didn't feel nearly as bad as he had let on. Now he was alone with the panel. He withdrew a long slender tool and placed one end in the center of the core. He left it there until the core flashed with blue sparkles. He then reattached the connection between the apex and the display. It was the simplest of repairs. The display began to emit a soft hum. He had a scan of the Hek stored in his resonator. Now he needed information about one more thing. Shu was calling to him from the entry passage. He had to hurry.

Shu came back through the door into the chamber. "Wait! What are you . . . .?"

Min took his hands and placed them, palms flat, on the display. He concentrated, opening his mind to the device. He maintained one word inside of his mind.

Cataclysm.

The entire display glowed with a blinding white light. Shu instinctively covered her eyes. Min's body shook, and his back arched as energy from the display coursed through it. After a few seconds, Min collapsed to the floor.

"No!" cried Shu as she ran across the room. Min lay flat on his back, his eyelids twitching with wild tremors. She touched his neck. The pounding was so rapid she almost couldn't distinguish between each individual pulse.

Suddenly, his eyes shot open and he took in a loud, deep gasp of air. Then, he was still, his pupils fixed. Shu knelt over him, waiting for Min to revive. He did not. She stood up and turned towards the panel. He had finished his job. She didn't need him any longer.

After briefly speaking with Shu, Lin and Dom walked in the direction of the stairs. Once they reached the top, they had a clear view as the lake spread out below them. They could see the others gathered around Cap on the walkway.

"Once they see us, they will come," said Dom.

"Maybe," said Lin, "but Shu wants us to go down to get them, so that is what we will do." Dom looked up at her, expressionless. "Come on!" said Lin, irritation creeping into her tone. She gave Dom a light tug on his arm and then started down the stairs.

The stairs were still wet from the rain, so Lin was careful with each step. Dom essentially leapt down the stairs, his feet only touching every other one. He quickly caught up with Lin. She stopped and put her hands on her hips.

"Dom, what are you doing?" she scolded. "Do you want to fall?" Dom stepped forward so the two were on the same step. Lin glared at him, the lake behind her.

"Do you?" said Dom.

"Do I? No, of course not. Now be careful." Lin studied Dom for a moment, puzzled at his behavior.

"Are you *sure*?" Dom's voice had dropped several octaves. "You are usually very . . . .careful . . . aren't you?"

Lin's eyes narrowed. His voice echoed inside her ears.

"What . . .do you mean?"

Dom leaned in close to her. "Haven't you wondered what it might be like to *not* be so careful?" His voice, although a whisper, rumbled like thunder.

Lin blinked a couple of times and took a step backwards. "We should go," she said without enthusiasm.

"We should, shouldn't we?" he said. "But this is more fun." He took a small step towards her. She shuddered and took a deep breath.

"Dom . . . ." she stepped back again. This time, her foot found nothing but air and she tumbled backwards. Everything turned upside down as she fell off the stairs. Just as she felt herself start to accelerate downwards, a firm grip seized her wrist. She was pressed against the cliff face, her free hand clawing for something to hold. Dom stood above her, nonchalantly holding her wrist in one hand. She looked down and could see the rocky base of the cliff far below her feet.

"See?" said Dom quietly. "Fun."

Lin was breathing rapidly as she neared panic. "Pull me up," she said finally.

Dom looked over his shoulder and could see Cap bounding up the stairway as fast as he could. He was calling to Dom, but Dom pretended not to hear.

"Maybe I should wait for him," sneered Dom.

"N-no. Now," insisted Lin.

Dom shrugged and easily hoisted her back up to the step. She quickly scrambled to the far edge, away from the drop off.

"You should be more careful," said Dom in his usual tone. "That would be quite a fall." Lin pulled her knees to her chest, unable to look away from him.

They waited until Cap arrived. "Lin? Are you all right? What happened?"

"She fell," said Dom simply. "She wasn't careful and stepped over the side."

Cap looked at the edge of the step and then at Lin. "Lin?"

"Yes. I was careless," she said matter-of-factly. "Dom helped me up."

Cap studied Lin for several moments. "I'm just glad you are all right. Try to be careful on these steps, they are still damp." Lin stood up and nodded. "I'm going back down to bring the others up. We can manage without the two of you. Go ahead to the top of the steps and wait for us there."

"Is everyone all right?" asked Lin. Her voice was now full of concern.

"Yes," said Cap. "They are soaked and some of the Charges spent a lot of time bailing water out of the boat, but they are all right." He noticed a look of apprehension on Lin's face. "Including the baby. Pol kept him well-covered."

"Good. I'd like to see him. Can I go down with you?"

Cap looked at Dom. "Can you wait by yourself?"

"Of course," he said flatly. He turned and began to walk gingerly back up the steps. Lin stood and watched him climb the first twenty stairs.

"Lin?" asked Cap. "Coming?" She turned slowly and started down behind Cap. She didn't take another look back up the stairs until she reached the bottom. By then, Dom was gone.

Shu struggled to maintain her composure. The discovery of the abandoned settlement had taken a toll on her. Now Min appeared to be comatose, or worse, here on the floor of the Hall. She hadn't anticipated that problem.

She stood up and approached the panel. She gently touched it once and it began to glow a faint blue. She then closed her eyes and focused. It was critical that she open her mind only to the data she was seeking. A lapse in concentration could result in a surge of information that might overwhelm her mind. Once she felt ready she placed both palms on the panel. The faint blue intensified only slightly as she stood motionless. After several moments, she pulled her hands away and opened her eyes. She covered her face with her hands as the tears returned.

There had been no dramatic ending to the Land Bridge community. They had simply left. Their food supplies were dwindling. Their ships on the sea side of the settlement were no longer seaworthy. They could not find food on the lake side as the cliffs required them to travel so far just to be able to go ashore. The Journeyers who called the Land Bridge home had stopped returning. As the hungry population decreased, they lost hope in the Journeyers. Instead, they placed their hopes in signs. Unusual creatures washing up on the beach. Strange colored clouds. Anything out of the ordinary meant something profound. Eventually, they had decided to dare the Hek by moving on to find food. Shu had no way to know where they went. She had no way to know where even to search for them. She couldn't help but wonder how many other settlements had been claimed by the same fate. For all that she knew, Atla really was the only settlement left.

Dom had stood in the shadows, watching everything. He wanted nothing more than to see what the display could show him. But not now. His time would come, and soon. After all, he was going to become one of them. Shu would teach him whatever he needed to know. After that, he would have everything.

THE END – BOOK 1

A NOTE TO THE READER

I hope you enjoyed **The Protocols of Uma**, Book 1 of the Journeyers' Tale. Independent authors like me are rather dependent on reviews from our readers. I'd really appreciate it if you would take a moment to provide a short, honest review on Amazon.com.

Book 2 of the series, **Blinding Sky**, is available in paperback, eBook, and Kindle Unlimited through Amazon.

If you'd like to find out more about me and my writing please visit my website:

www.johnbrageauthor.com

www.ingramcontent.com/pod-product-compliance
Lightning Source LLC
Chambersburg PA
CBHW051425170626
46809CB00006B/2330